THE AU DACITY

THE AU DACITY

RYAN CHAPMAN

SOHO

Published by Soho Press, Inc.
227 W 17th Street
New York, NY 10011

Library of Congress Cataloging-in-Publication Data

Names: Chapman, Ryan, author.
Title: The audacity / Ryan Chapman.
Description: New York, NY : Soho, 2024. | Identifiers: LCCN 2023045737

ISBN 978-1-64129-562-8
eISBN 978-1-64129-563-5

Subjects: LCGFT: Satirical literature. | Novels.
Classification: LCC PS3603.H37428 A93 2024 | DDC 813/.6—dc23/
eng/20231003
LC record available at https://lccn.loc.gov/2023045737

Interior design by Janine Agro

Printed in the United States of America

10 9 8 7 6 5 4 3 2 1

Daily am I myself the stakes
and I win myself every night.
—Walter Serner, *Last Loosening*

D'ailleurs, c'est toujours les autres qui meurent.
—Marcel Duchamp's epitaph

CHAPTER 1

"The necessary breakthroughs did not occur within the expected or justifiable life cycle of the product."

Guy received the text Thursday evening his time, late afternoon her time. He assumed it was meant for the company Slack. She had done this before: the dry nature of the missive, in addition to the formality of the grammar, contrasted with their clipped marital exchanges. Tonight was the Oxfam dinner, which V would have known. He replied with a question mark and drained his second flute.

As a veteran of the gala circuit, he knew he had ten minutes to eat before interruption by glad-handers and chummy acquaintances. The tuna tartare was a sensorial affront, given the slides of West African children warped by malaria and wefted by malnutrition. At least next week's Robin Hood gala wouldn't stoop to a *slideshow*. Though the chatter at cocktails was that everyone was skipping Robin Hood. Booking Yo-Yo Ma so soon after the Drawing Center . . . Much too much Ma, and certainly not the mood. He took another bite and ignored the scolding voice-over by the model/actor/activist. Yet another ingenue embarrassed by their frictionless ascent.

Roark Jefferson, seated to his left, pushed aside an untouched plate and sighed with glottal force. "The Drawing Center served steak. And *they're* on the ropes. This mess"—he mashed the fleshy pink ziggurat with a fork—"is just guilt made manifest by some aspirant more sous than chef."

Guy loved Roark. To the manner born and, like a wizened character actor, a man one couldn't imagine ever being under fifty. He wore bespoke pinstripe and Charvet shirting, which did a reasonable job of directing the eye away from the splotched complexion of an overripe banana, and he adhered to outmoded WASP traditions like only wearing sneakers on the tennis court. His family had accrued their wealth the old-fashioned way—that is, passively, as rentier moguls. Roark expanded his modest inheritance of Harlem brownstones into a quiet fiefdom and, at the age when most handed over the reins, multiplied his fortune by repurposing shipping containers as stand-alone rooftop apartments. This expansion of the housing inventory earned praise from the mayor and urban studies think tanks. Since Roark could not patent the concept, he stockpiled the global supply of coupling hardware for the containers, which braced the weight transversely. (Roark often corrected people on this point: the containers did not sit on top of the building, but "athwart" it.)

He had come out of the closet at seventy, which he celebrated with the establishment of an invitation-only cigar club in the Flatiron District: "Like the Yale club, but more selective."

Roark leaned over as the slideshow closed with what sounded like fake Satie; the pat outro did not send one reaching for the pocketbook.

"My boy," Roark said. "Did I see you at the Drawing Center? A week ago Friday."

Guy remembered the invitation. It was either held in the same event space they were sitting in now—a former bank from the gilded age—or in the LES, at the other gilded-age bank-turned-event-space.

"Couldn't make it," he said. "I Guggenheimed. We're an underwriter."

"Well," Roark said. "That evening I had an insight I'd like to share. With an aesthete such as yourself."

"A *failed* aesthete such as myself," Guy replied. His previous life fascinated the gala set. They lacquered his decades as a struggling composer with vicarious nostalgia. He didn't mind, was in fact grateful for how it assuaged his imposter syndrome after V's pole-vault up the tax brackets. And for how it assuaged other aspects: Guy was almost always the only Sri Lankan in the room, whether it was high school in suburban Minneapolis, conservatory in Philadelphia, or these august rooms. At fundraisers and dinners "In Honor Of" whomever he played the Good Time Charlie, improvising cocktails at the bar (the Ironclad Prenup, the Bahama S-Corp) or tickling the ivories on someone's Steinway. His piano was barely passable, even to his atrophied ear, and would have been shameful at the old alma mater. But the gala set gave him the benefit of the doubt. As was their practice and default position.

"'Failed,' come now." Roark waved away Guy's false

modesty. "The flame still burns within. So I'm browsing the auction—decent to middling. Ho-hum Elizabeth Peyton, a rushed Henry Taylor. Nothing like 2005, when I picked up my Wiley for a song. It's in the Montauk place—have you been?"

"To yours? Yes, the last lawn party." Guy disarmed the tuna with a third flute. He felt a tickle on his upper lip; a hair he'd missed shaving.

"Of course, of course. Anyhow. I realized that none of my contemporary works depict our people." He opened his arm to indicate the room. "The same applies for cinema, literature, popular song."

Guy leaned back in his chair. "You want more art about the affluent." From this angle, the long-stemmed calla lilies in the centerpiece appeared an extension of Roark's much-envied white pomp, amplifying the import of his speech and, when the uplights hit just so, giving the impression of a light bulb over his head.

"More art *by* the affluent," Roark replied. "No more of this reportage, these outsiders' chronicles."

"Aren't you writing your memoirs?"

Roark didn't hear the question. "In our society, we value individual life by the measure of one's monetary reserve." He put a hand over his wineglass at a waiter's approach. "Why shouldn't the highest-valued individuals be the ones telling the stories?"

"And they're not," Guy replied.

"Not like before. Proust. Montaigne, Wharton. All writers of means."

"De Sade, too," Guy said. "Didn't he torture sex workers?"

"I'm not talking morality here—"

"You guys are exactly right." A man with an oval, feature-less head peered around the centerpiece. He looked to Guy like that optical illusion of a face that could be seen upside down, the bald head becoming the chin, forehead wrinkles as tightened lips.

"Exactly right," the man continued. "Money is speech, after all, according to the highest court in the land. And we have the most speech!"

Roark pointed his fork at the man. "Mind your manners, Saul. This is a private conversation."

Guy was vaguely familiar. A hedge fundie who'd long grown accustomed to speaking without pushback or request for clarification and so felt comfortable with specious bullshit like "I'm socially liberal but fiscally conservative." As if there were any sphere of American life separate from money.

They ignored him.

"It's an intriguing idea," Guy said. He straightened and put his hand over his flute. "Implementation might be tricky."

"I thought of that. It should arise organically, hmm? After all, we're people too."

"We are people too. That is correct."

Roark nodded toward the screen above the podium. The Jefferson Development Group's anodyne logo flashed in a row of platinum supporters ("Close Friends of Oxfam"). Guy waited a beat for PrevYou. He could look up how much V's advisory group recommended she donate. But he decided he didn't care and it didn't matter in the end. A six-figure fillip out of a ten-figure purse. Ah, there it was: Nice Friends of Oxfam. He hadn't adjusted to the new logo, despite its ubiquity on the portfolios and notepads around the Manhattan place. The semiabstract drawing hinted at a crustacean, in the style of a single-stroke Picasso, which the consultant from Wolff Olins praised as "no-brow universalism." V had to connect the dots for Guy: "Crab, cancer. You don't get it?" Even when he saw the logo projected in Times Square to celebrate the Series H investment round—the squiggle floating above phrases like "from chaos, order" and "benign is divine"—Guy always saw it as purely gastrointestinal.

Roark folded his napkin and set it on his plate. "I'm retiring for the evening. Will I see you at Averman's?"

"Victoria might attend. I don't think I can tag along."

"Quite right. One invite per capita, no assistants, no partners. Which, given the holiday weekend, seems a bit strict."

V had mentioned Arthur Averman's conference before she left for California. She made it sound onerous, though she considered all nontransactional gatherings on par with jury duty.

"Enjoy answering all the big questions," Guy said. "Saturday I'm being fêted by the Brooklyn Phil."

Roark pulled a coat check ticket from his breast pocket. Given the weather, Guy wondered if the man had checked an umbrella, despite arriving by car.

"I hadn't realized the outer boroughs supported their own philharmonics," Roark said. "Well, good evening."

Guy thought of sticking around. See if anyone was up for a cognac in the semisecret lounge off the rear staircase. Then he remembered Averman's advice during the First Flush, nearly a decade ago: Don't stay too late, it looks desperate. Don't act like you won't have it next year. You will. You deserve it. You always have.

· · ·

GUY UNDRESSED TO his briefs and tossed his shirt in the hamper. The backup Brioni tonight; his fourth favorite tuxedo. Possibly fifth. He ran through his evening toilet while mentally rehearsing Saturday evening. If what's-his-name solicited ideas for the phil's schedule—out of politesse and, let's face it, obligation—Guy should have some names at the ready. Someone living. And young. Nobody who'd be mistaken for a peer in the group photo. Mason Bates—he was anodyne enough. Was Nico Muhly still drowning in commissions? Nico had impressed at Guy's spring salon, according to the compliments Guy still received two months later. When he relayed these warm feelings to V, she joked that chairing a family foundation had been his calling all along.

He voided his bladder and backed away from the flush's excess splash—an effect of the altitude and the summer winds buffeting the penthouse, one of the unforeseen drawbacks of New York's most advanced luxury supertall.

Quadrophonic chirping from his devices caught him mid-pajama. He picked up his watch: the PrevYou board was holding an emergency meeting, and they needed him to Zoom in. Guy caught his stricken face in a window's reflection: nearly five decades of assimilation and he was still the fearful immigrant. What had he done this time? The tartare at Oxfam? Had some witness to his indelicate hoovering posted a clip? Now he looked bad, ergo V looked bad, ergo the company looked bad, ergo the much-stalled IPO was in jeopardy. But if this was the case—if he'd blackened the brand's eye with a tactless gobble—surely Comms could handle it.

He texted "???" to V on his way to the main-floor living room, his shoulder brushing Post-its off a load-bearing column. The yellow squares were ubiquitous to the point of invisibility, covering the walls with illegible logorrhea she claimed were org charts, diagrams of chemical compounds, and experimental supply chains. Similar horror vacui filled her multiple offices and their multiple homes. More than once he'd taken the Post-its for the enthusiasms of an asylum patient, but when he did notice them, they provided a small comfort during her weeks away.

The projector rattled on start-up, which someone was supposed to have fixed. Guy signed into Zoom, and Jeremy Halloran's exsanguinated grimace appeared over the fireplace.

"Okay," Jeremy said. "We're still waiting on a few people. Everyone sit tight."

A dozen boxes popped into existence. The board member who invented the slimmer EpiPen. The board member from Cleveland Clinic. A few people Guy didn't recognize—probably corporate counsel. Everyone dialed in from a residence, save for Jeremy. He was in a conference room in the East Coast HQ, which, if Guy turned his head, he could see in all its glory jutting from the Jersey skyline. (On a clear morning the penthouse's shadow touched HQ for about fifteen minutes, which V refused to admit was premeditated.)

Of course Jeremy was in the office; his hours nearly rivaled V's. She'd recruited him early to be her CFO, wooing him from FedEx with a doubled salary and a barn-size block of shares. He had a linebacker's physique and a chess master's demeanor, spending meetings slumped forward and ignoring everyone until an impasse provoked a shrugging quotation from some paper out of the *Harvard Business Review.* He'd send the relevant PDF to everyone present—sometimes the whole company—and resume his silence. Guy had exchanged maybe a dozen words with the man.

Jeremy cleared his throat. "Enough of us are here; we're starting. Note that board members Lesser and Fitzpatrick are not present." His voice sounded scraped out. "Guy Sarvananthan, we're going to need your camera on."

"I'm slightly, er, dishabille, and I'm sure you don't need—"

"Camera on. Legal needs visual ID."

"One moment." Guy shucked his pajamas and pulled clothes from the hamper. He nearly tripped and hopped to the full-length mirror. The white bib-front shirt from before. A bit formal, but what did they care? He slid the tuxedo studs into the placket, tucked in the hem, decided to forgo the cuff links.

He fell onto the couch and turned on the camera hidden on the mantel. The board members rushed in at once, a caffeinated davening of bald pates: "A secular saint . . . The PrevYou family is here for you . . . A beacon for strong women everywhere . . . Strong *people* everywhere . . . The brightest lights dim too soon . . ."

Guy waved his hands. "What are you—Is Victoria dialing in?"

Jeremy silenced everyone's feeds. "There's news," he said. "About Victoria."

He screenshared a Google map. "At seven forty PST, Victoria's kayak was found in San Francisco Bay. Coast Guard and Search and Rescue are on the scene. Plus our people."

One of the lawyers unmuted herself. "The scuba team that repaired the Chinese fiber optic cable. We got them on it."

Jeremy gave her a look and continued. "Chances of rescue are highest in the first twelve hours. They can track tides, cameras on the bridge, that sort of thing."

Guy's vision shook. He felt like he was going blind. "Wait, what?"

"Breathe, Guy," someone said.

A prompt to accept a file transfer.

"Search and Rescue," Jeremy said. "Their initial assessment and agenda."

Guy's vision quieted. He wasn't going blind. But nobody would make eye contact with him, save for Jeremy. The former Secretary of State typed on his phone. A second later his paraphrased Auden appeared in the chat: "Victoria was our working wk, everyone's working wk."

The lawyer cleared her throat. "We have to state the following as per the charter Ms. Stevens drew up for use in situations such as this—such as these. We acknowledge its indelicate nature." She read from a tablet. "If the CEO is considered auto absentia by a majority of the board, willful or not, this constitutes a violation of the morality clause of the standard PrevYou employment contract and forfeiture of annual bonus—"

"Wait. Wait," Guy said. A mosquito flew across the screen.

"It doesn't mean anything," Jeremy replied. "Legal has to say it. Let them say it."

"Willful?" Guy asked.

Jeremy directed his reply off-screen. "It means suicide. If investigators claim she took her own life she doesn't—you don't get the Q4 payout. It's a technical issue."

"She retains her majority of Class B shares," a board member said.

The lawyer chimed in. "Dolphin rescues are rare, but not an impossibility."

Jeremy motioned for them to shut up. "Don't panic. We'll find her. She's just offline for a few hours, that's it. Most likely tipped over and swam to shore."

Guy had cheered her finish at the Boston Marathon. She ran with a bloody toenail and beat her PR by seven minutes. "Suicide? Have you met Victoria?"

Jeremy snapped his fingers at the screen. "Hey. Hey. Look at me. Breathe. Now look out your windows. See that sky? Concentrate on the sky. Everything's going to be fine. Or not fine—different."

A chat message from the former Secretary of State: "'Failure is simply the opportunity to begin again.'—Henry Ford."

Another board member spoke up. "Can we move to the next agenda item? There are restructuring protocols we have to—"

Jeremy muted him. "Guy, if you want to be there, that can be arranged. The jet's fueled and waiting at Teterboro. And, ah, we respect your wishes completely, whatever they are."

The lawyer raised her hand. Jeremy sighed and nodded.

"Have you heard from Ms. Stevens in the last twenty-four hours?"

Guy shook his head. "She's due back tomorrow. We don't check in unless there's a delay."

Several board members unmuted themselves and began arguing. The Comms guy accidentally screenshared his desktop, which displayed 709 unread emails and an open tab on LinkedIn. Someone named Li posted in the chat about turtles eating the body tissue of drowned sailors. One of Guy's tuxedo studs fell from his shirt and clattered on the coffee table. Li's message disappeared.

Guy tried to speak but was drowned out. He messaged Jeremy: "V did text about a product cycle. around 8."

An instant reply: "omw."

Nobody on the call noticed Jeremy's sign-off. Guy exited and checked his phone—nothing from V—then autonomically walked to the foyer terminal, ordered a martini, and unpaused whatever he'd been playing that afternoon. A confirmation beep: three minutes, to be delivered by the residents-only restaurant on the thirtieth floor, which for some reason was always faster than the residents-only bar on the seventeenth floor.

German trilling filled the bare penthouse. Oh, no: Schumann's op. 42. Death and widowhood. Lamentation. And didn't he try to kill himself? A leap into the Rhine's biting waters—that was it. Guy swiped down on the terminal, becalmed momentarily by the blurred wheel of names, and tapped at random. An album of chamber work by Ned Rorem, the lusty demigod back at the Curtis Institute of Music.

A martini, though? It felt vaguely salutary and therefore inappropriate. He needed a ruminative liquor. Scotch. He ascended to the second-floor living room and smell-tested the decanters on the bar cart. Poured two fingers of the peatiest liquid, hoping, without being conscious of it, for alchemical probity; at the first wincing sip, he realized he had been repeating the word "fuck" in a crescendoed trance.

The PrevYou tower across the Hudson flashed, or its crown of lights flashed, and a sleek white helicopter rose from within the penumbra with a slight wobble and canted east over the river to alight at the newish Pier 90 heliport. Guy forced down a second sip. He watched the dot that was Jeremy cross traffic and wend up the blocks. Guy poured another finger and returned to the terminal, approved Jeremy with the lobby, and then blinked with deliberation.

The elevator opened to Jeremy dictating a press statement on his phone, oblivious of the sleepy attendant next to him holding a felt-topped tray and coupe glass. Guy raised his scotch and pointed at Jeremy. Jeremy registered the waiter and silently declined.

"She's okay, right?" Guy asked. "This is a scare. An accident."

Jeremy started to reply, and then noticed the rows of Post-its. He ran a finger down the columns, then read them right to left. The elevator chimed, and the livery-clad waiter nodded goodbye; Guy was pierced by a rare envy.

"Show me what's on your phone," Jeremy said while

pocketing a Post-it. He read V's text, looked at Guy, then back at the phone. His neck veins danced.

"It's bad?" Guy asked.

"I suppose she wanted you to know. The cat's out of the bag. No: the tiger's loose in the day care." Jeremy moved to the kitchen. He removed his wallet and keys from his pockets and lined them on the center island.

Guy looked at the text again. "The 'product'—that's Caduceus, the new booth OS? It's been delayed before."

Jeremy rested against the counter, then reconsidered and straightened his posture. He started spinning invisible dials with his hands. "Elena's cancer cure, all that 'capturing lightning in a petri dish'—Victoria faked it."

Dr. Elena Corral, hired after successfully treating the First Lady for what everyone else deemed a terminal diagnosis.

"Impossible," Guy replied. "Elena cracked it just before, you know, her vacation."

"You can say she died. And it is possible. She told Victoria we were still years out from Phase III. Then she contracted a lung infection in Tibet."

"But she wasn't, I mean . . ." Guy thought about the funeral, Victoria's steadfast confidence.

"Our guys hit a wall eighteen months ago, so Victoria brings in Corral. Silos her work and tells the board we're weeks away from a cure. 'The end of cancer, finally in sight.'"

Guy leaned his head on the glass. His unfocused gaze fell on the perforated rods circling the window ledge, part of the Cloud Halo amenity: an on-demand fog for erasing one's view of the other supertalls of Billionaire's Horseshoe. V liked to

activate it from her phone when she touched down, a meteo-
rological note to say "home soon." The halo reminded Guy of
a ring toss; the tabloids, in their typically lurid fashion, compared it to a cock ring.

"But not in sight," Guy said.

"Yeah, we hit the ceiling of our investors' patience. Hiring
Corral was a last-ditch effort."

Guy could see it. She learns they're still far from a cure.
PrevYou's burned through its cash reserves. Then: an opportunity. "So V tells the world Elena cracked it. Turns her into
a martyr, says they'll roll out the cure after internal testing."

"More or less. But there is no cure."

"Wait, so—"

"Yes."

"But that means—"

"Yes."

"And she—"

"Yes, yes, and yes. It's as bad as you think. Or worse.
Madoff. Fukushima. A zombie Madoff, Ponzi scheming inside
the reactor core."

"She knew the whole time?"

Jeremy correctly guessed which cabinet hid the refrigerator
and inspected its contents. "No, Mr. *Stevens*, it worked perfectly for nine years, and then she defrauded investors for no
reason."

"She wouldn't—she's brilliant, I know—"

"All due respect, you don't seem to know your wife much
at all." He left the fridge open and replied to something on
his phone.

Guy felt hammocked by vertigo. Vertigo and nausea and something vaguely splenetic. He lay on the floor.

One of their first dates. An Italian spot in midtown. He was still living in Philly, and she'd convinced him to drive up. He circled the blocks in vain until succumbing to a parking garage's exorbitant rates. What did she wear? What did they eat? So much of that year was a blur. He remembered being led to a private table in the wine cellar and informed that Ms. Stevens was en route. Rachmaninoff's op. 3 bounced off the bottles.

When she arrived he casually bragged that he'd once performed the prelude, back in Minnesota. She said, "I know," and then asked, before taking her seat, why he was still single "at his age." He gave a potted summary of Philadelphia's slim offerings and his two-decade affair with a married violinist, begun while students at Curtis and terminated a few years back. V asked her follow-up so baldly he didn't take offense, or not at first: Did his status as a Sri Lankan immigrant materially hinder his relationships?

Guy quoted his father. He was an American. Then he asked her why she was single, emphasizing "at her age" out of petty and justified redress.

She took a long, slow sip of water, maintaining eye contact before replying. She'd met the love of her life at Stanford. They married soon after. Two summers ago he failed to overcome a malignant tumor. She took a sabbatical from the search giant, nominally in mourning; in fact she had been developing something new. Something transformational. Romantically she was uninterested in flings or anything short-term. At the time Guy was stuck on her phrasing: her husband didn't suffer from a tumor, nor die from one. He'd "failed to overcome."

V pulled an iPad from her purse and slid it across the table. If he wouldn't mind taking a look at this PowerPoint, he would learn what she's seeking in a partner. As he read—one slide consisted of an eight-columned table of traits like "stolid," "debt-free," "strong ACLs"—she talked about her recent "eureka" concerning the systemic errors in cancer research; her tone implied a rehearsed speech. *The incentives were all wrong. The research centers don't coordinate, big pharma's not focused on prevention, the databases are outdated . . . And, of course, the subject was incredibly depressing.*

But she'd figured it out. An insight during her last triathlon. With a fair bit of investment she could install a network of robotics-driven "booths" in population-dense areas. Each booth would perform common medical tests; in five to eight years the aggregate and proprietary dataset would help her leapfrog the systemic scientific and commercial problems. With a fair bit of investment, some patience, and the right personnel, she saw a path for eradicating the country's second leading cause of death.

His expression must have betrayed his skepticism. The idea was sound, she said. She just needed a partner to live and breathe the idea alongside her. Someone who—and here she broke eye contact—could adjust their situation to her own. Without friction and without complaint.

He bit into a garlicky breadstick while the Rachmaninoff looped. Her courtship felt more like recruitment, which wasn't so terrible. Abstractly flattering, even. And he could love someone who didn't love him in the same fashion. America had prepared him well for that.

He handed her the iPad and looked at her. Fully and straight on. He had no idea what she saw in him. Then, later, now.

Jeremy clapped in front of his nose. "You have a mosquito." He looked up and clapped again.

Guy abraded his head into the wood grain, his hair velcroing into the planed grooves. "You knew this whole time? How could you go along with it?"

"I keep forgetting you've never had a real job. To answer your questions: Yes, and I thought we could pull it off. We have eighty-seven of the world's best oncologists on payroll. Failing that: acquisition. But our valuation kept skyrocketing, so after a while it was, like, who could afford us? Merck? Yeah, maybe Merck."

Guy sat up. Bile in his gut readied a coup. "You people . . . You're scum . . ."

Jeremy ignored him and texted at speed. His phone emitted stroboscopic activity. "Yeah, boo-hoo, everyone's culpable, woe is me." He paused. "You're distracted. Remember: Victoria is the priority. We will find her; she will right the ship. She always does. A lot of icebergs in the old rearview."

Guy swallowed to quell the bile. It half worked. "I wish I believed in God right now." He immediately regretted the scotch-fueled confession.

"I'm told religion is very helpful for people in your predicament." Jeremy squatted and placed his gigantic hand on Guy's shoulder. Guy waited for a squeeze.

"What would Victoria say?" Jeremy asked.

"We're just one miracle away. And—"

"'—And the world is full of miracles.' Exactly."

"That was written for her. She never believed it."

"True. But I thought you did. You always seemed to us as Mr. Go Along to Get Along. Constitutionally supine."

Guy wondered whom he meant by "us." He breathed in Jeremy's aftershave. The man's grip was meant to comfort him, but it felt theatrical, as if the physical connection was itself disconnected from any real physicality. Lightly menacing too, how it pinned Guy down. Reinforced his flayed volition.

"I'm headed back to the tower," Jeremy said. "Are you joining Search and Rescue?"

He would. Had to. The very visible husband of Victoria Stevens? He must be there. To look pained. To worry, on-site.

He attempted to stand, couldn't, and accepted his intractable mass.

"Mm," Guy said.

"Sorted. Wheels up at seven." Jeremy stood up. "And if the press contacts you—which they shouldn't, if Comms gets on top of this—give the Glomar response: you can neither confirm nor deny, etc., etc." He walked to the fridge and closed its door, then seemed to hear the Rorem for the first time. The playlist had moved to an organ rondo.

The necessary breakthroughs did not occur within the expected or justifiable life cycle of the product.

"Why now?" Guy asked.

"Why now what? The accident? I'm with you there—nothing

Victoria does is accidental." Jeremy pocketed another Post-it; Guy thought he saw a drawing of a cactus. "I suppose she'd want you to know. Someone leaked the fake cure to ProPublica."

More than betrayal. Utter collapse.

Jeremy continued with discomforting equanimity. "This hack Berkheimer'll break the news Monday. Probably Monday." He showed Guy an email on his phone. A fact-checker asking about PrevYou's $1.52 billion in investment, the four thousand medical booths, how much of the Stevens Family Foundation's endowment was comprised of investor capital . . . and then his own name, in naked sans serif.

Jeremy then reread the email himself. "So we have three days to find Victoria and—"

"Right the ship. Can't you give the usual defense? Hearsay, bitter ex-employees, all that."

"Doesn't work with a missing CEO. And they have internal documentation, a ton of sources. Elena's lab reports. Not even the legal might of his holiness David Boies can save us." He caught himself. "Don't tell Victoria I said that."

Guy felt cleaved. Guillotined and basketed.

Jeremy paced the living room, predicting FDA and SEC investigations, mass defections, board revolt—the stuff of C-suite nightmares. Guy opened the app for their properties and swiped through the camera feeds. The Aspen ski-in/ski-out A-frame. The Hudson Valley acreage. The Mayfair pied-à-terre. All empty and lonely. Even the last feed, a bird's-eye view of his huddled self and Jeremy's yo-yoing about.

Guy heard something about frozen assets.

"The Foundation's too," Jeremy said. "It's a charity, but it's still a tax dodge. Only temporary. Victoria will solve all of this. Meanwhile, dip into your liquidity."

The acid spread into his chest. Numbness in both arms. "I think I'm having a cardiac event."

"You're not. Calm down. What are you, fifty?"

"Sixty-three," Guy said.

"Americans are living longer, richer lives all the time. Many paths are open." He drummed his fingers on his stomach. "Okay. Expect a statement from Comms." He crouched again to Guy's level. "It's an unenviable position, but not a wholly untenable one."

Guy exhaled. Thick air pricked every inch of his skin. As a teenager he'd been fascinated by a Midwest chain of dry cleaners promising "one hour martinizing," a process he fantasized as expensive and brutal. That was how he felt: martinized by the universe.

Jeremy swiveled and rose in one elegant motion, then walked to the elevator. "Remember, Teterboro at seven. I'll meet you out west."

Guy found he could stand, found his legs taking him to the rooftop, found his hand dialing V's phone. Straight to voice mail. He dialed again.

How could she? But that wasn't the right question. It wasn't how, but why. The unknown why encompassed all that he didn't know, an exponentially growing known unknown. The unknown why was one of those hyperobjects he'd heard about at some gala presentation. It was like climate change, something so large and inchoate one couldn't process its scope. He couldn't remember what this meant for humanity, but it felt right: V was a hyperobject.

As for him, these revelations detonated whatever certainty he may have had about himself—which, he always thought, was a serviceable amount, given his general incuriosity—not to mention detonating his sense of the past and his plans for the future. It was all too much and beyond his control. So yes, he too was a hyperobject.

He paused on the landing in front of her exercise bike. He may not know her as well as he thought, but she certainly knew him. She knew he would deafen himself to the cacophony of all this. She had likely plotted his next forty-eight hours; despite all, there was a perverse comfort in being predictable.

The screen highlighted shots of her most recent ride. A bridge under early evening skies. Red pillars, support cables swooping past like angel's wings. Endless ocean below and a metropolitan skyline to the left. Green hills in the distance. The Golden Gate. The camera looked down at the white-caps and the surprisingly strong current. She would have storyboarded it. Checked the tide charts. Gone on dry runs. Stowed a getaway car on the opposite shore. And then? Where would she go?

V was out there, somewhere, and without a trace of regret. She was the least introspective person he'd ever met. Least ret-rospective, too: Victoria Stevens had no use for the past. She directed her entire being toward enfolding the present into the future, a tangible future she alone could grasp. Nothing metaphysical, but real, and right there.

And yet. Maybe nothing so nefarious. A little kayaking to clear her head. A plan to make it right, to tell Guy about the fraud. They'd been through so much. They could weather this. Surely. Then a rogue wave far from shore. Panic. Shame. Thoughts of Guy. More shame. Darkness.

The screen recited her stats. Some Olympian told V she was "on fire." Guy retched.

Come Monday everyone would assume he had been in on it. How could he not be a party to such malfeasance? How could he suspect nothing from his side of the marital bed? Only a fool would be so hoodwinked, and Guy had taken great care not to appear foolish. Sure, he'd once confused Royal Ascot for men's neckwear. And he'd once criticized private equity in mixed company. How he wished for one brazen public gaffe, something exculpatory he could point to and say, "See? I was an idiot! Of course I didn't know what was going on."

Alas. Come Monday his past actions and the actions he took herein and henceforth would be interpreted ex post facto as a finger in the eye of every one of PrevYou's victims—*her* victims—as well as a general finger in the eye of the public.

Once word got out. So many words would follow: Coconspirator. Defendant. Pariah.

Guy felt his entire life in his bladder. It felt punitive.

What he needed was movement. At this second and inside this second. Movement and aimlessness. He wrapped himself in a trench coat, descended to the lobby, ignored the doorman's greeting, and turned east.

The Stevens Foundation. That would be scuttled. Naturally: the charitable arm of one's wealth depended upon the existence of wealth; a percentage of zero was still zero. But he could tell the staff. Give them a head start. It was about all he could provide, gift-wise, in his newly reduced pecuniary circumstance.

Or, not yet. Not just yet. Jeremy's talent for secrecy rivaled the Manhattan Project—clearly—so only a few people knew of her disappearance. And the moment Guy told his staff, an avalanche of hysterical, all-caps censure would follow. He wasn't ready for all that. Queue it behind the other terrible truths he'd have to eventually internalize.

A fire truck sped past, taxis in its wake trying to make the light. He zigzagged south, then east again, into the center of the island. Tomorrow he'd wander a patch of San Francisco Bay while scuba teams looked for a body they'd never find. Or worse: a body they would find.

He could guess what V would say right now. The great empiricist. Did he have to internalize? Must he process? Guy questioned the short-term benefits, refused to indulge long-term thinking. Roadblocking his ability to understand might be the simpler, greater act of self-protection.

He could hole up in the penthouse. Embrace denial. What followed denial? Anger? Anger sounded good too. He could toggle between anger and denial. Wait for V to glance over the parapet.

Columbus Circle. He'd walked the last block with his eyes closed. The city surged, even at this late hour. A hi-vis cordon of rollerbladers flowed around a whistling delivery man in the bike lane. Japanese youths tittered over an inside joke. Horses on standby, an earthy fecundity below. The percussive sounds of a teen stubbornly ramming a Citi Bike into a broken dock.

And at the park entrance: a PrevYou booth. One of a couple hundred in the city. The bulb over its door lit up, and a white-haired woman exited to join a tourist group in matching fanny packs. He approached and his organs vibrated, as if magnetically attracted or repelled by the booth itself. In his hand he discovered a bottle of Japanese whisky; must have toted it from home.

He hovered his executive access card over a pad bearing the slogan "Preview your new life," and the door slid open. He clinked the Super Nikka against the doorway in consecration and helped himself to a large mouthful.

The hardware engineers nicknamed them Bessies, as in, "We need to lose ten kilos off the next round of Bessies." He didn't get the bovine reference; the booths looked to him like a shrunken bouncy house, or maybe those public toilets in Shibuya. V insisted they be rounded on all sides; "right angles connoted severity." PrevYou was warm, nonjudgmental. She'd hired aeronautics designers, reasoning that they were special-ists in rounded interiors who'd also been trained to futurecast design trends by the long lead times of jet production. The finishing touch came from an end-of-meeting suggestion by an unpaid intern: Why not paint each booth to match the dominant color palette of its neighborhood? This small detail contributed to the booths' reception as in situ miracles of pre-ventative health.

V promoted the intern on the spot, fulfilling her long-held wish of replicating a possibly apocryphal story about

Walt Disney, who, shortly before opening his first theme park, personally demonstrated the rides for the operators and employees. Seeking feedback about the Pirates of the Caribbean, a fresh-faced youth with a Creole drawl raised a hand to say the set lacked the authentic fixture of every Louisiana twilight: lightning bugs. Disney took the note and elevated the boy to corporate. Or something like that. The story provided color to V's fundraising pitches, and she was known to embellish.

At least Disney delivered on his promise. The Bessies scattered across North America and Western Europe still performed their battery of robotics-assisted examinations, but their greater purpose was now entirely vestigial.

He entered the womb-like chamber and ignored the voice prompts. No, he didn't wish to monitor his glucose, biopsy a mole, or receive a mammogram. He ran his fingers over the wall panels. Inhaled the lemony scent, the bottom note of Lysol. An ideogram display praised the benefits of regular prostate checkups.

What had Jeremy said? *Many paths are open.* Not for Guy Sarvananthan. The assets were in her name; lawsuits would take everything else. He might have stashed some art in a freeport. That would have been prudent. Or watches. They traveled well, could be pawned for a couple million.

He was retirement age, with a bad ticker, no professional skills, and, any moment now, toxic search results. Caught in the storm sans umbrella. Or life raft.

Teach piano again? There was a galling thought. He could return to that Philadelphia shitbox, adopt another skeptical Tabby. Drum up tutees through the alumni network.

Composing was out of the question: his last commission was a partita for voice, never finished and nominally about Y2K.

Maybe take the Amtrak to the middle of nowhere. Play dueling pianos in some third-tier city. Somebody would recognize him eventually. He fantasized other lives, the years and decades, highlight reels of America's frenzied self-hypnotic. Every scenario bent itself into a Möbius strip. There was no forward for him, not anymore.

Fuck, Victoria. You really left me with nothing.

He drank more whisky and pressed buttons until a bench extended from the wall. He could lie here as long as he liked; his access card would override the time delimiters.

A sheet of paper taped to the ceiling informed him that Dan Smith would like to teach him guitar. He watched its soft fluttering, listened to the park's hawked wares and strangers' laughter. Some of the whisky escaped his mouth and spilled down his face. He focused on the sensation of its journey.

• • •

THIS. THIS WAS the ideal zone, the twilight between sleep and waking. If he could only exist in this zone forever.

He sat up and tested his hangover. Not terrible. Low fogginess, a balance just out of true. Sweat on his neck and face. He should have tried harder last night. An upended life demanded strenuous bludgeoning.

His belly yawped, and he tongued scarred cheek meat. Spat thickly on the composite flooring. Thunderclouds massed under the wobbling yolk's silky membrane like a tardy portent. *Tardy.*

Guy checked his watch. Only an hour late; the plane wouldn't leave without him. They couldn't, not really. The bayside presser needed its husbandly window dressing.

The thought of flying three thousand miles to fake a search party produced another thought of V, who was most decidedly not there, and this thought produced a one-second supercut of Thursday evening.

He fell out of the booth and stumbled before regaining his footing. The aluminum frame of a hot dog cart caught the morning sun and temporarily blinded him. He needed extirpation, a righting of wrongs, or even a wronging of wrongs. Guy beelined to the cart and interrupted the vendor's reprimand of ambivalent pigeons.

"Hey. How much for the water?"

"Bottled water, five dollars."

"No." Guy pointed at the tureen full of dancing wieners. "The hot dog water. How much."

"Bottled water, soda, hot dogs, chips. Can't sell the water."

Guy pulled out his wallet. "Listen. I'm going to give you . . . eleven hundred dollars, and you're going to give me that tub of hot dog water. And pot holders if you have them. I'm not even going to keep the tub, I just need the water. You'll get it back in a minute."

The vendor assessed Guy and tonged the wieners. "Plus thirty-four. I'll have to toss these."

"Eleven hundred dollars. They're a sunk cost."

"Deal."

The vendor gave him a wad of napkins to hold the bin. They absorbed the condensation and warmed his palms. Guy returned to the booth, balanced the tub on his leg, and res-canned his card. His thigh scorched through the fabric, but he was above pain now, focused and purposeful. The pocket door slid open. Remembering to lift with his back, Guy took one step in and hurled the steaming water onto the readout screens. A pleasant glitching commenced; the loosed hot dogs bounced dumbly.

A scrum of German pensioners stared and reached for their phones. He pointed a thumb at the booth and the odor of burning plastic.

"*Alles gut*," he said.

He returned the empty tub, true to his word, and felt it wise to leave the scene. Vandalized booths automatically alerted the local authorities.

Guy didn't feel better, but he felt different, if only for the moment. He redialed V, ignored the panicked messages from his money manager. Let the rumor mill churn. The truth was so much worse. His phone dinged: a *Forbes* alert on the Cost of Living Extremely Well Index. He returned the phone to his pocket. No prepper's hideaway in Auckland for him. Not anymore.

He halted outside his building. There was nothing for him in California. V would be found when she was ready to be found. Or, though, although, however . . . He banished the alternative from his thoughts.

He could opt out. Why should she be the only one? If the public wanted to tar and feather him, let them settle for the corpse. As for posterity, this was the Anthropocene. Clima-tologists gave posterity a fifty-fifty chance of survival.

His doorman ignored his appearance and greeted him warmly. Guy handed him the whisky bottle and patted his shoulder. As the elevator made its silent ascent, Guy whispered, "I'm finished," then repeated it as a consoling dictum.

But it wasn't true. V's actions denied him an ending. The final act of the opera *Guy Sarvananthan*, an American rags-to-riches tale for the ages, cut short by philistine arsonists. He'd been abridged on a primal level, as if his very thoughts were. Never again would he complete a. He was full of. V, his V, a true.

He ran his hand along the corridor, sweeping the Post-its from the wall, and stood in the empty living room. His life had been measured and found wanting. What was left, then, but to run a bath and open a vein? When he considered it, when he broke it down—step one, step two—lassitude crept in, like the adolescent ability to render the smallest chore a herculean effort. People weaker than him killed themselves all the time. How did they do it? Did the decision produce the resilience to follow through, or was it something more innate? He supposed this was one of those moments when one was put on their mettle. He felt instead a great absence. This confirmed the troubling fact that, alongside his failures as a husband and as a composer, he was not the suicidal type.

He circled the first floor, then wandered into his office. The smallest room in the place. He nodded at the vinyl collection. His Curtis degree. A wedding photo on the desk.

The sword drew his attention. He removed it from the wall mount. Despite the spotting on its blade, the ceremonial piece was damned impressive, with an ornate hilt and, resting below it, a dark brown scabbard with gold filigree. A faded inscription near the mount noted Queen Elizabeth had bestowed it upon his father in 1954, during the optimistic era of the man's military career and two decades before their emigration.

He shuffled to the living room and dropped the sword on the sectional. Perhaps he needed a slow farewell. With prorated toxins Trojan horsed by pleasure-inducing drink and drug. Yes, Guy thought, as he nudged V's laptop off the coffee table with his foot. The sybaritic route. A fire hose of serotonin to combat his grief.

Because he was grieving. A widower in spirit, if not the letter. Or perhaps not grief alone. Looking around the penthouse, he detected a new sensation: good old sphincter-tightening hatred. Clean and free of nuance. Grief was a process, hatred all childish simplicity. No wonder bigots had such confidence. Hatred shuffled aside higher-order thinking and provided a sense of purpose. He would exit on his own terms, in high neon.

The terms, the terms . . . he could bathe in the milk of human kindness, be it proffered, purchased, or rented. Rub elbows and brush shoulders—other points of contact too. The question was where. New York had everything, an ideal spot for locavore suicide. He went to the kitchen and idly separated bananas from their stems. The open cleaving resembled a shorn iceberg. He peeled one and explored the furrowed underside of the pliant skin. Pressed tongue to fruit. There was no taste, just texture.

Guy brought up their shared calendar on his phone. Her team hadn't yet cleared her appointments, which were color-coded according to an indiscernible methodology. In dark purple: Arthur Averman's Quorum.

The Quorum. Three days on a private Caribbean island, surrounded by his people. The perfect setting for a final hurrah. Averman expected Victoria, but surely Guy could attend in her stead. And the PrevYou jet could deliver him by happy hour.

CHAPTER 2

When Neil Armstrong placed his hand on the door lock of the lunar module and looked to Buzz Aldrin with a "here goes nothing" expression, while that third guy, the backbencher whose name nobody remembers, lolled in the orbiting shuttle—at that moment ProPublica would get the mission canceled.

PrevYou is finished. And a mere three months from the breakthrough. Six at most.

Millions will die of cancer—that's on ProPublica. The blood is on their hands, on their home pages.

All I ever wanted to do was help people.

Jeremy will know what to do. Keep the wolves at the door. Free up cash for the legal defense fund. The old smoke, the old mirrors.

Maybe offload the Bessies to J&J? They'd love the revenue stream. Selling the dip will hurt, but optionality is compromised.

The cabin will suffice. Its back porch abuts the park. Might even be within its borders. What's the word—grandfathered.

Grandfathered into the public land, like those resettlement fetishists outside Jackson Hole. The back-to-the-landers in Central Maine.

I could look it up, but no. No phone or laptop until the next eureka.

How likely is another one? Answer: as likely as I determine. I have the tools and the ability. This, whatever it is, it's a setback. Eureka waits on the other side of a fixed number of thoughts. Within the Zone of Utmost Throb.

Commit your energies, Stevens. You are sharp of mind and fantastically anabolic. Focused in a land of focus. A land for "cathexis," as Big Mike would say.

Can't they see the work was for them? That it was all an immense act of generosity?

I will be pilloried in the commons. A humbling. Something to be wrenched for pathos in the biopic.

And yet. An opportunity. *The* opportunity.

There is nothing Victoria Stevens cannot bear.

The A.M. run was passable. Sunrise two minutes later than the almanac said, so I waited on the porch for the sky to lighten enough to see the road. It's a vista of open nothing.

Two minutes was not enough to review yesterday's Post-its, so I drank another sixteen ounces of magnesium water and loosened my ankles. Wrote my name in the air with my big toe. Something about the air affects the joints, though that could be age.

The sunrise took forever. Once that yellow band crested the ridgeline I set off. The cold dissipated by mile three. My right outstep needs work. Plus there are fewer than a hundred miles left in the shoes. Get the boy to order a new pair.

The road is still unforgiving. Like running on hardpack— no bounce at all. But I stay between the ruts of the tire tracks. I can guarantee an efficient line. Plus the ruts force me to pay attention. A sprain would be lethal.

And if I did die? Everyone would claim suicide, given the eleven-figure write-down and the imminent dissolution of a company once called "a unicorn's unicorn" by Kara Swisher. But that is what objective observers do. They speculate while others accomplish.

The line between the ruts creates a nominal buffer from the humped earth on either side. The boy said rattlers hide there. He also said to avoid any snakes with diamonds on their heads.

The boy's a Joshua Tree native. He loitered after the grocery delivery enumerating all the tourist deaths over the years. Watch out for the flash floods, he said. A sudden wall of water, strong enough to carry boulders in the current. Get to high ground or you're fucked.

The most common cause is the simplest: people get lost. The desert swallowed hikers with a primitive regularity. The park service's much-touted Lost Person Behavior algorithms only go so far. It's a scalability problem. You try locating a delirious and dehydrated pin in a haystack the size of Rhode Island.

While the boy ticked off other dangers—he fixated on the varieties of scorpion—I thought of the Quick Shop at the end of the road. Its corkboard near the carts festooned with missing persons flyers. Plus a few hand-drawn invites to jam sessions and "second-wave" ayahuasca ceremonies.

A nice shorthand for this place: find yourself, or wander off and die.

The boy's name is Juan. Probably twenty.

The run. I kept to the plan, turning back after expending two-thirds of my energy. But I'm still gauging my levels at this elevation. Ideally I would strain myself in the last mile and nearly die making the cabin. Ideally very nearly die. I will learn the signals of near-death, and then ignore them. Remember what Coach Adams said: physical limits are actually mental limits. The brain's governor tells the body to stop well before it should. An act of self-preservation. And nothing more than the mind getting in its own way. Push past it.

(Father hated this philosophy. Said a Calvinist shouldn't be teaching high school students cross-country. But he overindulged all of *his* governors, so what did he know.)

The lactic acid and the wobblies hit around mile fourteen. Pace slowed—I won't break my PR out here. Remember the goal is distance, not speed. Or, not distance: exhaustion.

Difficulty around mile fifteen—reverted to ball-to-heel. Coach Adams wouldn't approve. Invoked a visualization exercise: the ground as lake surface, dipping my forefoot, finding it too cold and retracting quickly.

Positive results.

I always liked the name "cross-country." Marking fresh dominion, step by step.

Legs gave out thirty yards from porch. Crawled to the outdoor shower. Acceptable nipple chafing. The thermometer read ninety-one.

Exhaustion is only part of the goal. The goal is attaining the Zone of Utmost Throb. Where all constraints fall away. The considerations of everyday life, everymonth life, everyyear life—they fall away too. Only then will eureka occur.

Drank the recovery drink. Ate the toast. Wrote out daily list of fears. Added "iatrogenesis," crossed it out. The unforeseen long-term problems of the breakthrough are no longer a concern.

Habits persist. Without Mai Ling's A.M. readout of the overnight social posts—the waterfall of "cunt" and "bitch" and other first thought/best thought ripostes to my latest public statements—there was a noticeable 8 A.M. sluggishness. Additional matcha required.

This diary seems to help. I will keep at it until eureka. At the close of day I will burn the index cards. A record of the present, then, and only a record of the present.

A.M. session:
6 in clarity
5 in productivity

8 in focus

No migraines

Stacked the tchotchkes and the armchairs and Jeremy's family photos in the indoor shower. I should perform another sweep and clear out any objects that might distract from eureka. Jeremy framed my first *TIME* cover, the one with that terrible headline—JOAN OF SALK. People should know better. Sainthood dooms.

Also: hide the board games. The Navajo blanket. Keep the dartboard and the sudoku book.

Don't falter. You don't need consultants. You don't need blue flame thinkers, or new white papers, or adaptive methodologies.

During A.M. break I browsed an old issue of *NatGeo*. Surreal to see advertisements—when was the last time I encountered one.

Learned of stotting gazelles, who jump high when they sense predators nearby. The predators were not identified—maybe leopards—and the jumping stumped evolutionary biologists. Why advertise your presence to your enemies.

A.M. break included twenty minutes of calisthenics and pelvic floor stretches. The upper back needs work. Send the boy to get a foam roller.

Forgot to mark today's turnaround point: a pile of lichen-covered boulders ten yards east of the road. Maybe a half mile past the teddy bear cholla. (The Deep Time aspect of the desert is a little unnerving, but the lack of change makes for handy markers.)

The boy dropped off groceries before P.M. session. Still feels odd to handle cash. Juan needs no encouragement to talk: he shared local gossip while he filled the pantry. He says his income derives from managing vacation properties; I imagine it's drug dealing. (Declined offers of DMT.)

He is a lonely person, but he doesn't realize it. His friends went to UC schools or found employment in Palm Springs. When I mentioned the Foundation's scholarship program for BIPOC youth he parroted some Bax line about the "the multilevel marketing of postsecondary ed."

I haven't recorded how we met. He stands out in his cowboy getup. So unlike the tank-topped hoi polloi who'd pull up stakes if they could afford the Greyhound. He appears to spend his evenings doing circuits of the neighborhood and performing lasso tricks while heavily stoned. An ideal gopher.

He's unintelligent, but observant. When I proposed the compact he asked if I was important. I told him about PrevYou and our mission.

He gave the standard reply: his aunt died of breast cancer. I waited for him to connect the dots, but had to tell him yes, everyone has an aunt who died of breast cancer. That's why I'm important.

He narrates his life. Storing the foodstuffs, he'd say, "This bulgur's the best," or "These strawberries have been tasting great lately." (I explained he meant flavor, not taste. It's their scent he was remarking upon. He asked about the bananas, but I changed the subject.)

We sat on the porch afterward. When I remarked on the welcome quietude, he said low-flying planes used to buzz the town and annoy everyone. Military flight paths, since redrawn.

He asked to Bluetooth his DJ mix, but I declined. The silence is generative.

He indicated the columns of Post-its and asked what I was working on. I asked if he knew the name of the man who broke the sound barrier. He ID'd Chuck Yeager. Then I asked him if he knew who the first commercial pilot was. He said he didn't know. I said, "Exactly." Unsure if he understood.

Few people seek the nexus of high ambition and higher risk, and even fewer have the competency. It's not about flying a plane. People had been flying for half a century before Yeager. It's about being the first to exceed what had been previously thought the limit of human potential.

Juan talked about his future plans, none of which are worth transcribing. Seems happy to continue as a human ellipsis.

He asked where I was born, so I told him the map story.

At ten years old I pulled the local Rand McNally from our meager home library and did what everyone does: I looked up my house. There was a moiré red dot over Tacoma's north end, almost exactly over our address. The map legend didn't explain it, so I asked Mother. She informed me this was an intentional printing error by the publisher: If the dot appeared in competitors' maps, they could sue for plagiarism. (She meant copyright infringement, but the point stands.)

A giant corporation decided my neighborhood could be completely obscured. A nondestination. Certainly a place worth leaving for a young girl who felt capable of more.

The boy gave a suitably mind-blown response. I didn't tell him Big Mike's reply to the story, from our first coaching session. He said I was misreading the anecdote. Think of it as a gloss on the Napoleon myth. Where the future emperor was birthed on a rug depicting the conquests of Caesar, Rand McNally had selected my childhood home—of all of the streets in the US—as the site of their bona fide.

I wish Big Mike was here. I was fortunate to receive his counsel at all, after his hot streak coaching Jack, Sheryl, and Reed. Put off retirement just for me. Sure, he dressed like a nine-hole duffer, charged an unconscionable block of shares, didn't say shit for the first session apart from "Go on" and "Why."

That one session, just working on posture: "Keep your head immobile. Project assurance. Project finality." Something about West Point cadets not being allowed to look down while they ate. Or was that Annapolis.

The weekend intensives. "Narrativizing" random episodes from my past into a coherent upward arc. Repeating the arc like a prayer. Memorizing it. This was the first success brick in the PrevYou foundation.

(And not without cost. On my annual visit to Truckee, Daniel said he caught my *60 Minutes* segment. The parasailing anecdote had happened to *him*; Father thought I was too small for the harness. What other parts of my biography are not my own.)

Daniel always extolled the off-grid life.

Guy would hate this. I wonder what he's doing at this moment. Reeling, yes. Wallowing, yes. He'll take all this much too personally. Treating the end of his world like the end of *the* world.

That's fine. Complacency weakens the spirit. He could use getting his bell rung. I don't expect heroics—he's not the type. Anything other than his usual resignation.

Just being alive in America, every day you have a one in a million chance of dying from unnatural causes. My runs increase the chances tenfold. Still fractional and easily dismissed. Then add in the other factors. Heat. Exhaustion. Lack of emergency services.

If you're going to push forward and travel where nobody else will, you have to ignore these thoughts. Knowing what to ignore was an underrated success brick. And it's key to entering the Zone of Utmost Throb.

CHAPTER 3

He took in air. Compared to Manhattan's concrete sentries, Averman's island was a state of nature. Or, relatively: They'd landed on a fresh tarmac carved out of the jungle and skirted by a comically long hangar. To the left, rows of idling Jeeps. Above, a sky the size of a sky. And all around, an atmosphere rehabilitated with newborn oxygen.

This felt right. Nobody here would know his circumstances, not fully. He'd sent Averman the barest outline of V's disappearance. There would be perfunctory inquiries, a show of bereavement—*To lose one's wife! So suddenly! And not just any wife, but Victoria Stevens!*—and then Guy would be given room to fully embrace his denial. He'd carouse and collapse; they'd look the other way.

The Quorum: a punctuation to his misspent life. He would enact a prohibition against self-awareness, against awareness of any kind. Guy would exist simply. And then, after public revelations forfeited the simple existence, he would exit simply as well.

He waited on the airstairs as the pilot collected his bags. He inhaled again, as deeply as his phlegmatic respiration allowed, stopping at the wet rattle in the lower throat.

A simple existence required discipline. To live without thought was challenging enough; add rigorous self-sabotage and you court failure. But he'd been firsthand witness to the continual challenging of the limits of human capacity. V said it was a matter of wherewithal. And while he lacked her brains and brio, he could imitate her unyielding will.

Oh. A glandular swell under the jaw. He turned and voided onto the black airstrip. It was improbably milky and—good news—free of blood.

A rude moue from the pilot. Uncalled for, really. Guy was so obviously a wreck, so obviously freshly upended, one would think a little sympathy was in order. The pilot had that exsanguinated Gaelic look; maybe a proverb from the old country? But no. He just bent forward to check if the vomitus had spotted the plane. Guy returned to the cabin, gargled vodka from the galley, spit, realized he still could still taste yesterday, and took a quick, bracing pull.

The pilot waited near the cabin door. "I'm to return Monday at sixteen hundred hours, sir?"

"Let's take things one hour at a time."

The pilot stifled a look and returned to the cockpit. Guy filled his hip flask and tried the stairs again, with good results. Someone had already loaded his luggage in one of the Jeeps. Two sun-kissed youths approached, both clad in teal jumpsuits—Averman Teal, which he'd paid Pantone an undisclosed sum to invent. The boy and girl radiated possibility.

"Mr. Stevens, Arthur Averman welcomes you to the Quorum," they said in unison.

"Mr. Sarvananthan," Guy corrected.

"Of course," the girl said. "Allow us to escort you to your vehicle."

A quiet frenzy of staff, security, and ground crew conferred in the hangar. There had been a miscommunication, it seemed, or possibly several. The bodyguards kept pointing to rows of cots in the corner. And near the Jeeps, a naked Bennett Benatti, waving hello and performing light stretches. Guy waved back and, for some reason, gave a thumbs-up. A trio of Averman's staff waited on the luxury automotive heir, holding a white towel, a garment bag, and black espadrilles. Benatti finished his routine and dressed as Guy approached.

"I expected your lovely wife," Benatti said.

"Indisposed. You're stuck with me," Guy replied.

Benatti left his shirt half-buttoned to display his tattoos of Old Masters facsimiles from the family collection. Probably the only heir at the Quorum, Guy thought. Most were incredibly conservative, loathe to donate a penny more than what was expedient taxwise. Whereas one-percenter transgression was Benatti's raison d'être.

He opened a gold cigarette case. Guy motioned for a smoke.

"Not stuck with you," Benatti said. "All due respect, your wife is super boring. Work, work, work. You I like. We will cavort? Maybe 'solve global problems.'"

"I don't want to think about any problems," Guy said. He took a slow drag. Like licking the books of God's library. "My goal is ruinous intake."

The glowing youths directed them to a pedestal with a tray of amuse-bouche, explaining the clear liquid was Averman's concoction for "post-flight refreshment with infusions to stimulate focus." Guy passed; Benatti drank two.

Guy pointed his head toward the huddle of personnel. "More frantic than I expected."

"Everyone's arriving now," Benatti said. "Arthur wanted to stagger us, but we come when we come, no?"

Benatti put on a white linen blazer, then slid a leather driving glove onto his right hand. Guy likened the affectation to men who got a single earring when they hit fifty.

He couldn't recall the last time he'd driven. His license expired ages ago.

Jeeps arrived as others departed, carrying Quorumites one by one to the main compound. The drivers, much like the rest of the jumpsuited employees, seemed culled from the lacrosse fields of the Ivy League.

The girl gestured toward another pedestal, with markers and sheets of paper. She explained they were to write a one-word reply to the sentence *Humanity is _____*. Guy's honest answer wouldn't do. He went with *afflicted*; Benatti drew an exclamation point.

"Excellent," she said. "Now Mr. Averman would like you to peel the sticker and wear your response on your chest. This ritual will—"

"Forgive me," Benatti interrupted. "But we do not wear stickers."

The girl retained her smile and directed them to their Jeeps. Benatti tossed his cigarette and Guy did the same.

"Let's ride together," Benatti said. "I'll take front."

Guy climbed in while the driver radioed to someone at the compound. The legroom was lacking, which would normally annoy him, but the nicotine bloom kept his spirits up.

They careened down a red-dirt path barely wider than the vehicle and flanked by squat palm trees. Robust jungle left only a column of sky; Guy saw the next wave of circling Quorumites, awaiting permission to land. How big was this gathering? A hundred? Two hundred?

Benatti was talking about his new girlfriend and angling his phone toward Guy. Intimate selfies from what's-her-name, *The Voice* winner whose repertoire consisted solely of the last couplet of "The Star-Spangled Banner." Lifelong bachelors liked to share these updates with Guy, as if seeking approval.

When did he and V last fuck? A month ago? Now it would be their last fuck, as in never again. She might have warned him. One final romp, with their repertoire of gags and friendly edging. V disarmed utterly during sex (or he believed she did), her grunting chromatic and unselfconscious. He knew the spots: visit the clavicle, avoid the hip bone, hum down the perineum. She would tap his shoulder to advance to the next position and, almost without fail, orgasm with three large shudders. Their circuit lacked variety but never rose to the level of complaint.

Which didn't mean much now. Their plateau was, in fact, a slow decline—easy to mistake when your schedules so rarely overlapped. With her work, travel, and general single-minded-ness, what might be an evening's conversation for others took them weeks.

"Do you smell that?" Benatti asked. "Lavender. That can't be natural here."

"Mosquito repellent," the driver said. "Mr. Averman dusted half the island."

Guy noticed stitched letters across the shoulders of Benatti's jacket, also in white: "Mistakes Will Be Made." The new slogan for a Rome-based periodical he'd recently purchased. Guy coveted the sartorial subtitle.

He moved to inspect himself in the driver's rearview. Must be presentable, up to a point. Guy's hair, teeth, and skin still advertised his access to the best products and methods. Nothing could be done about the eyes. The past twenty-four hours had accelerated the discoloration, as if he'd smeared camouflage around them.

The past twenty-four hours. Christ.

The Cucinelli polo couldn't do anything about the paunch, but it artfully hid the love handles which continually flummoxed his personal trainer. They were something of a birthright: Sarvananthan men, though blessed with good hair and high metabolism, could neither figuratively or literally outrun the soft middle of middle age.

His body was aging faster now. It knew the money was gone and the jig was up. They said fame arrested one's maturity at whatever age the person broke through; with sudden fortune it was one age's that became cast in amber. He had looked fifty since the First Flush. No longer. He rolled his head on the swivel of his neck. Today he would age a lifetime.

"Are you ready to do the most good? Are you ready to finalize your legacy?"

Averman's voice—from where? The questions repeated with the same inflection.

"Speakers, hidden in the brush," Benatti said. "He does the same thing at his companies."

The driver made a joke in Italian to Benatti, possibly about soccer, and they were soon debating something of grave importance in Turin. Guy concentrated on not sweating out the booze.

The Quorum was a fitting last fête—he'd met Averman at his first one. A fundraiser for the Central Park Conservancy. Back then Averman was like an avuncular mentor, despite their proximity in age. V had setup the Foundation and told Guy his job, more or less, was to solo navigate the circuit. Be a face. Charm, smile. Learn the unwritten rules.

Guy had thought the Curtis Institute's black-ties would be adequate training for the gala crowd, but he was quickly at sea. How did one stand at these things? Was he just supposed to walk up to random people and introduce himself? Then a tanned and toned arm interlocked with his, an arm belonging to a magnificently coiffed Australian beaming with naked gusto. Guy later learned Averman fed this state through adrenaline-spiked family outings with a cadre of X Games athletes; he'd just completed two weeks in a self-made sloop up the Amazon. Averman had a vague and modest idea of himself as a legendary figure—common enough among Guy's new cohort—reinforced by the man's inability to simply *be*. The world was a sleeping bear he couldn't resist poking.

Averman's attitude immediately calmed Guy's nerves. As did the zoological tour Averman launched into, pointing to a redhead in a white caftan gesticulating wildly inside a circle also in white caftans. "That's Petra Bax, libertarian blowhard extraordinaire. Who knows why God gave her money. Like a baby with a handgun." Though Averman hadn't lived in Sydney for decades, his voice retained the wide accent of the antipodes. "And never go to one of her 'summits.' People quoting the Federalist Papers and talking about century rides on their trail bikes." He nodded toward a lounge filled with people in aggressively experimental clothing. "The young heirs. They're intellectually lazy, humorless, and indiscreet." He winced; Guy silently hypothesized an extramarital misstep. "High statistical likelihood of squandering the family fortune and whiling away their dotage in the pool houses of distant cousins."

Averman never picked up on Guy's intellectual laziness, which surprised him. Guy thought it fairly apparent. He never saw the benefit of growing as a person and long suspected its alleged correlation with success—a skepticism reinforced by V's rise and the First Flush. The only real shift in his beliefs was the inevitable one, that their largesse was preternatural, which happened to match everyone else's outlook in their rarefied orbit. He acknowledged that sure, the people who would correct him on this matter were incentivized not to by his ability to disperse capital their way. Stipulated. But his conviction held: he had become the person he was always meant to be.

Until.

"Are you ready . . . ?" Another Averman recording Dopplered by.

Guy unconsciously checked his phone and startled at the

waterfall of Jeremy's messages. His brain would not allow itself to cohere the letters into words and the words into meaning. He pocketed the phone, then unpocketed it. Thought of V's cold dispatch.

He should send a final text. Something curt and wounding. She'd expect some transliterated sobbing, a witching-hour accusation or two. His thumb absently tapped the screen while he considered the spectrum of replies. Every one of them expected and ineffectual. He checked the screen; his thumb had typed a string of Fs, Gs, Hs. He cleared them out. There was nothing to write.

He cocked his arm to throw the phone, then stopped and tapped out a message to the Foundation staff. Why not.

> *You should all find new jobs. By Monday, if possible.*
> *No time to explain.*
> *Be good,*
> *G. S.*

He hit send and flicked the phone into the deep green. The driver noticed and didn't react. What a professional. Auspicious for the days ahead. Alive, Guy felt alive.

They passed a faux-weathered sign welcoming them to ARTHUR'S FOLLY. To Guy's knowledge the name had never stuck, even after Averman commissioned a Netflix travel series on the island. It sounded more befitting a pontoon than a Xanadu—you shouldn't be cheeky with your private Eden. They slowed behind a line of idling vehicles. After ten seconds Benatti exited the Jeep.

"We must be around the corner," he said. "Let them sort this out."

Guy nodded at the driver and followed suit. Benatti's instincts were shared by the other Quorumites: every Jeep was similarly empty, save for luggage and Styrofoam coolers. They walked the bend and the road widened to a circular drive with a blue-tiled fountain, chatting Quorumites, and their host, perhaps fifteen feet up in a shining scissor lift. Guy recognized about half the crowd. Mostly American, maybe a dozen women.

Averman bullhorned in their direction. "And now we have Mr. Guy Sarvananthan and Mr. Bennet Benatti! Welcome, gentlemen!" He wore the same outfit as his staff, and from this distance his head appeared monochromatic: the deep tan on his wide face matched the sun-bleached gold of his shoulder-length hair.

"*Il duce! Come stai?*" Benatti exclaimed, saluting.

Averman made a sarcastic gesture somewhere between "hang loose" and "rock 'n' roll." He swung the megaphone toward employees creating a shaky tower of Globe-Trotters and Rimowas. "The luggage should already be in their assigned suites. This accumulation is displeasing. How we begin is how we proceed!"

Benatti and Guy walked to the fountain and away from the chaos. The other arrivals milled around a registration setup, backslapping and catching up; Guy spotted Roark. Just beyond, marble stairs led to a whitewashed high-ceilinged structure with teak trim. When the island appeared through the jet window, after Guy had awoken from a nap blissfully free from nightmare or spousal apparition, he catalogued the sandy beaches, dense jungle, tiered steppes, and the craggy black swoop of a dormant peak. It all conformed to the default mental image of a private island, razed and rewilded into a capstone idyll, albeit with fewer buildings than Guy would have thought. He'd also expected the busy design of Averman's hotels, with their dessert-bar maximalism that, to Guy at least, tended to curdle into architectural temporizing. This was quiet. Austere. Averman wanted them clean and focused.

"Gentlemen, we begin." Roark joined them at the fountain in a white linen three-piece.

They all nodded. Benatti distributed cigarettes.

Guy gestured at the crowd and found he was listing to the right. "Roark. What's your over-under on Averman pulling this off?"

"If he does," Roark said, "it'll be the first major contribution from the Aussies since Hewitt took Wimbledon." He turned serious. "I'm sorry about Victoria, Guy."

Guy held his inhalation, pictured the smoke filling his respiratory tract. How did Roark know? What did he know? Ah—Averman. He must have updated their mutuals sotto voce.

"She . . . she would have wanted me to be here."

"Not one to cry over spilled milk?" Roark asked.

"Or flipped kayaks."

Roark whispered into Benatti's ear. The Italian stared at Guy, then past him, then at him again. Averman boomed that the swordfish needed icing.

"She is there," Benatti ventured, "and you are here. Hence the ruinous intake."

"Hence," Guy said. He remembered his flask and took a nip.

"Yes, well." Benatti pursed his lips and exhaled, then motioned them to follow him. They skirted the scissor lift and the luggage tower—the same height, Guy noticed, but Argo-like, refreshed with new pieces—and walked onto the lawn between the main building and the jungle to the left. Low-slung residences in Santorini white extended down the plateau, where sinewy palms emphasized the blank sea beyond. Averman's staff buzzed around and between the buildings like atoms. Or like electrons inside an atom. Whichever was scientifically accurate. Guy nipped again.

"Do you fellows notice anything about our accommodations?" Benatti asked.

Roark nodded. "Those two are new construction, built for the Quorum. And the suites are ground level so nobody can claim a better view."

"Ever the egalitarian," Guy said.

Benatti sniffed, as if Guy had passed gas. He pointed to the farthest residence. "Ah, but they only look the same. I have it on good authority those rooms come with new Totos—the ones with the, what do you call it, stool analysis."

The staff cast dark glances at Benatti's smoking; he didn't notice or didn't let on that he did. "And some rooms have authenticated Noguchi lamps. The others are repros."

Roark attempted a hierarchy of the amenities—all agreed on the primacy of the deluxe shitter—and pointed to a staff dormitory camouflaged by thick flora. Guy felt an initial scrim of anxiety fall from his person. This was why he'd come:

the lingua franca, the high judgment, and the presumption of never pleasing anyone else.

They returned to the circular drive, where about forty Quorumites were milling about. Averman was now delivering orders at an auctioneer's pace, his usual bonhomie usurped by impatience. There were schedules to amend. Late arrivals to process. A flat tire "two clicks south." Guy remembered the *New Yorker* profile where Averman celebrated his sixty-fifth birthday by paying the Navy SEALs to take him on practice exercises. ("Best broken arm yet.")

Roark turned to Benatti. "Guy and I are coming from New York. You?"

"Punta del Este," he replied. "I am celebrating the conclusion of the merger. In fact—"

Benatti darted to a crate of coolers on wheeled metal racks and began flipping open their lids. There had been a long-running family struggle at Editto S.p.A.—something about bringing Benatti's empire in line with his cousins' regional telecoms—and an acquisition by Daimler would guarantee sinecures for everyone's eventual great-grandchildren.

As much as Benatti livened up a room, Guy never envied him. When you're born with that much you've already used all the good luck you'll ever receive. What's more, short of curing blindness, you'd never best your ancestors' achievements; Guy had seen this dawning realization lead to crack-ups in more than a few dynastic layabouts.

Benatti returned with a bottle of champagne and shot the cork toward Averman, whiffing by a yard, then dabbed a bit of foam behind his ears.

"*In bocca al lupo*," he said. "May those German pricks fund my Lake Como expansion." He held up a wet index finger; Roark and Guy declined.

"No! Absolutely not!" Averman barked at an arriving group. "Zone of trust. This was made explicit." He hit a button and the lift accordioned down.

Three people climbed out of a Jeep while a fourth passenger remained seated. Roark said they were the MIT kids, a trio of postdocs whose breakthroughs were on par with John Bogle's invention of the index fund. They could be triplets: matching curly black hair, roughly the same height, olive skin, wearing white T-shirts and bands of smart bracelets.

One of them called up to Averman. "He's integral to our algorithm testing. He'll stay in our suite the entire time."

Averman handed his megaphone to an employee and hurdled the crossbar. "Zone of trust," he repeated. "I must insist." He opened his arm to signal the other Quorumites and walked over. "Our accord is strong yet fragile, built from years of groundwork and the cooperation of the greatest minds in the world."

While keeping his eyes on the MIT kids Averman reached into the car and reattached the passenger's seat belt. "I don't know your plus-one. Nor do I care to. Get rid of them."

The passenger radiated discomfort while the MIT kids conferred. They nodded and the Jeep drove off.

Averman clapped his hands. "Okay! Sign in with Jessica and get situated. Drinks on the veranda in seventy-eight minutes."

Benatti threw his cigarette in the fountain. "If you'll excuse me, I'm going to talk to Arthur about one of those Totos."

After he left, Roark lowered his voice. "What have you heard about a secret conclave?" He stared straight ahead, as if they were being watched.

"Secret how?" Guy asked.

"A Quorum within a Quorum. Where the real action is."

The insecurity of these guys. "Well, Roark," he said, with sugar in his voice, "I wouldn't know anything about that. And if I did . . ."

"Joke all you want. Some of us are here on business."

"Pitching your Governors Island project during the discussion on female genital mutilation?"

"Don't be naïve," he snapped. "Any man who leaves here without new partnerships should kill himself and spare his board the shame."

"I have other priorities," Guy said. "And your conclave idea is probably just a rumor."

The crowd at check-in dissipated, so they walked to the table near the marble stairs. Averman's executive assistant Jessica mapped directions to their suites ("Ooh, you both got good ones") and reminded them of the cocktail reception. Roark waddled off to take a phone call.

Guy patted his flask and remembered his plans. "Jessica, I wonder where one may procure cocaine and amphetamines for the weekend."

She tapped at her tablet, all crisp demeanor and general precision. "All set, Mr. Sarvananthan. It will be delivered to your suite by dinner."

"Oh, and a quick shave. Send someone down before drinks. And a pack of Camel Reds."

"I'm afraid the Quorum is smoke-free, Mr. Sarvananthan. But we'll have a barber sent right away."

"Thank you."

He was directed to his residence. The suites ran down one side; on the other, a column of large picture windows. In his room he found a handwritten note next to his bags: *Let's save the fucking world!!!*

Heavy fricatives came from the walls: grey noise, V's favorite. They must have programmed it for her arrival. He found a control panel and muted it.

The suite was a soothing mix of tightly threaded rattan and off-white suede, with an overly curated bar. He'd need to send for more; man couldn't survive on gin alone. Or die on gin alone. Next to the stoppered Watenshi and an ice bucket sat a green juice in a chilled highball glass. Delivered seconds before his arrival.

He unpacked his polos and linen trousers, keeping two inches of space between the hangers, and lined the horse-bit loafers near the door. He tossed his sleeping mask on the bedside table, next to an issue of *Celeste*, the glossy magazine Averman published for his wife, about his wife. What started as a one-off anniversary present had grown into a puckish take on AmEx's *Centurion*, with stockists in London high streets and collaborations with designers of cruelty-free resort wear.

He unzipped the padded ski bag and pulled out the sword. It was smart to bring it. A comfort blanket and, if things went truly awry, handy for parrying threats. Back in New York he'd thought about brandishing it at the Quorum—an eccentric's open carry. Now he saw that wouldn't do. Best to keep it a secret.

He stowed the dulled heirloom and assessed the bar cart, sampled the juice. Nutrients surfed his veins and brightened his being. Clarity encroached from the periphery. Oh, no. He poured a big boy gin, knocked it back, and checked the bathroom. The usual buttons on the toilet—rosewater bidet, heated seat—but no stool analysis. A subpar Toto.

The patio looked out to lawn and sea. Various staff ran by transporting lobster crates, pillows, croquet sets. They were uniformly young and athletic and about as racially diverse as Guy expected. Not a Desi in sight, but otherwise like a Ralph Lauren ad conscripted into hospitality.

It was too quiet. He searched for Brahms on the wall console. Op. 118 felt appropriate. He thought of an anecdote Roark had once told him, how MLK would call Mahalia Jackson at all hours and request his favorite hymns.

Glenn Gould's version of op. 118. That would do.

Guy was a year out of Curtis when Gould died. Faculty and local alumni held an improvised memorial at someone's house in Chestnut Hill. He immediately regretted attending. The eulogies were stilted, overreaching. A musical studies professor said if the Russians attacked, he'd take the maestro's Brahms LP into the bunker. A soused oboist hinted Gould had faked his death. Another argued the pendulum would swing back: restraint would be in vogue again. Professors who'd caught a performance transmuted their past annoyances—Gould's posture, Gould's clothing, Gould's humming—into the fundament of secular sainthood.

Guy hadn't seen the next generational talent at the conservatory, but there were plenty of virtuosos. He could recognize it instantly, whatever the instrument or style, a recognition below consciousness which consciousness fought to articulate. That level of talent was a true gift, a richness that could be enjoyed dumbly—that is, enjoyed without any knowledge of its innovations or method, and with inexhaustible obsession. One of the other composers possessed this talent. A sickly boy from the Gold Coast whose name Guy could no longer recall; he did remember—could, in fact, not forget—the spinal purr of the boy's chamber piece. Like discovering a new language one could not yet speak but intuitively felt reached heretofore impossible levels of articulation.

It took time for Guy to discern the limitations of his own talent. Composing short pieces for orchestra masked some of it. Here was the pinnacle of aesthetic experience: twenty-seven world-class musicians articulating a sound comprised of discrete, bounding fluidities. Nothing compared to the simultaneity of its breadth and depth. Whereas the song cycles he composed practically shouted their deficiencies. One could not hide oneself behind piano and voice.

Naturally he was fond of those years; naturally that was inevitable. Though he admitted to a level of naïveté, Guy was clear-eyed enough at the time to avoid self-delusion. By his last year at Curtis he understood that he'd peaked young and at modest elevation. He would never become one of the handful of composers with a career. In the years following graduation he stuck around and found contentment—or something just below it—in his rotation of piano students (respectful, college-bound tyros); an on-and-off affair with Gretchen Baumer, assistant concert master for the Philadelphia Orchestra; and, when he could afford it, pilgrimages to the festivals at Lucerne, Salzburg, and the rest.

A staff member ran by his patio, halted, waved at Guy, and walked toward him. She stopped again, rethought her approach, and dashed around the corner. Thirty seconds later he heard a knock.

"Mr., um, Sar-van-than?" she asked, and flipped through a portfolio stuffed with leather pouches.

"Sarvananthan. I'm him."

"Here you are, sir." She handed him a pouch and ran off.

He laid out the vials and glassines on the bed. Best to save the coke for nightfall. He swallowed two blue pills and made another drink. Turned the volume up and browsed the inlaid bookshelves. Patrick O'Brian adventures, photography books, World War II histories, Delvaulx's *Nautical Works*, and, prominently faced-out, Averman's bestsellers. His debut had been adapted into a Korean soap called *Big Man Big Heart*, according to the cover. Guy inspected the back copy. Apparently the charismatic titan of industry had first dictated the memoir's outline into a voice recorder atop Everest. Did people really believe that? Guy reshelved it and came to the most recent publication, a glossy hardcover titled *No Man Is an Island, But It's Fun to Own One*. V once said it had caused a minor dustup for its erasure of the triangular trade.

Her own business memoir was quickly negotiated and long delayed. They used to laugh about it: the woman who hated looking back, forced to synthesize her past. He once asked if they'd Ubered from their City Hall wedding to the Ace Hotel in NoMad—this was before the First Flush—or if they'd taken the subway. Her reply: "The past consumes too much bandwidth."

V, invading his thoughts once more. A neuroscientist once told him memory wasn't interested in its conception. When you recall a moment, you're not getting the original, some preserved flash with all its particularities. It's merely the most recent iteration, changing in the present through the act of recollection. Moreover, it's all incredibly fallible, open to present feeling and influence. Better to think of an individual memory as an ever-evolving concept.

In the coming hours and days his brain would likely dis-inter long-buried memories, mulishly forcing himself to encounter himself. He was a man in free fall; it made sense. But if the memories were colored by his free fall, perhaps this absolved him from interrogating them for a point—or worse, a lesson. Treat them as random images lobbed by a desperate subconscious into . . . processing? Was that the goal? That meant change. Improvement. He had no intention of either.

Hell, there may even be some fun in it. If his brain insisted on fighting the disequilibrium to spotlight All That Has Come Before, or All That Might Have Been, perhaps his free fall might reconfigure the memories into new and unrecogniz-able shapes. Perhaps his disequilibrium might even *befriend* his brain; alcohol was a social lubricant, after all, as were the pharmacological sweeteners on his bed.

He slapped his face and washed his hands. Curled his toes into the jute rug. Paged through a coffee-table book about the island, where an architect extolled "nature as nature intended." This apparently required a godlike swipe of the vegetation and the planting of seven cypresses outside Averman's quarters, symbolizing his chief revenue streams.

A foldout map confirmed Guy's impression from the jet. The island resembled a puzzle piece, with circular bays and rounded peninsulas. The grassy steppe of his residence also contained the sprawling central hub, athletic facilities, three outdoor pools, and a bocce court. Other delights included gardens and greenhouses; a fruit tree with varieties of pear, apple, orange, peach, banana, and kumquats grafted into an efficient cornucopia; and all that jungle, with paths and cairns for forest bathers. Foxglove too. Even a man-made ecosystem needed its poisons.

The north sported a novel bit of geographical cosmetology. A monolithic and imported sliver of limestone leaned against the grey cliff face, having been sheared off the Olana estate in upstate New York. A sidebar noted its sentimental value: the site of Averman's proposal to Celeste, back when they were young and, after the implosion of his first hotel development, briefly destitute.

Another knock on the door, and soon Guy was recumbent on the patio under a teal apron while a staff member scrutinized his cheeks and neck.

"Full shave, sir?"

"No, just this hanger on, above the lip." Guy pointed with his drink and sploshed some gin onto his face.

The unflappable barber toweled him off. "Very good."

The barber still went through the motions, laying out his

razors and creams. He spritzed Guy's face and produced a hot towel from a small Styrofoam box. Head back, with a partial view of the sky, Guy took in the familiar scent of the barber's deodorant. What was it? Something with anise—Old Spice. His father's aspirational purchase from the local Target during the three-day stretch between arrival in the United States and a fatal heart attack, which occurred mid-interview for a position in the catalog department of Sears & Roebuck. It was sudden but not unexpected, a common morbidity among Sarvananthans, and the cruelty of its timing, in Guy's mind, was eventually laundered through an emergent Midwesterner's optimism: at least his father didn't die the week before. No, he'd collapsed on America's doorstep, a grand achievement after years of maddening bureaucracy, dead-end calls to various embassies, rejected bribes, unexplained deferrals . . . and then that catalyzing stroke of luck, arriving not by the connections of a sterling military career, but through his wife.

Guy's mother, who only ever wanted to practice law, was forbidden to do so by *her* father, who demanded she choose between teaching and nursing. She went for the former, and this skillset finally unlocked America, whose mid-1970s shortage of preschool and kindergarten teachers partially informed a larger immigration quota of subcontinentals. She co-ran a robust Montessori in St. Louis Park, the middle-class Jewish enclave outside Minneapolis, and they lived in nearby Richfield. If the location was undesirable—his father balked at the stories of tundra conditions—she reminded him their other option was Toronto, farther north.

Guy and his mother took to wearing his father's deodorant

in memoriam and out of pragmatism. When it ran out they silently agreed to keep the red tube in its rightful place on the bottom shelf of the medicine cabinet.

His mother mostly referenced the death in monetary terms—the high cost of funerary services in this alleged land of opportunity—and in the redistribution of household duties. Guy later understood she grieved privately, taking long drives while carpeting the driver's-side floor mat with soaked Kleenexes, or with a tight group of aunties who ran a catering business out of one of their kitchens, cooking banana-leaf-wrapped lamprais for the birthdays and graduations of the Twin Cities' Sri Lankan population. His mother specialized in love cakes and would refill a water glass with Diet Coke as she worked and complained about the "one step forward two steps back" shuffle of her new life.

When he pressed the issue one night over Hamburger Helper, she replied his father had simply used his lifetime allotment of heartbeats—fifty-eight years' worth—as she would too someday, and if they were going to thrive in America they shouldn't waste one minute crying over misfortune. His father was in heaven, boring God with talk of the untapped potential of the national cricket team, and that—she enunciated decisively, with a mouth full of ground beef—was that.

Guy found his school work comically easy compared to the Colombo regimen—they didn't even enforce corporal punishment! But he had difficulty making friends, and the Minnesota winter conspired against his social life. Take the simple act of entering school. The second he crossed the threshold his glasses fogged up, blinding him no matter whether he wiped them clean, removed them, or waited for the condensation to dissipate. Thus he was cursed to hesitate inside every entrance, making pinched expressions and hoping nobody was nodding hello or—however improbably—motioning for a high-five.

Then there was his general inability to walk on the icy sidewalks, a skill his fellow students seemed to perfect at birth, like Inuit children flensing seal meat. (He believed Eskimos lived in northern Minnesota for an embarrassingly long time.) He was prone to overcorrecting, bending forward at the waist and throwing his center of gravity about, a shameful ballet that both attracted and repelled attention. Finally, there were the painful effects of winter on his cock. This was most acute whenever he came in from the cold and had to urinate. Something about the outdoors stimulated his bladder, and he would fumble with numb fingers through layers of clothing, praying he wouldn't piss his pants, unbuttoning the fly of his Lee's and releasing the torrent with a still-frozen, shrunken cock that stung sharply until it accustomed to room temp. The generalized effects of the routine surely contributed to his difficulty losing his virginity to one of the comely Scandinavian or Teutonic girls.

Though if he were honest, the cold cock wasn't nearly so detrimental as his reputation of an asocial weirdo, established by a rather public dropping of his water glass in the lunch line—he had it in his hand, wondered what it would be like to drop it, and simply dropped it. Everyone disregarded this as accidental, until he repeated the action three more times. A counselor recommended "healthy outlets" for his confusion and anger but wouldn't give specifics. He heard tales of class-mates' acts of rebellion: stealing street signs, doing whatever the burners did behind the Southtown Mall. Guy never received an invitation.

Which isn't to say it was a lonely adolescence. The Sar-vananthans were welcomed by their neighbors, mostly 3M retirees with extreme fealty to the sportscasters of WCCO—mentions of KFAN were met with silence. He spent many nights at the Knutsons, playing their modest collection of sheet music on a workaday upright. The Germans, of course, but also Copland and Gershwin. He credited Shelly Knutson for alerting him to his talents. Not enough musi-cianship for conservatory—she was realistic, for which he was grateful—but the improvisations showed promise. Per-haps composition? This comported nicely with young Guy's self-image as a budding anti-capitalist, born of misplaced rage at Sears & Roebuck. Much later he would learn of the bankruptcy of the original "everything store" and feel intense bodily elation without understanding quite why, time being what it was—what it is—and really, who among us is that in touch with their childhood selves?

Though "self" was imprecise. From what baseline might he measure his changing self against? He perverted himself through memory, and he couldn't stand outside himself to glean the knowledge of this perversion—or at least, glean per-spective on the size of the perversion. There was no record to consult. He'd never been a diarist, and he didn't have any lifelong friends.

All the better. He was freed from the obligation of

consistence, absolved for all near-term hypocrisy and selfishness. To cherry-pick oneself: what bliss!

The barber applied a cold towel to his face and asked about the nose hair. Would he like a touch-up? Guy declined. Let them be wild.

He thanked the barber, sat up, and managed the slight dizziness. A white leviathan appeared in the water. He asked the barber if he was seeing what he was seeing.

The barber rolled up his equipment. "We're not allowed to comment on it, sir."

The object resolved into a passing megayacht with ungainly mods pimpling its decks. A glass dome covered the stern, with trees inside and what looked like sand dunes. A small figure arced up one on an ATV, held in midair, and disappeared down the backside.

Petra Bax. Crashing the Quorum.

Guy stood and fell backward, saved from knocking his head on the concrete by the barber's quick reflexes. Excellent: the pills had kicked in.

• • •

HE SAW A few more familiar faces en route to cocktails. Perhaps the college-reunion atmosphere might hold through the weekend. Surely nobody would be so uncouth as to go on about genocide or whatever during the brainstorms. Would there be brainstorms? How was Averman organizing things? Likely modeling it off Davos, with McKinsey input for legitimacy. Guy entered the main building and followed signs to the veranda. He passed a human-size glass vitrine, humming with electricity, with a striated hunk of ice floating inside.

He could hear the Quorumites before he saw them. Dozens of voices slightly louder than warranted, out of confidence or competitiveness: an atmosphere of projected excite. In the coming hour the men would unconsciously match their pitches to a pleasant flatness, the women floating an octave higher.

The veranda ringed a courtyard and pool, with Greek columns, overhead fans, misters, and bar stations. Averman and Jessica stood at the fulcrum of the semicircle like newlyweds in a receiving line. They spoke heatedly as Guy approached.

"Arthur, thanks for having me," he said.

"Mr. Stevens!" Averman said. "It is a pleasure to see you, if under regrettable circumstances." He whispered to Jessica, who turned her tablet toward him. "I'll keep Victoria in my prayers. In the meantime, we stocked your kitchen with your wife's preferences in nut milks and energy drinks. Let Jessica know what you want and she'll swap it out."

"No need, no need." Guy felt aglow. His chemical imbalance was just right, doubling the boundaries of shapes and edges. Jessica's ponytail bobbed like a cresting orca.

He indicated the crowd. "You should be proud, looks like everyone came. More women than I would have thought."

Averman tapped Jessica's tablet. "There would have been zero if I adhered to the net worth requisites. But it had to be done. We don't want to put in all this effort only to debate prostate health, now do we?"

"I suppose not. Unless you have prostate cancer."

Averman blinked a couple times. "I have had prostate cancer. Didn't you see my documentary?"

"I don't really watch movies." Guy saw Averman had affixed one of the *Humanity is* ____ stickers on his arm but couldn't read the handwriting.

"Well, I'm glad you're here. Great things ahead! We'll really expand the envelope this weekend. Now go mingle. We'll start soon."

On his way to the closest bar he saw Roark dressing down a caterer, possibly for the entertainment of the young tech guys. At the center of the crowd Benatti performed close-up magic while waitstaff dodged his gesticulations, orbiting in an unwitting pas de deux. Mary Ellen Park stood a few feet behind Benatti, attempting to learn his technique. Guy was surprised to see her in attendance.

He ordered a gin and tonic. The bartender indicated a tabletop card.

"Can I interest you in a Quorum Nitro? It's our specialty batched cocktail with infusions to stimulate focus."

Guy read the ingredients list; they'd misspelled turmeric. What was Falernum again? "Is this NA?"

"Yes, sir. It's highly sessionable."

"Tell you what. Never use that word again, and I'll order a Quorum Nitro with a double pour of Belvedere."

He tranced out to the bartender's deft mixing and hard shake. Behind him someone boasted of his "discerning ass" and critiqued the canework on Averman's Jeanneret chairs. Another voice lamented the "cavalcade of East Coast olds."

Yet another complained how unexclusive the place felt. Without turning around Guy toasted these beautiful people. He noticed a green bug writhing on the cocktail's clear surface and happily gulped. A hint of aftershave in the taste.

Guy consulted the Quorum schedule mounted on easels next to the bar. Tonight: Welcome Speech with Special Guest Appearance, followed by Welcome Dinner and Free Time. Tomorrow: two Quorum sessions, Informal/Unstructured Breakouts, and Free Time. Sunday: Same. Monday: a final Quorum session, Champagne Toast, Departure. He would have to play along, attend a few sessions. Guy knocked back the remainder of his drink, ordered another, and wandered the crowd.

There was a festive, expectant air. A time outside of time. The Quorumites laughed into shoulders, bumped hips, cupped elbows. He wanted all of it. Here was energy. Here was humanity.

Ah, Colby Wright and Jed Weiss. Teetotalers but otherwise decent fellows. Weiss was a legendary salesman, dropping into new fields, creating value from thin air, and exiting as the bubbles burst. Known as the unofficial mayor of Tel Aviv.

Wright was similar to Guy in that they both led philanthropic foundations, though Wright was imminently qualified, as a former president of two HBCUs and past head of corporate giving at Barclays. They'd become friendly after years of being seated at the same tables on the circuit. With his shaved head and lean runner's body, Wright reminded Guy of those posable wooden figures used to practice life drawing, a comparison deepened by Wright's stoic, motionless response when colleagues punctuated sentences with "man" or asked if he knew Obama.

Weiss stuck his hand out. "Who are you with?"

"Stevens Foundation." By Guy's count this was the third time they'd met. "Family operation."

"Your wife's Victoria Stevens?" Weiss looked momentarily puzzled.

"She brings home the bacon, then I give five percent of the bacon to underbaconed nonprofits."

"Hey," Wright asked. "What residence you in?"

"Uh, three, I think," Guy said. He pointed it out. "Whichever that one is."

"That's four," Wright said. "Your windows're pitched more southwesterly than the ones in three."

"So?"

"So the building hasn't settled yet. So your glass door is loose in its track. Tomorrow the transatlantic current will send the wind knocking. Good luck sleeping through *that*."

"And three will be nice and quiet."

"Believe it," Wright said.

"I could just roll up a towel, bunch it around the door."

Weiss flinched. "Or," he said, "hear me out. I'm in five. Switch with me and you'll sleep like a baby. Without the hotboxing."

Guy said, "Appreciate the concern, gentlemen, but I'm not changing suites. It's already been consecrated. And if tonight's a success, desecrated too."

"Speaking of desecration," Wright said. "Did you see Bax is here?"

"I saw her boat pull in."

Wright shook his head. "You saw her boat go *by*. Averman won't let her dock, so Bax anchored at the property line. Or the waterline—you know what I mean. She's running sorties all night on these cute little rafts."

A dizziness reared up and buffeted Guy from all sides. An effect of the amphetamines and alcohol, some disruption of the inner ear. He directed Wright and Weiss to a high-top and rested his elbows in a way he hoped looked casual. It was too early in the evening for a public collapse.

He hadn't experimented with drugs until late in life. With V's weekslong absences he was left to his own devices and soon absorbed into the tech set's hallucinogenic weekends in Big Sur. Whereas the young heirs would gift him uppers, looking to convert the amiable new old guy—this, after Guy avoided coke throughout the entire 1980s. They'd find an after-party; he'd return home and butcher a Scriabin sonata.

"Bax's hosting a party?" Guy asked.

"Yeah, something like that. Roulette, poker, baccarat. Croupiers from Monte Carlo."

"I detest baccarat," Weiss said. "More homework than gambling."

Guy told them about the sand dune.

"Her new pet project," Wright said. "She wouldn't shut up about it at my last IHO dinner. A full-on bio dome with desert, rainforest, menagerie. Whole nine yards. I might play a few hands after dinner."

"Always bet on black," Weiss said. He waited for acknowledgment. "Wesley Snipes? *Passenger 57*? You two have no appreciation for cinema."

A figure walked the edge of the gathering, some asocial Quorumite. Guy watched him while Weiss and Wright talked poker. A white-haired Asian man in flowy robes, hands clasped behind his back, head down, ignoring all. Then a bouncing Averman caught Guy's attention. Pinballing between groups, injecting bridge-building quips with an expression just shy of maniacal.

"So what are you pushing for tomorrow?" Weiss asked Wright.

Guy gestured to the bartender to bring another drink.

"Water rights, hands down," Wright replied.

"I'd have thought education," Weiss said.

"Would you have. That's the foundation's mission, but here, this weekend? Zuck and LeBron can fund the schools. Water is *the* issue of our young century."

Guy recalled the early days of hanging his own shingle, with a hundred million from V to get started. Enough to play around with disbursement, get a feel for it. He assumed they'd focus on cancer research. On-brand and apolitical. Ape the Jon Huntsman method of spraying cash into oncology centers. But V steered him elsewhere—like everything apolitical, the field was so well-financed it was impossible to measure impact. Perhaps biography, then. Could the foundation support Sri Lanka's Burghers? There they had the opposite problem: not enough applicants. There were more anarchists in North America than Burghers globally. V said this was a blessing: "Nobody asks, 'Is it good for the Burghers?'" They were a nothing people without an identity.

He had even consulted Wright, apologizing for using him as his one Black friend as he used him as his one Black friend. Wright noted that while the Burghers were the result of subjugation, as European colonialists took native wives, their offspring received better education than the Sinhalese and the Tamils and, with these opportunities, became an elite class of their own. Wright's solution was to widen the scope. And so the Stevens Foundation became the sole nonprofit specializing in Sri Lanka, save for the eight others so minor as to be nonexistent. Guy funded land mine disarmament, cross-cultural dialogues, and the annual repair of the five thousand steps running up the Sri Pada mountainside. This last project was by far their most beloved, winning plaudits from the Hindu, Buddhist, and Christian pilgrims.

The only hitch: all of it only consumed a third of their required disbursement. They did end up sending a bunch to the American Cancer Society. Plus a million to Curtis for the Sarvananthan Composition Scholarship for South Asian Americans, renamed the Sarvananthan Scholarship for Asians due to lack of qualified applicants. The inaugural recipient was most unimpressive: a Thai percussionist who gave single-word answers to the alumni newsletter about the "common approaches" and "unique perspective" she shared with her benefactor.

"What about reparations?" Guy asked Wright. The bartender delivered his drink, with another green bug.

"What about it? Look around you. There's no way in hell this group could tackle systemic racism. Might as well let Uber run the MTA."

"I'm going with UBI," Weiss said. "It's safe, and I think I can get enough people on board."

Wright took on a solemn expression. "Guy, Averman told us about Victoria. They'll find her."

Weiss toasted with his seltzer. "A formidable woman. She always accelerates through the yellows, you know?" He lowered his voice. "My oldest nephew pulled a runner after Choate, lived in the woods with this granola girl. The Pinkertons found them within two days."

Guy attempted an expression he hoped conveyed gratitude for their sympathy. He could see her: Driving a rusted pickup through rural landscapes. Keeping a low profile. Paying with cash. A beachside hut in the Yucatán. Or camped out with her prepper brother in Truckee.

Weiss coughed into his hand. "You're not worried? About the optics?"

Guy's drink leaped into his sinuses. "Optics? Which ones?"

"Well . . . you. At this." Weiss flicked a bug from his shirt. "Some would call that cowardly."

Guy assumed he replied, something about multitasking and doing the most good for the most amount of people, and then realized he'd merely opened his mouth.

Wright gestured at the schedule and tried playing peacemaker. "What would she have proposed? Did she tell you?"

He was being generous. They had no real interest in Guy's contributions to the Quorum. Guy was a tourist and hadn't distinguished himself enough to earn a vote.

If V were there, and she came clean about, well, everything, she would have said breast cancer. It wasn't even that much work. Twenty billion in preventative care would lengthen the lifespans of tens of millions, with knock-on effects like a few additional basis points to GDP and more gender equity in the C-suites. But there was just no money in it. As V pointed out to well-meaning interns and bushy-tailed protégés, preventative care abraded against American values of gleeful short-termism and the freedom to destroy oneself.

A Gulfstream VIII coming from the north arced widely overhead.

"Tonight's guest," Weiss said. "What do we think: Macron? Fed Chair?"

"Averman's a star fucker," Wright said. "It'll be an athlete."

Mary Ellen entered their circle. "Check the geotags on social. It's gonna be that guy from the action movies." She held up her phone. A gargantuan man squeezed into an all-white jet cabin with a half dozen children in the background. The caption read, *About to meet my good friend Arthur Averman and #fixtheworld! Let's do this, fam!*

They raised their glasses to acknowledge Mary Ellen's detective work. Weiss asked how she was faring.

"I was cornered by the Millers." She bent her head toward John and Joan Miller, a couple in their eighties who wore matching tailored outfits and, more offensively, always shared their drink, passing it back and forth while carrying on. "They just discovered Marcus Aurelius."

Guy was slightly afraid of Mary Ellen. Adopted from Seoul by a God-fearing white couple in Mobile, she had coded a dating app at Yale that matched people based on their fears, proving with its wild success that it was a better indicator than shared interests. She then invested her buyout millions in a far-reaching surveillance e-commerce platform fronting as an aspirational lifestyle brand. Guy had caught her spiel while tagging along to one of V's "women in business" gatherings: Mary Ellen's eureka moment came when she discerned her fiancé's infidelity from a midnight jump in his exercise tracker during a business trip. She publicly vowed to never depend on a man, and to outearn every man she met.

If Guy remembered correctly, her company's brand personification was a woman named Olivia whom employees invoked constantly: "Would Olivia like this email header?" "How do we convince Olivia to try the capsaicin-infusion in her neti pot?" Olivia was between thirty-two and forty-eight, worked out three times a week, had 2.3 kids in private school—but supports public education—vapes sativa on Saturdays, and has weekly sexual intercourse with an age-appropriate spouse who inserts a single digit into her anus on birthdays and anniversaries. (This last detail was why Guy could remember her presentation so well.)

Mary Ellen probably hadn't laughed unselfconsciously since adolescence. Which was not to say she was without imagination. For a spell of childhood her family lived out of a beige conversion van; Mary Ellen celebrated her IPO by tracking down the van and installing it in the lobby of her Los Angeles headquarters. The vanity plate read OLIVIA$.

"We're debating Quorum causes," Wright said.

"Good luck with that," Mary Ellen said. "You do know there was a Quorum in Mumbai last week? They got the Saudis onboard, if you can believe it. None of the Chinese. Whole thing's driving Averman nuts."

An awkward moment passed. Finally Wright spoke up. "So why come, Mary Ellen? Averman was quite insistent. Plenary sessions only work when everyone buys in."

"Relax, I'll go to the sessions. But I'm here to work." She turned mock-conspiratorial. "Putting together a new venture."

"You're still based out of San Diego?" Wright asked.

"Increasingly, yes," she said. "Solid workforce, no congestion, few disasters."

"I'd miss Carnegie Hall," Guy said, just to say something.

"I don't know how you stomach New England," she said. "Too many blowhards with roman numerals after their names. All that dynastic rot."

Averman cleared his throat through a PA system. They all turned toward the veranda entrance. Guy didn't realize how crowded it had gotten; from his vantage in the back he saw nearly a hundred Quorumites. He could discern the factions by the backs of their heads: conservative looks for the finance and corporate types, longer styles from the tech sector, shaved heads and shaggy manes from the retirees. Guy was on the outer circle; he could step back and be hidden by shadow.

Averman stood on a platform in front of a bar station. "Ladies and gentlemen, welcome to Arthur's Folly!" He prowled the stage like a big top barker. "I won't be long, I know some of you are ready to eat. But let me just express my optimism about this weekend. We have here the brightest and most successful minds in the world. Historians will look back on this gathering and say, 'Bretton Woods? What the fuck is that?'"

A few chuckles.

"You're all just as excited as I am, I know. But let me ask you something. What is the Quorum? Well, it's big. It's bold. It's about touching the entire world, transforming the entire world . . ."

Guy tuned out the rest; Averman's sincerity gave him goosebumps. He leaned back to glimpse the pool's spotlit blue. A late-night float might be nice. That same solo Asian crouched near the ladder, pointing a small electronic device toward the lawn and ocean.

An actor Guy half recognized was now onstage, shadowboxing Averman and talking up the Quorum's mission. Was this the one who wanted to run for office? There was some talk of a presidential run if the next sequel hit two billion. The actor tore off his suit jacket and button-down to reveal a tight T-shirt emblazoned with "Quorumite" in thick teal. He side hugged Averman for a photo, then tore off the T-shirt to show his impressive upper body. He loosed a Tarzan yell, jumped offstage, and snaked through the crowd, high-fiving Quorumites on his way into the main building. Guy heard a Jeep rev up and drive off.

While people continued their applause Mary Ellen leaned over to Guy. "He books his appearances in thirty-second blocks," she said. "No photos either, after Epstein."

"How about that?!" Averman bellowed. "He's what we're all about here. Decisive action! Real solutions!"

Someone in the back yelled, "What about all these goddamn bugs, Averman?"

He turned serious. "We're on it. Bats come out at dusk and eat most of them. Okay, back to the Quorum. Do you all realize that the people in this room have as much wealth as eighty-five percent of the US? Think of what we can accomplish!"

One of the MIT kids next to Guy said, "Ninety-two-point-six, actually."

"I know a lot of you are eager to get started," Averman said. "First, some housekeeping notes. I'll be leading sunrise yoga right on the lawn there, and there's tennis and lap swimming too. See Jessica if you need equipment. But remember, we're here to work!"

A smattering of lighthearted booing. Averman waved it off and continued his spiel.

Guy turned to Mary Ellen. "A good turnout, you think?"

"Mm. You heard about Jerry Nguyen."

He had. It was the gossip of the fundraiser on . . . Monday? Monday was a lifetime ago. "I fear imploding one's deep-sea submersible will become an increasingly common cause of death."

"He hadn't updated his will after signing the pledge," she said. "It was literally sitting on his desk."

"So nothing for the Quorum?" Guy said.

"It all goes to a donor-advised fund. The wife's pet projects."

"Well, Southampton's parks need the money."

She tittered and clinked her glass to his. Averman launched into a story about getting the veranda blessed by some holy man.

Mary Ellen said it was just as well Nguyen didn't attend. "He was an *ergo sum* guy. You know, people who go to these things just to prove they exist."

Guy assumed she thought of him similarly. He was mildly cheered this didn't seem to preclude back-of-the-bus snark. While Averman pantomimed giving CPR to the holy man, Mary Ellen explained their host had recently learned his career breakthroughs exactly aligned with cheap money and an unusual amount of investor liquidity. He'd had more luck and been given more second chances than anyone present.

"It's obvious," she said. "Averman wants so much for the Quorum to succeed that it's guaranteed not to."

Averman finished; Weiss began an extemporaneous toast.

"I read your *FT* interview," Guy said. "You don't really hold meetings on the toilet, do you?"

"Time's a finite resource," she replied.

"You couldn't conference call or something?"

"I could, but it's psychological. My subordinates have to make eye contact with me while I evacuate."

"How's your staff retention?"

"Don't be smart. LBJ used to hold bathroom meetings all the time."

"At least he closed the door." He swatted a bug from his face.

"So I'm a bolder leader than LBJ?"

"Sure, that's what I'm saying."

Now one of the tech guys was talking, invoking the poet Mary Oliver and a memorable Nike commercial.

"You look awful, by the way," Mary Ellen said.

"It's all this unhealthy living." Guy emptied his drink. They were standing on the periphery. He underhanded the highball glass onto the lawn. It flashed for an instant as it caught the low sun, then rolled under the deck loungers.

". . . Guy? Is Guy around?" Averman called out. He motioned for Guy to come up front.

What was this? He was a nobody. A bit player. Oh—Victoria. The jig was up. Berkheimer published his story. He'd made it a full two hours.

Guy blank faced all the way to the platform. Averman put his arm around Guy and addressed the crowd. "As many of you know, a dear member of our community is not with us this weekend. Victoria Stevens was one of the first to sign our pledge, and she's a model for so many of us. 'The end of cancer!' We wish her a speedy rescue and recovery."

Jessica handed Guy a microphone and mimed tapping it. He looked out at the assembly; nobody wanted this. Pure killjoy.

Averman continued. "I'd like to ask Victoria's partner Guy here to say a few words. Remind us of the importance of her work, and the work we'll do this weekend." He stepped back and whispered, "Go on."

What to say? A semi-enthused rah-rah? He could tell the truth; there was an idea. No, that's just the booze talking.

A rush of giddy anger. V dismantled their lives, and he was still forced to carry the water. "Victoria was, *is*, one of a kind." He coughed. "She never let anything get in her way. And she always wanted to make her mark."

He looked to Averman to see if that sufficed. Averman gestured for more. Guy mimed a drink; Averman shook his head.

"I think if she were here right now, that's what she would say. This weekend, make your mark. Don't just think blue sky.

Think, um, blue galaxy." Sweat beaded his lips. "Now let's raise a glass to the future. No, to the present. And to my wife, who is truly unbelievable."

Desultory cheers. Averman thanked Guy and ushered him offstage.

Wright met him at the bar. "Make your mark?" he asked.

"I'm not good off the cuff," Guy said.

"Lucky for you nobody was listening." Wright ordered a Perrier. "I predict more bloviating at dinner. Want to skip it and hit Bax's with me?"

Guy thought about scuba divers in San Francisco bay. Helicopter spotlights. Sonar grids. Then he thought how clear these thoughts were, how sharp, and how abhorrent that felt. He needed to dispel himself from himself.

"I'm in."

CHAPTER 4

Successfully accounted for two-minute sunrise lag. After mile fifteen my vision shimmered and the pain bloomed into an elevated homeostasis. The Zone of Utmost Throb was perceptible, but brief.

I may need to dehydrate more. Make a note to temper the magnesium water.

Invoked new visualization exercise, though not intentionally. A specific memory from the last Founder's Day, Emeryville campus: riding the golf cart through that quarter-mile corridor in the atrium, the one that curves inward toward the end. All the employees lined up on both sides. Like a gauntlet. Everyone cheering. Louder cheers with every honk of the horn. The events team topped the previous Founder's Day by tying strings of cancer ribbons to the bumper.

I remember optimism. I remember hope. Corral hadn't yet given up.

At first the executives and managers led the chant of

"PrevYou," which showed a predictable fealty and lack of imagination. Somewhere in the procession this evolved to "Fuck cancer," likely from Sales; in the last third, mostly filled out by new hires and the interns, they'd found the logical conclusion and chanted "Fuck death."

A loop of the memory sustained my last mile. (No crawling today.)

Need to clear wall space in the guest bedroom—the living room is covered. Tonight I should fall asleep after P.M. sessions, seated in front of the Post-its, with the lamps arranged around me in a half circle.

> Speaking of, yesterday's P.M. session:
> - 6 in clarity
> - 5 in productivity
> - 8 in focus

I've modified Big Mike's technique and gone with color-coded rows, indexed thusly:

> Industry
> Historical Milestones
> Total Accessible Market (if known)
> Major Players and Market Share (if known)
> Obstacles
> Gaps
> Opportunities

———

I mustn't foreclose any idea at this stage. Early green shoots include hybrid teledoc-euthanasia (notable obstacles: deregulation for the domestic market, national allergy toward end-of-life care) and good old Arctic drilling (notable obstacles: geopolitical strife, high barrier to entry).

Must not falter. Maintain trust in the process.

A.M. session:
- 5 in clarity
- 2 in productivity
- 6 in focus

Obviously not ideal.

After A.M. session I rotated the lounger on the porch away from the firepit and fully toward the vista. Figured an initial quarter-hour sit.

Truly soundless. Wholly soundless. And a disturbing lack of change in the landscape. I extended the session.

I recalled those summers with Grandpa Hochstapler, the punishing house chores. Mowing that endless yard. Turning the jack posts in his basement to keep the house level. It took all of my strength to twist the metal rod a quarter turn, elongating the column an eighth of an inch. While he stood and monologued, arms crossed. The origin stories of inventors, saints, explorers. People who risked all.

More than once I screamed from the effort. More than once he replied, "Don't be ashamed of exertion."

———

The porch session lasted four hours and thirty minutes. Robust vectors of new thought.

I have not recorded the boy's suggestion. He ingests psylocibin mushroom tea and goes through the car wash in his father's pickup truck, four or five times in a row. Cannot imagine achieving eureka through something so prosaic.

I did ask Juan to cease washing his back. In four days there should be whiteheads to work on.

I once read that good journalism contains a verifiable fact in every sentence. Maybe eighth grade. I remember Father's favorite talk radio sounding different. Empty. Same with the minister's sermons at First Lutheran. I tried to combat the impoverished rhetoric with my everyday speech. Mom said it was unnerving; Daniel said I sounded like a robot. In all likelihood I only kept it up for a day or two, but it feels momentous now.

Guy has no habits. He abandoned the piano. Grew needlessly self-conscious about it. There was that evening, celebrating the hundredth UK booth. He pretended to indulge me, theatrically finishing the bottle of champagne and spending an eternity positioning the bench. Then a deep breath and . . . scales. He tittered like a preschooler pissing on a bed of flowers.

Still, he obliged me, in his way. Voice memos of his old compositions, hummed and sung and then uploaded to the shared drive. Waiting for me at the end of a long day in Frankfurt, in Mumbai.

I hadn't thought about the Foundation yet—obviously it will have to close. That's unfortunate.

The boy came over to administer the foam roller. He asked about my life in that polite way. From behind his narcotic fog he may even despise me.

He asked if I missed my job. I described the thrill of overseeing the millions of moving parts—now cruelly arrested—but he didn't understand. I told him about Heraclitus and the world's secret harmony. How I missed orchestrating capital and ideas and labor into a new coherence, organic and alive. Nothing is more beautiful than a corporation that outlives its founder. It's a gift to the future and instrumental to the shaping of that future.

Take art: you can look at a painting, or not. There is no looking away for the employees and customers of a going concern.

The boy replied corporations were the antithesis of harmony. He's still very much a boy.

He did share something amusing. While he tended to my glutes he said he has tasted his ejaculate. I asked for clarification and he said, "I, you know, know what it tastes like. Most guys don't. A thing about me is, I'm open to new experiences."

I didn't doubt this aspect of his character, but the way he sought to affirm it apropos of nothing amused me. Reminiscent of Guy in some way.

———

The boy's air of naïveté is also familiar. Taking everything at face value. You put that much trust in the world, it's going to backfire.

Guy should be grateful. Truly. In our time together he was—at best—a placid helpmeet. A solid partner, yes. Trusting, yes. Did he ever wonder how far would he have gotten on his own?

Jeremy once said Guy was "passive to a fault." But I don't know. From what he told me of his youth—moving to America, being orphaned by age twenty—his rapid acculturation was inextricable from that bone-deep geniality. A friend to all, enemy of none.

I remember the inaugural booth test. This would have been the first West Coast campus, the one in Oakland with the sinkhole in the parking lot. Guy insisted on flying out. He wanted to be in the chamber too. It was a standard pelvic exam, but I think he had in mind something like a sonogram, where the husband has a role to play. As the robotic arms did their thing I told him of my first eureka. It was all in the dataset. A million patients in five years and you would advance oncology forever. He held my hand throughout and gave an involuntary squeeze when the console delivered the results in my own voice. (I explained it was a placeholder.) He shed an actual tear and told me I was incredible.

What must he think of me now.

After our session the boy and I went to the yard. He demonstrated his rope tricks. He asked my opinion of the cannabis industry, but I think he was trying to square the circle of his ethics and income. The compromise of legitimacy, I suppose.

I shared the adage from the Y Combinator days, about the inseparable bond between money and medicine. How the heart attack, the leading cause of death in America, was first theorized around 1800 but couldn't be proven: no fresh bodies to dissect. Someone would die, an anatomist would state their case to the next of kin, the next of kin would protest. If you sliced open the dearly departed, how will the soul ascend to heaven.

This impasse lasted eighty years until a St. Louis doctor thought to give the mourners some cash. Consent followed forthwith.

I consulted the boy on the light switches at the entryway. They're wired counterintuitively, such that two are redundant with the switches in the kitchen, and the overhead light and ceiling fan are set at opposite ends of the panel. He said he had some electrical experience and could fix it tomorrow.

Remind him to pick up extra moisturizer too—the eczema's been flaring up.

The boy asked me to take photos of him for a girl in LA. He posed shirtless with his lasso and with the desert at his back.

I thought of the photo my college boyfriend took of me, standing naked in his dorm room, using a Polaroid camera he took everywhere freshman year. God, my skin back then.

After the Series A round of investment I emailed him and asked him to burn the photo. I had no reason to think he wouldn't comply, but when I received no response, I delegated to security ops; they said he died in a car accident the year before.

After Grandpa passed, Father swapped the basement jack posts for permanent lally columns before listing the house. He said they should have been installed years before; there was no reason for the excess labor. Father could never see the bigger picture.

It still feels odd to spend an entire day in athletic apparel. The silk blouse, black trousers, and Prada sneakers are stowed in the closet.

The same getup for nearly a decade.

I'll wear it again, to be sure. After eureka.

Forward, forward.

CHAPTER 5

The raft comfortably seated their party of six and was substantial enough to handle the nighttime chop. A relief—Guy hadn't thought of seasickness until they were already zipping toward the glittering white mass. From their low position he could only see the top curve of the bio dome at midships, lit from below to offer the sight of small birds limning its transparent shell in bent figure eights. As far as he could tell they didn't touch the glass; they must have adapted.

He was glad to escape dinner. Roark had cornered him, reeking of cigars and asking if he'd heard anything about the Quorum within the Quorum. Then Roark complained about a New Jersey development's engineering delays and soil contracts.

A wall of spray hit Guy's right side. Wright was reminiscing about the last time he went "four-bying" in the Moroccan Sahara. "It's wild out there, man. They'll let you do fifty if you detach the governor. Serious air."

"Is that dangerous?" Guy asked. In Minnesota, death by

snowmobile was common enough to warrant an ongoing tally by the nightly news.

"Incredibly," Wright yelled, and gave a thumbs-up. The ocean mist looked good on his bald head. Guy's looks were site-specific, benefiting from collared shirts and the cleanest-cut mien. He'd learned this in his distant bachelorhood after a wincing photo snapped during a shirtless, sweaty round of beach volleyball; his context was all wrong, like a banana in a snowstorm. He took care to never be seen in disarray again.

The water darkened as they left the man-made sand shelf. Instead of casting toward the bow, the raft swung wide, letting them take in the breadth and majesty of the megayacht. This was likely at Bax's direction. Guy never saw the appeal of boats or boat culture.

After a quietish moment of engine noise Wright scooted closer. "Don't take this the wrong way," he said. "But don't you want to be local when they find Victoria?"

Guy imagined a decrepit hospital ward and a plaster-cast Jane Doe. Then a Coast Guard spotter's flashlight chancing on a body in a dark wet suit, bobbing face down. He wanted to tell Wright he had his reasons. What if he brought him into his confidence? If anyone here would sympathize, it would be Wright.

"We're both deeply committed to philanthropy," Guy said evenly. Wright took the hint.

The guide at the outboard motor recited in a tired monotone: "Gentlemen, you're looking at a fully operational sea steading vessel, built by Ms. Bax's own team in a first-of-its-kind joint venture with Feadship. It contains the largest private seed library in the world and a temperature-controlled menagerie of a hundred-plus species living in ecological harmony. It is also the first superyacht to use Ms. Bax's Fidelis-Nav system, a network of low-orbit satellites free of input or interference by the NOAA."

The guide took a deep breath. "There is a forty-seat cinema, two karaoke rooms, no-limit gambling, a lazy river for tubing, two squash courts, lap swimming, a tough mudder course, and, last but not least, All Flags Flying, the twenty-four-hour entertainment revue . . ."

Wright elbowed Guy.

"Spot bet. Ten K says Bax mentions the college dropout thing inside of five minutes."

Guy last saw Bax in the waters off the Cannes lido, where she was toasting her latest fellowship recipients: humanities PhD students recruited away from academia, under the condition they contribute to Bax's journal of Ayn Rand scholarship. Guy had heard the publication, nominally under the aegis of DeVry University, was an ubiquitous eyesore in the mail cubbies of undergraduates and the waiting rooms of shrugging orthodontists.

"Bad odds," Guy said. "No bet."

Twenty or thirty skippers came into view, anchored close like remoras. Several sported yellow flags with the "Don't Tread on Me" rattlesnake.

"Who are they?" Guy asked.

"The flotilla," the guide said. "Followers of Ms. Bax's travels and philosophy. Most of them live on board."

Wright shook his head. "I miss the days when retired white folks just bought RVs and tooled around the flyover states."

They slowed at a wood slat platform in the bow, where a few people waited to disembark. Their party hopped aboard, exchanging greetings with Quorumites returning to the island. Guy recognized Bernard, the fashion magnate, and they exchanged a friendly nod. Ah, France: the only country in the world where one could amass a fortune producing high culture.

They climbed the ladder to the lower deck and came upon cigar smokers loud with chortle and phlegmy cough. At the center of their circle was Bax, in a Breton shirt, pressed white trousers, and bare feet, miming a sailing mishap or a ropes course.

"You have to be nimble. Otherwise: boom!" She exhaled a hearty whoo, then noticed Guy's group and put both arms up, V-for-victory. "Welcome to my stately pleasure bio dome!"

A server with a wooden display case around his neck offered them cigarettes and cigars. Guy selected a gold-tipped Parisian brand he swore had gone bust. "Thanks for having us aboard, Bax."

"The pleasure is mine!" she said. He'd forgotten about her intense eye contact. Up close he noticed the papery skin under her eyes, pale against her orange tan like two strips of war paint.

"The *Amor Fati* has rooms and services for all kinds. Light up, old Joe, light up."

The staff boy sparked a zippo for Guy and Wright. It tasted powdery, with chicory for sweetness. After his second inhalation Guy was certain it was laced with something.

Bax clapped her hands together. "Okay! Ground rules for

our new guests. Be respectful, stay out of my office, and no black-soled shoes. It scuffs the decking. And for our Quorum guests, I'll ask you to refrain from using the word 'legacy' while aboard."

Someone asked Bax where they'd been sailing.

"In short? Everywhere," she said. "We've logged over a thousand days circumnavigating this great big world. Could be a record. Probably a record."

The marathon charter was improvised after the hull destroyed coral off the Brazilian coast; Bax didn't know it was a designated UNESCO Heritage Site. Her tone-deaf response multiplied the bad press: "It's no different than you people hitting a mailbox with your Honda." She paid the fine and then put out a statement vowing to live for five years without touching land, free of "terrestrial tyranny."

A Quorumite to Guy's left cut off the end of his cigar. "*Amor Fati*, huh? Boats are supposed to be named after women."

Guy had never met Nietzscheans until the First Flush. Only besotted teenagers and the comfortably wealthy invoked destiny in casual conversation.

Bax performed light jumping jacks. "This isn't a boat, *Jonathan*, it's a floating nation-state. We have a working farm. A clinic with a GP and two nurses on retainer." She turned to the new arrivals. "You like gambling? We picked up some circuit pros in Marseille. Experience the thrill of losing to a guy with two World Series of Poker bracelets!

"Cards not your thing? We have everything. Explore, explore. Crash overnight if you want to. Just find an empty bedroom. Tomorrow we fish for marlin."

"Is it true you have a tough mudder course?" someone asked.

"Can confirm. It's there principally to keep the staff in shape. Though I participate too. Remember: complacency is a killer! No university will teach you that. I learned that on my own, at the best university: adversity."

"I'll take you up on the poker," Wright said. "But no sleepovers. We got the kickoff session in the A.M."

Bax let out an exaggerated groan. "Averman! What a bore. No imagination."

"So what's your long-term plan?" Guy asked. "Sail off into the sunset? Retrace Magellan's voyage?"

She moved to performing squats. "We did Magellan last year. As for the future, Mars is looking more and more viable. Plan B's Geneva. I have a lakeside property I'm overhauling."

"I could never find anything to do in Geneva," one Quorumite said. "The restaurants close at, like, nine."

Bax didn't appear to hear him. "They respect genius over there. Nabokov. Chaplin. Godard. All retired in Switzerland."

"Well, genius white guys," Guy said. He looked to Wright, whose expression said, *Not worth it.*

Bax stopped. "Exactly the kind of shit you don't have to hear in Switzerland."

The cigar smoker chucked his end over the side. "And how do you want to go, Bax?"

"Gout."

"That isn't fatal," Wright said.

"It is when left untreated," Bax replied. "Come on, I'll show you the poker rooms and the disco."

Their group swept through hallways, down staircases, past a weight room, possibly up the same number of staircases, and, nervously, through an apiary; Guy was immediately lost. The cigar smoker complained about being kicked out of a Koch retreat for questioning their lobbying around the estate tax; his revenge, a new think tank called Real True Americans for Prosperity, hadn't rattled them sufficiently yet. Guy repeated "Good for you, man, good for you" to the cigar smoker.

Someone handed him a drink and another gold-tipped cigarette. It felt like they'd been walking for miles. He realized he'd been whispering the phrase like a mantra—"good for you, man, good for you"—and in this realization had another: perhaps there was something in his cigarette pushing him in a new direction. Elevating him onto another plane.

• • •

HE CAME TO on a black velvet banquette in a Weimar-themed cabaret. Mirrored walls, low-top tables, and squat kerosene lamps dimmed by red lampshades. The banquette lined the room; through thick smoke he could make out figures gyrating inside the plush abyss. Bax sat in a corner in guru pose, lecturing a group of sleepy apostles.

". . . It's why nature is always shifting, always evolving. To define it is pure folly. Is the orange 'natural'? It doesn't grow in the wild, of course—it's a hybrid. Should humankind forbid ourselves this wonderful fruit? Why forbid anything? We must let go of our old conceptions of the natural world. Yes: millions will die from climate change." Someone raised their hand, but Bax gave him a look and pressed on. "Suffering will compound. More will suffer and those who do will suffer in ways unimaginable to you and me. This isn't new. After the Holocaust everyone said, 'Never again.' Then Cambodia. Rwanda. East Timor. The Uighers. People will always suffer. And other people will always look away.

"What's changed," Bax said, surveying her audience, "is the cost of looking away. It's become expensive. So the question is not, How do we preserve every individual life? The question must be, Who will survive? And not just survive, but thrive! There are winners and losers in every transaction. Our future is no different. We must concern ourselves with our best, our most imaginative, our most talented."

A murmur of agreement. Guy wondered how many times the passengers had heard this before. A Weill piece started up, strangled by bass. Maybe he could ask for something less obvious and more distracting. One of Julius Eastman's torrents?

Eastman. There was talent. An outsider's outsider. People imagined composers lived well; probably because they imagined some conductor at Tanglewood, flapping his arms in a tux with tails. That was to say, people imagined composers without imagining much, without putting much imagination into it, because most composers died like Eastman, penniless and unheralded, even the composers who deserved heraldry—not to mention the pennies, tens of thousands of pennies, if one ignored whether artistic achievement "deserved" financial recompense. Guy didn't kid himself. Capitalism was capitalism, everyone conflated artistic worth with commercial viability—a conflation almost laughable considering how neglected classical music had become. And this, in fact, was the paradox Guy felt keenly and also felt nobody understood. Composers were paupers who depended on the largesse of Guy's cohort—Guy's former cohort—who all did live well, really well. The most extreme practitioners of living well since Croesus.

Consider Eastman's case. A homosexual Black contemporary of new old-guard grandees Philip Glass and Steve Reich. Died homeless. His compositions saved by his sister, and only then by accident. A homosexual Black composer in defiance of the white establishment—an establishment Guy knew well from Curtis, quite possibly the best conservatory in the world, though wholly closed off from the contemporary, at least in the early eighties when Tchaikovsky still ruled the curricula. Yes, Eastman was in defiance of everything, titling his humming-bird pieces "Evil Nigger" and "Gay Guerilla" and daring the establishment to say in public the words they only said in private, words he certainly heard during his own time at Curtis. Then as now Guy was thankful not to be a homosexual Black composer, even if he had never approached Eastman's talent, even if he had plateaued early and low. Whereas nobody knew anyone from Sri Lanka. Much less a Dutch Burgher, much less one with a complexion that in winter blanched to almost passing for white.

Whatever "white" meant—no matter whom or how often he asked, Guy never received a convincing response. He once asked Victoria and she paraphrased Potter Stewart's line on obscenity: you know white when you see it. A typically straightforward and uncomplicated reply. Guy didn't buy it because, while straightforward, it didn't answer his question. He sometimes passed because people *didn't* see it and *didn't* know it.

V's reply—initially satisfactory, ultimately free of substance—was typical of her in a truer sense than he appreciated at the time.

When had he asked her? He could place the memory but not the chronology. Certainly during their annus mirabilis. Perhaps at one of those Michelin-anointed meccas with paragraph-long entrees and two-word desserts. He'd paused as the second course arrived, unaccustomed to continuing racially sensitive talk in front of waitstaff. He later learned this was the precise environment for such talk—waitstaff would never tip off Page Six. The restaurant was one of many spaces built for the comfortable exchange of polite infelicities and high-flown impudence.

Anyway. That was all over. If he must die like Eastman—alone, penniless, unheralded—then this spree, this balmy paradise, would do just fine.

Bax dispersed her group and slid over to him.

Guy tested his mouth. "Why not attend the Quorum, Petra? You and Averman are talking the same things."

She faked a laugh. "A fool's errand. Good luck finding consensus with a hundred men who made their fortunes by being disagreeable."

"So why come? Why . . . all this?"

"Why wouldn't I, old Joe? Everything I hate is here."

Guy never understood the persecution complex, that need

to be motivated by spite in all endeavors. The gyrating figures moved toward them. They were lithe and light-skinned,
with curtains of long black hair, all wearing black silk boxer
shorts. From his vantage and the makeup of his brain chemi-
cals Guy could not determine their sexual characteristics. One
crept closer and stretched on the cushion next to him. There
was something familiar about her face, which was fuller and
more yellow than the pink of her neck. Another one sucked
on Bax's thumb.

The one next to Guy flipped over and looked up at him
with a knowing smile. Ah, that was it. Mona Lisa. Same with
the others.

Bax nudged him in the ribs. "What do you think? They're
all surgically enhanced. In the Louvre there's the glass parti-
tion, the tourists, all that headache. Here you can do . . .
whatever you want. And no, I didn't get a bulk rate."

The Mona Lisa kept her tight smile and nuzzled his crotch
like a cat.

Bax continued while her Mona Lisa sucked her fingers.
"One of the poker guys wanted catamites, but I can't see how
that would work. Teenagers really kill the vibe."

Guy nodded and attempted a sagacious expression.

He remembered his first exposure to pornography. There
were the smudged photographs of Indian women in tapestry-
rich boudoirs, passed between the furtive St. Joseph's boys
during recess. The nudity was somewhat drained of its luster
by the subjects' classical poses and the pages' heavy striation
from repeated folding. As Guy later learned, if it's vibrant,
degrading pictorials you seek, come to America.

During the latchkey hours of senior year he liked to wander the neighborhood, counting the black POW MIA flags jutting from the split-levels and humming whatever Copland piece he was practicing at the Knutson's. One day he spotted a manila folder at the edge of a patch of forest. The folder had been clumsily buried and, judging from the small bite marks in the corner, pulled free by rodents. Someone had scrawled *Work Stuff* in thick marker. Inside was a well-thumbed issue of *Playboy* sporting a close-up of a white woman's posterior in cutoff denim shorts, with the lupine colophon rhinestoned on the pocket. The photo spreads were a hazy memory; he could easily recall the shape and weight of the travel-size Neutrogena moisturizer he later bought for his much-abused cock. All of his guilt manifested in the stern expression on the elderly face of the drugstore cashier who rang up his purchase. *Oh, he knows*, Guy thought then (and, if he were honest, still thought). It wasn't far-fetched to credit the intuition of a man with decades of similar exchanges with sweaty-palmed adolescents within biking distance.

A Mona Lisa crawled toward him on the banquette, maintaining that ambiguous and unnerving expression. Guy knew he should feel aroused. This was, in a certain sense, the most aesthetically pleasing offer of its kind, and what's more, he'd heard plenty of stories of men who countered approaching death with libidinous riposte. Jokes of a myocardial infarction in the arms of one's mistress, between the legs of one's mistress.

Victoria had hollowed him out, taking everything—his will to live, yes, and apparently his sex drive with it—but perhaps if he went through the motions, the blood would rush from pure habit. The Mona Lisa attempted to undo his trousers but couldn't work the hook-and-closure from his slumped position. He stood too quickly and pitched forward onto a pile of bodies. Polyglot cursing and unguarded yelps. Various hands lifting him back up. A heavyset and shirtless man in a Yankees cap loudly whispering, "That's why I don't drink. I just sip."

Bax handed her Mona Lisa an envelope and called out to Guy. "Quite a tumble there." She motioned for him to follow. "Let's get you some fresh air."

A few steps, an elevator, and they were back on deck. They faced the open water with the island at their back. Bax whistled an old pop standard as they walked toward a group playing shuffleboard.

"I may not be cut out for life at sea," Guy said. Someone put a cigarette in his mouth and lit it.

"Nothing is better than standing at the helm when we dock in a new port. I imagine I'm captain of a mighty Navy ship. Coming home after a lifetime of impeccable service."

The cigarette cleared his head. He took stock. Was he sufficiently fucked up? If he could take stock, did that mean no? "Things aren't so good, Bax. I'm on the verge of a profound life decision."

"I was in your shoes after the tragedy at Burning Man. Great things follow periods of strife."

The shuffleboarders waved at them.

"The short one has been with me since Brazil," Bax said. She spit over the railing. "My mobile island of misfit toys."

They came to a cabana bar and a kidney-shaped pool. Sounds of frivolity from above, or below; Guy couldn't tell. Above the liquor an ornately framed box held what looked like four lab vials suspended in air.

"What's that?"

Bax went behind the bar and started smelling the plastic bins of citrus. "That? My little art project. They're self-portraits: each vial contains a seven-year span of my body's cells."

Guy reached for the closest bottle of gin and poured himself a glass. "Go on."

"The human body regenerates its cellular makeup every seven years—does this smell fresh to you?"

"Toss it."

"My cleaning people collect the dust from wherever I'm staying, and at the end of each year I have a lab filter out the nonorganic material. I use Perkins Labs—did your wife ever contract with them?"

Guy shrugged.

"Perkins adds what's me to the vial. Every seven years I start a new one."

"They're self-portraits."

"Yes; I just said that."

"When did you start?" Guy poured himself another and dropped an uncut lime into the glass.

"When I could afford it."

"No, I mean, how did you mark the beginning and end of the seven-year period?"

"You mean, how did I pick which span was a version of me?"

"If your first self ended at age seven, did you wait until you hit a multiple of seven? Otherwise you may be collecting three years of older you and four years of newer you."

Bax rolled a lemon to test its ripeness. "Cells don't understand time."

The shuffleboarders came over with beers in hand. Burst capillaries spread across their faces like river deltas.

"You with the island people?" the short one asked.

It took a moment to catch his meaning. Guy sipped and tongued the lime into a full revolution inside his glass. "I'm a citizen of the world."

"Smart-ass." He was missing a few front teeth. He winked at Bax, who ignored them. "Welcome aboard the new *Mayflower*."

The second one piped in. He was easily six foot six, and his face looked recently sandblasted. "You look like a techie. Silicon Valley?"

"Former philanthropist. Before that, composer." He might have said piano teacher, considering the years he'd put in. More honest and representative.

"Let me ask you something," the tall one said. "Who's the youngest guy in your little group over there?"

Guy figured it was the MIT kids. "Thirty-two? Thereabouts? We're very diverse in our demograty—demographs—demography."

"So you get together, you pick a cause, you pool all your money. Don't you have to wait until the youngest guy keels over before you can get to work?"

"A piss-poor system, if you ask me," the first one said.

Bax rooted around below, tossing basil and mint into a bin.

"I believe implementation is Monday's agenda," Guy said. "Averman's been researching successful tontines throughout history. And there's an idea of electing to give away up to half within the next fiscal. If Averman can lobby a tax exemption."

The first shuffleboarder made a dismissive *pfft* sound. The second said "This fucking guy" under his breath. Guy felt a foggy rage in his chest, too amorphous for action. He also felt bored.

He leaned over the bar. "Hey, how do I find the poker room from here?"

Bax clarified: there was a classic room, and a non-fungible room, for the truly adventurous. She gave instructions, which he immediately forgot.

Guy wandered the halls, turning toward the sounds of chatter. The muffled sounds of D-major guitar brought him to a karaoke room. He peered through the porthole glass: a couple staffers, a gang of Quorumites, two sleeping Mona Lisas. The lyrics flashed on a screen with a tropical island in neon Day-Glo. The men swayed in a drunken chorus line and sang both lead and backing vocals, doubling the already loose call-and-response:

"I'm gonna go out in the street and do whatever I want!"

"I'm gonna go out in the street and do whatever I want!"

"Oh shit!"

"Oh shit!"

How could anyone enjoy such brute chords. He continued his search, going down another level. Card sharks likely preferred the underwater atmosphere.

All noise fell away. It was like finding himself on an empty block in daytime Manhattan. A little spooky, a little thrilling. Except not so thrilling. He didn't wish to be alone; the whole point of the weekend was people and distraction. Perhaps he should return to the cabaret. Find companionship with a Mona Lisa. He'd never been with an escort, save for an aborted encounter in a Fishtown brothel after a particular lengthy fight with Gretchen.

His sentimental education was scattershot, unambitious. Gretchen told him as much at some point in their tryst behind her husband's back—a colleague of hers in the Philadelphia Orchestra whose administrative title Guy never cared to learn. He met her in their second year at Curtis, when he confirmed the limit of his talents and she, a star violinist, was preparing for respectable orchestras. That a chair opened locally was sheer luck. The two of them established a routine born of a mutual understanding: they had a chemistry in bedroom matters and, for whatever reason, nowhere else. This was cemented by a Poconos holiday/trial in cohabitation that ended with neither acrimony nor deeper attraction. Guy was never sure at what point he'd become the other man. He and Gretchen were dating, then less so, then she was seeing someone new. And there followed new parameters.

They were to meet at hotels or Guy's apartment. They would not be seen together apart from alumni functions and concerts. Either one of them could end the affair at any time, which would trigger a sixty-day communication blackout. He would use protection.

He tried dating other people but found it too much effort

in the face of his arrangement with Gretchen—a terrible long-term strategy. The years passed and he never performed the real work of finding a real partner, with all the requisite vulnerabilities and leaps of faith. At one desperate point in the early nineties he looked up Fiona Rzepko, the hard-partying pianist who'd taken his virginity freshman year. Her Chopin's second sonata was legendary on campus—exceptional in an environment of precocity—and her ability to dismantle trickle-down economics midway through a vodka blackout was incredibly erotic. In the decade since graduation she'd disappeared into the Berlin scene with rumors of a long-delayed record under contract with Warner Classics.

So it was. He and Gretchen conducted their rendezvous once or twice a month, he scraped by with tutoring work, and then, after her successful pregnancy spelled their immediate termination, Guy found himself nearing fifty without much of an adult life. There followed a hazy, empty period, until a former student called: Was he interested in an easy nine hundred dollars playing her friend's wedding in Allentown? They couldn't spring for a hotel, and she needed a confirmation ASAP. He was free; he was always free. And at a point in his career when playing a wedding was no longer so ignominious, provided nobody from Curtis was in attendance.

Victoria knew the bride from Stanford. Within a year she and Guy were living together in Manhattan. Within three they were married, and she'd raised her record-breaking round of angel investment for PrevYou.

A rough-looking member of the flotilla stumbled down the hall toward Guy, his face sunburned and Fu Manchu'd, with a sociable belly straining the hem of a guayabera. He gave Guy the old once-over along the lines of "Where are you from, *really*?" as he yawed side to side. Guy moved to let him pass. The man mumbled "thinkyerbetternme" and leaped forward as if to give him a bear hug. Both men fell against a door, which opened into a small cabin. Luggage and bedding was strewn about, and there was a sour odor of room-temp dairy. The man, tangled in the sheets, still tried to maul Guy. His threats were indecipherable from under the fantastic amount of spittle frosting his mustache. Guy scooted backward, accepting soft blows to his head and chest, and threw whatever was at hand: a woman's mule, a broken children's mobile, a tube of sunscreen. The assailant growled and rose up, then lost his footing in the comforter and tripped onto the mattress. Guy waited a beat. He heard snoring.

He kept scooting into the golden glow of the en suite. The sink was lined with makeup, pill bottles, wooden toothbrushes, three different colors of mouthwash, and a sheaf of glassine baggies. He splashed cold water on his face, taking care not to get any in his mouth. Swallowed two ibuprofen (maybe) and hoovered two lines of cocaine (medium certainty) and then hoovered two lines of cocaine (high certainty) and tilted his head back to rush the drip. He used the belts from the bathrobes to truss the heavy sleeper, who ripped some truly noisome flatulence as Guy rotated him about. Guy returned to the bathroom and wrote *SORRY* on the mirror in lipstick.

He gently closed the door and continued down the hall. He felt . . . different. Possibly better.

The desert. He needed to see Bax's desert. He wouldn't ride

an ATV—he knew the impracticality of an attempt in his current state—but something ameliorative might be achieved from the vista. All that sand under a night sky. He hadn't seen a desert since that conference in Abu Dhabi, which barely counted. He spent the weekend indoors and under heavy coolant.

The sounds of high revelry directed him left, then right, and finally to a pair of swing doors with panels of bolted red leather. He entered to find a pirate's treasure of watches, stapled contracts, necklaces, dusty bottles of wine, and a Fabergé egg teetering atop the green felt of an oversize poker table, around which were seated eight men carrying on eight conversations. Behind them sat Quorumites and flotilla folks whispering play-by-play commentary. The cigars couldn't mask a thick staleness in the air. Someone put a highball glass in Guy's hand. He asked a young guy seated near the door what was going on.

"This is the non-fungible room. Probably thirty stacks in the pot, and Minh's got to raise or fold."

"What's with the papers?"

"It's fucking crazy. One's a deed to a horse farm in Kentucky. The other is an ownership certificate to a minor Warhol."

Guy peered around and saw Wright seated behind the pile. "Even a minor Warhol's worth more than three hundred grand."

"Yeah, there was a fight about that. And another about digital wallets. It's not a perfect system." He took a long hit from a vape pen.

One player shouted down the others. Guy thought it might

be Minh. "You know what Stu Ungar said in '81, right? He wins the bracelet, and someone asks him what he planned to do with his winnings. Back then it was like four hundred K."

"Three seventy-five," someone yelled.

"Right, right, three seventy-five. So Ungar turns to the person, he yawns, and he says, 'Lose it!' Can you believe that!" This was incredibly funny to about half the room. Guy realized he'd been snapping his fingers allegro agitato.

"Shit or get off the pot, Minh," someone yelled.

"Christ, what's your hurry?" he said. He pulled up a suitcase, opened it on his lap, and after a bit of rifling retrieved a small leather-bound portfolio. "I raise you twenty-five. This is a Rhodesian 1901 hundred-pounder, near mint, with authentication from David Feldman. Plus the auction report."

Wright sighed. "You can't bet with stamps. Only retrogrades collect stamps."

Minh put up a finger. "It's within the house rules. And stamps are highly portable. You won't find me stuck with a wine cellar in a flood zone."

A Quorumite next to Wright interrupted. "The bet stands. James, your turn. Just fold. We know you're going to."

"Can we return to what I was talking about?" someone in the corner asked. Everyone ignored him.

James folded, and the next player tossed in his ex-wife's engagement ring. Minh took the pot with two pair, kings and jacks. Wright threw his cards down and motioned to Guy. "I'm heading back before I lose my shirt. Carpool?"

Guy remembered there was something he wanted to see but couldn't recall what. He did register that more Quorumites would be departing, and these choleric flotilla folks carried a whiff of violence about them. He nodded at Wright.

There was a queue for rafts, so they idled on the lower deck. Wright checked his phone while Guy tested his balance. He was exactly as fucked up as he wished to be.

"Before we get back, let me ask you something," Wright said. His voice dropped. "Everything okay at the Stevens Foundation? Five of your people reached out for a job today."

Guy was aware he had a wide, foolish smile. He couldn't stop grinning. "No shop talk, friend. Those are mainland problems. Though I recommend our ED, Andrew Enriquez. Can't say why until next week."

"Be straight with me. I don't go in for the cloak-and-dagger shit."

"Next week, next week. Get in the Quorum spirit. Be Quorum."

They climbed down the ladder, received their gift bags, and stepped into the raft. The ride back was direct but more turbulent, either from the tide going out or the boatman's ambivalence. The raft heaved up and down, slapping the water like a dropped elevator, everyone's insides falling on a time delay. Wright's eyes rolled back. Guy remembered recess at St. Joseph's and jumping from the swings at the peak of the arc, the midair second telescoping into eternity, the world blurring save for coarse sand rising to greet open hands and bare shins, followed by mild opprobrium from the bald Jesuits. Perhaps his adult inebriations were simply attempts at recapturing that feeling.

The raft mercifully slowed and docked at the south beach-front. They inspected the gift bags—an orange stress ball, a rope bracelet with a shark's tooth, and a signed issue of Bax's academic journal—and left them behind. Wright waved goodnight and peeled off for a spot to recover.

Surely Averman installed a swing set for his grandchildren somewhere on this island. That's what he needed right now. Just to look at, maybe sit for a minute. He tested his person; his tongue felt too large for his mouth.

He walked the ipe-slatted path toward the main building. The breeze carried sounds from the semidark residences: nightcaps between friends, Zoom calls with spouses, sudden laughter at a dirty joke, Benatti's whistling.

He took a forking path away from the residences and trailed along the edge of the steppe. A vent of ocean air cut through the humidity. Averman had planted mature trees along the ridge, like flags at a peace summit. One of them was, incredibly enough, a jackfruit tree. He hadn't seen one since childhood. An uncle from Kandy once said this was why there were no truly poor Sri Lankans: "Here a man can live off jackfruit. All the nutrients he needs, free and plentiful. You want to see real poverty? Go to India."

He thought of his first night in the States, as he and his father crammed around the small glass dining table in his mother's apartment. It was part of a complex of four-story buildings whose layers of red brick and beige concrete gave Guy the impression of giant club sandwiches.

His father, believing jet lag was on par with the flu, continually refilled his coffee to adjust to local time. "Right," he said. "We're not Sri Lankan anymore, we're American. And being American is number one."

His mother knew better than to interrupt, but Guy's sleepiness was close to indolence. "Why is it number one?"

"Nobody knows," his father said. "Just as nobody knows what being American means. Everyone fights over the definition."

Guy thought of his friend Yanni, who had stepped up her envy-laced barbs in the weeks leading to Guy's departure. "I heard Americans hate foreigners."

"Your friend is ignorant. All Americans are foreigners. The ones who forget this don't hate us, they hate themselves."

"How do you know so much about America?"

"Because I'm your father."

Guy thought the man was simply projecting the reality he desired, which had seemed to work out so far. A very American trait.

His mother remained the stubborn realist. "Nothing's changed. Back home we worked, we ate meals together, we saw friends. We'll do the same here."

"There's negroes," Guy said. He tried to remember the other boogeymen in Yanni's lecture. "And Jews."

"That's true," his father said. "You stay away from them. Mexicans too. You're all competing for the same slice of the pie."

"What about white people?" Guy asked.

"What about them?" his mother replied.

"What about their slice?"

Her mother poured cream into his father's mug. "Their slice is so big they can't eat it all. They can't even see the end of it."

His father laughed. "That's why they all have diabetes!"

A large bird bolted from the jackfruit tree, startling Guy. He slipped on a patch of moss and nearly fell ass over teakettle before catching his footing. The millisecond of panic was enough to produce a thin sweat. Jesus. He kicked the moss off the path, considered it, then kicked it back where it was.

The black mountain silhouetted against the night sky, like a Magritte painting or a special effect. It would be a great time to see a shooting star. It would feel important, prophetic. Or a comet. A comet would be even more prophetic. Were they the same? He should know this. In any case: here it came. Right now. Right . . . now.

A high trill sounded ahead. A snake hissing. Or fuller—a rushing. He advanced slowly toward a short figure crouched on top of a bench facing the ocean. A frenzied collection of shapes, like a holy vision. A sodium lamp flicked on behind them. The shapes cohered into a person, specifically Mary Ellen, specifically Mary Ellen urinating.

"An abundance of nature, and you choose the furnishings," he said with an unfortunate hint of slur.

She finished and hopped down. "Revenge. Arthur comes out here to watch the sunrise."

"What did he do?"

"It's what he said after dinner. He—never mind, it's between the two of us. Tomorrow he'll relax in my dried urine and that will be that."

"I could assist, but you'll only get a few drops."

"You're listing quite a bit there, sailor. Benatti force his grappa on you?"

He steadied himself on the bench. "Bax. I think she drugged me."

"Nothing is worth having to put up with her speechifying. It was worse when she was Peter, if you can imagine it. All that talk about 'struggle.' She's from Brentwood."

"There are no libertarians in a foxhole. So this is a working vacation for you?"

"Of course it is." They headed toward the residences. She nodded at the main building. "Do you honestly believe that group will reach consensus? They have a keyhole view of the world's problems."

"And you don't."

"I don't pretend to either way. I make money."

"As the world burns?"

"Mama said do what you're good at while you have the means and the time."

"It's at least something, Averman's goal."

She stopped and looked at him again. Her stare had a discomforting effect, like a sock bunching between his toes.

"You shouldn't correlate mastery in one field with competence in another," Mary Ellen said. "Behavioral ethicists aren't better at making ethical decisions in their own lives. They actually make worse decisions than the average person."

"They're just better at rationalizing their mistakes?"

"Something like that."

"So your plan is, what. Accumulate, then die?"

"Listen to you. Who told you it was about the money? We're all just finding out how far our abilities will take us. Or most of us, Mr. Stevens."

"I found my limit at twenty-one. Trust me, ignorance is bliss."

"God, you're sad. Does this shtick work with your wife?"

"I'm low-maintenance."

"Long-term, men grow to resent their more successful female partners. It's better for my health and well-being if I stick to sport fucks."

They observed two staff members diligently removing fallen palm strands from the edges of the steppe. Mary Ellen summarized her last real date, which occurred two years ago with a Tokyo-based financier whose idea of a pleasant afternoon had left her feeling half-dead (picnic).

"Plan on sport fucking here?" Guy asked.

"Unlikely. You guys don't realize this weekend is one big lifetime achievement award. Questions about legacy you haven't had to contemplate—actually contemplate—until now. I predict a lot of irritability."

"There's always denial. I'm a great fan of denial."

"Only plebes get away with that. You don't have the luxury when shareholders depend upon you staying upright."

They arrived at the main building. Mute staff wiped the marble steps and photographed their accomplishment.

"Well, good night," Mary Ellen said. "I'm this way." She didn't wait for a reply and walked to the far residences.

He wasn't tired, and sleep carried the risk of dreams. He needed a dense blackout. And the ability to make this plan meant he was nowhere near close to achieving it. He made for the veranda. Every now and then staff would dart by, a bit of shadow and then gone, delivering towels or preparing for the morning's festivities. Several people were solely dedicated to removing the dainty piles left by birds nesting in the crossbeams. He slalomed these crouched cleaners and stopped at an alcove with a glowing screen mounted above a small display, like one might find in a historical museum. Must have missed it before. The screen looped a muted video of a tweedy fellow with the chyron *Professor of Caribbean Ethnology Studies* and production values of a *Jeopardy!* Clue Crew segment. Animated ghosts flew by; a cartoon child representing the island's displaced tribe waved happily. Guy waved back.

The veranda's bar stations were still well-stocked. He made a negroni—the Campari would settle his stomach—and nearly sliced off his thumb attempting an orange garnish. He threw the offending citrus over his shoulder and wandered with his drink, circling the pool and its row of recliners. The annex of the main building ended at a two-story blank cube nestled into a shallow slope. Staff polished its teak trim and spot cleaned faint blemishes, taking closeup photos of their progress as they orbited. He heard them complain about increased salt in the air; it somehow added to their workload. He walked the cube's perimeter. Ah: an amphitheater. This must be where Averman would conduct the sessions. Its oceanside wall was open to the elements; a line of samovars gently rattled in the breeze. Above them was a massive painting half-hidden in shadow. It looked both familiar and new and depicted a kind of exploded stadium with seat grids, architectural renderings, and zipping lines in blue, white, red, and black against a desaturated yellow. Guy dipped his finger in his drink and flicked a red drop toward the lower left corner, then toasted his contribution and drained the glass.

Was he peckish? Perhaps. He could be convinced to snack. It would be advantageous to give his body some carbohydrates to balance the sugars. He walked down the annex and came upon a staff member leaning against a stack of coolers and scribbling in a tiny notebook.

"Hey, help me out. Where's the nearest kitchen?"

The kid startled. Guy realized he was the first Asian he'd encountered on Averman's staff. Cambodian, maybe Vietnamese.

"The kitchen," he repeated. "Nighttime comestibles."

The kid slowly tore a page from his notebook, balled it up, and put it in his mouth. Then he pointed down the hall and motioned to hang right.

After a wrong turn or two he followed the smell of fresh bread. In the kitchen a dozen people worked in silence. They were as uniformly attractive and racially diverse as the daytime staff, but with a Francophone air about them. He watched their top-notch mise en place. Baking and slow roasting, braising and steeping. And sidestepping: they sluiced around one of the MIT kids like river around a boulder. She was blending something dark brown and viscous.

"Milkshake for your sleepover?" he asked.

The MIT kid shook her head. "Nondairy. Not a shake. It's a mycological blend for concentration. We're on a coding tear."

"You do know it's Friday night."

"The Friday before the first session, yes." She looked up at Guy. "Are you inebriated?"

"Not as much as I'd like." He tapped the shoulder of a passing sous-chef. "A baguette, and a bottle of bubbly. Something vintage. Whenever you can." He turned back to the MIT kid. "Guy Sarvananthan, by the way. Stevens Foundation."

She lifted the blender cap and smelled its contents, then resumed blending. "Nice to meet you."

"What are you coding?"

She poured the drink into a large plastic bottle and inserted three large metal straws. "Only the program that'll eliminate all the inefficiencies from this whole process." She caught herself. "Not to disparage. He's a great man. But this"—she indicated everything around them—"is improvisatory theatre. We have a better methodology."

Someone put a plate of sliced bread rounds and a chilling bottle of champagne in front of him. He squeezed the bread and it quickly bounced back. Nice and fresh.

"This will implement whatever we decide on?"

"No."

He waited for her to continue, then saw she was wordlessly counting. At ten she turned and walked away. He followed, having no better option.

Her residence happened to be his residence; they were neighbors. Perhaps the three of them bunked up together. She indicated the door and he opened it for her. The suite looked like a South Beach coworking space, with multiscreen setups on folding tables and modernist furniture in all white. Guy noted their daybed had pebble grain leather, where his was full grain. He wasn't sure which he preferred. They'd taped caricatures of the Quorumites to the walls, but he didn't see himself. The taller MIT kid was staring closely at a whiteboard blacked out with dense scribbling, while the shorter one tapped away at a workstation in the corner.

Guy set his plate on the coffee table and poured himself a flute. The amount of concentration required for this simple task told Guy he was approaching his ideal state. The champagne was nice and orange, but it would go flat quickly. All the more reason.

The female one whispered to the tall one, who waved him over.

"First things first," she said, "this is early beta. So don't pass judgment on the initial results. Secondly, this is based on objective meta-analyses, so don't take offense if your pet cause is unranked or whatever."

"I have no pet causes."

The tall one circled something in red, took a long sip of the coffee drink, and joined the female in their pitch. The third one also chimed in. "What we did is enfold the top fifty thousand 501(c)3s and their non-domestic counterparts . . . sentiment analysis from social . . . real-time news from trusted outlets . . . stripping out the false positives . . . the usual macroeconomic drivers and a century of census data . . . only US outcomes as a function of the dataset . . . Europe and Africa by Sunday . . ."

"So this picks a cause?" Guy interrupted. He leaned close to the whiteboard and tried to decipher the tiny script. The tall one underlined *overindex black swans?*

The short one said, "For the current minute, yes. We got

lucky with the dataset. Global ills are both persistent and predictable."

They gathered around his screen. It refreshed with a paragraph of text at the bottom.

Guy skimmed. "There's a charity for the relatives of KKK members?"

All three answered in turn: "Yes . . . no . . . yes, but . . . They are at this moment the most vulnerable population with respect to food deserts, access to education, economic prospects . . . The effects of radicalization on cholesterol . . . And a thousand other metrics . . . You have to account for the second-order effects of the donation . . . Eradicating malaria, for instance, empowers Boko Haram."

"Can't imagine this will be an easy sell."

"No, that's not . . . We just said it's buggy . . . still working on it." The short one looked exasperatedly at the female one. "Who is he?"

"The husband of Victoria Stevens."

"Oh."

The tall one kept scribbling on the whiteboard. "The doyenne of private-sector medical research."

"Mr. Averman told us about her accident," the female one said. "Terrible timing—I mean, terrible in general. A terrible thing. To occur."

Guy thought of his conversation with Mary Ellen. "Let me ask you something." He pointed to the monitor. "Isn't the obvious answer climate change? Why doesn't it spit that out?"

All three snorted. "Because it demands buy-in from the public sector . . . and international cooperation . . . a generational timeline . . . serious Benthamite calculations of acceptable population loss . . . without precedent it breaks the algo . . . out of scope . . . maybe the Roman Empire, but it's too qualitative . . ."

Guy felt the rush of alcohol. "To clarify, then, we're not saving *the* world, but saving *a* world." He chewed the bread thoughtfully. "How long did it take you three to come up with this?"

"We've been iterating the basic concepts . . . A lifetime of work . . . Tuesday. We started in earnest on Tuesday."

"Could you create a similar algorithm around avocation? Like, the reason to get out of bed in the morning?"

"Yeah, the answer's forty-two . . . You can't get a one-to-one output like that . . . Maybe the best avocation for the most amount of people . . . Doesn't take a genius to see it's farming . . . No, engineering . . . You're both wrong . . ."

Guy poured another glass and settled on the daybed while they squabbled. He could have been a farmer. Up at sunrise, a day of hard labor, then early to bed. Planting, sowing, reaping. The cycle of the seasons. There would be resistance, sure, initial racism from the good ol' boys at the VFW. But they'd see him put in the work, and at the autumn harvest they would clap him on the back and say, "When you showed up we thought you had a snowball's chance in hell. But you did it, Guy. You farmed the hell out of her."

The musicians at Curtis—now those were laborers. Gretchen went five years without missing a day of practice, even when she broke her femur in a skiing accident.

All this was surprising when he first arrived on campus. He

had inherited his father's notion that success entailed overcoming a single obstacle—in his case, arriving in America, though he died before he could see his mistake—and for Guy, matriculation guaranteed success. He'd made it, right? Apparently not. He had to compose his first longer work. And then await its grade and eventual reception. And after that? More obstacles. That's all America was for most people, a series of new rungs on an interminable ladder. For most people.

He felt the urge to play. There was a piano somewhere around here. Didn't he see a baby grand in one of the lounges?

"Hey, stop arguing." The MIT kids turned his way. "You guys want to hear some music?" He mimed playing the keys.

"Like, live music?" the short one asked. "By you?"

"I'm quite good. Or I used to be."

The female pulled the bread plate toward her desk. "We'll keep chipping away at this, thanks."

"Godspeed, you crazy kids." He left the bread and took the champagne.

He tried a different annex of the main building. Then he heard his name. Jessica appeared in paint-covered overalls and shouldering a tote bag full of produce.

"Mr. Sarvananthan, I have an emergency call for you." She pulled a tablet from her bag and tapped a few buttons.

Ah, here we go. A wave of sangfroid hit him in the face. He killed the bottle while Jessica signed in. She held the screen in front of her face. Jeremy's haggard expression faded in.

"We've been trying to reach you. You should be here at

search and rescue." Jeremy was on a beach at twilight, surrounded by duck-walkers in full scuba. It looked like quite
the operation.

"I am consumed by grief. Walloped by misfortune." Shards
filled the throat.

"Status update. No Victoria. Yet. We found a water
shoe—that's promising. And I've been researching some very
avant-garde debt restructuring—"

Jessica stifled a sneeze.

"Am I on speaker? Goddammit . . . No news about the
other thing. We still think Monday. You need to check in
with Comms tomorrow. Every hour."

Guy nodded along. Nodding was good. Jessica slipped on
an earpiece and whispered to someone about a 5 A.M. news-
paper delivery and "a roe restock."

". . . And get your crisis PR people to liaise with ours,"
Jeremy said. "Remember, it's a moving target. Could be
Monday. Could be sooner." He looked off-screen and made a
"wheel's up" motion. "There's also an update re: complicity."

The shards pooled in his skull. "Re: complicity. Re: the
innocent husband."

"Who knows what who knows about what, and who knew
it when? But yes. Complicity. Liability. However many lawyers you have, double it."

So. The fall guy. He could see it. Could not believe how he
hadn't seen it.

A yearslong trial, a harsh sentencing, a prison cell. Then
nothing. He'd gone from Colombo to the land of liberty and
from billions to ruin. Quite the American story. And the Sri

Lankan one—there was that insider trading case, with that moron from Galleon Group. Raj? Raj. A bitter poetry there: not even his downfall was original.

Jeremy was still speaking, incredibly. ". . . Which is why your excursion south is, is, *inopportune*. You need to be here."

"Jeremy, I hear you. I hear you and I see you. It's just that my complicit and liable self needs to be less complicit and liable. And less self." Guy gave the red X a hearty push.

Jessica snapped to. "Anything else, Mr. Sarvananthan?" If she'd surmised anything amiss, it didn't show. He shook his head and she departed.

In her stead appeared a floating Berkheimeresque face, generalized Caucasian and also—or perhaps redundantly—not quite a face. He walked forward into it.

Courage, Guy . . . Nope. Not quite. To the suite, then, for some material courage. Maybe a straightener.

He used the subscription card from Averman's magazine to lay out "happy hour" lines: not too thick, not too long.

Jeremy, Jeremy, Jeremy. Didn't Guy's behavior scream Do Not Disturb? He should ask Jessica to take a message. No need to interrupt this last little holiday.

He retraced his steps to the main entrance and found the piano. It blocked floor-to-ceiling glass and a wedge-shaped opening to two arms of the residences. He tried A above middle C. In tune, but resonating with an ugly bounce—installed just for looks, then. He fell onto the bench.

When was the last time he'd played? He eased in with Satie and, despite heaviness in his left hand, rediscovered the old muscle memory. The Jesuits had forced him to become a righty, which he later appreciated for the ambidexterity. Now his swollen fingers resisted him. The ease at Curtis! He didn't even think of his hands back then. They were mere extensions of his racing mind. He'd pop NoDoz during all-nighters, part of a frictionless line between idea, body, and sound as he churned out chamber pieces in his favorite basement practice room. The faculty feedback was often the same: technically proficient, a bit undercooked, and too in thrall to its influences. At first he thought he could compose his way out of it. The inviolable truth of *Sitzfleisch*: if he put his butt on the bench for four years he would emerge a mature talent. Or a talent with a glimpse of maturation.

The first half of his second year was the peak of early possibility. By spring his mother had passed and his teacher was hinting at a switch to music ed at Temple. He saw the rather circumscribed future awaiting him. Not an unhappy life, to be sure, but decidedly smaller and decidedly adrift.

No, that wasn't how it happened. He switched to someone's étude and granted that he was retroactively giving himself far too much credit. He could have done anything after graduation. Sure, he graduated bottom of his class, which meant table scraps, jobs-wise. But he had inherited a little money; he could earn one of those ten-month certificates advertised on city buses, bluff his way into Cisco or IBM. Everybody thought subcontinentals worked in IT anyway.

But it required reinvention. Fortitude. The truth was he had never thought of anything but composing. His mother hadn't pushed him toward medicine or law. She said a nation as capacious as the United States would deliver a salaried position for the most obscure desire. And while there was a grain of truth to it, she didn't live to see its necessary precondition—that of talent. While he told his professors he was too grief-stricken to concentrate, he confessed to Gretchen during their second reunion that it was nothing more complicated than a journeyman's knack. He was an enthusiast, not an artist. (Her slight recoil at this admission led to their third breakup.)

And so he entered his twenties with a few skills and not much imagination, hewing close to the narrow parameters of the self he'd set before reaching the low ceiling of his promise. Thankfully the classical music world welcomed stubbornness and an arbitrary adherence to tradition. He found an apartment in Franklintown, bought a used upright, and asked his former professors to connect him with anyone looking for piano tutors.

He tried to remember one of his own compositions but couldn't find the line. A whisp of melody just out of reach. He switched to Brahms.

He might have earned a business degree. The Penn campus was a mile away. In the eighties everyone was getting rich doing nothing. By now he would have the house, a wife, and a sensible SUV. He would derive meaning from his work. Or, if his work was meaningless, he would derive meaning from the backyard grilling and weekend boating. He'd become a happy mediocrity.

Alas. Instead of embracing the Reagan revolution Guy bet on the wrong horse, favoring the Gipper's predecessor. He and his mother watched Carter's "malaise" speech the summer before he left for Curtis. She said she'd already experienced enough pessimism from her leaders, thank you very much. Guy loved it. He'd been told he would have to work twice as hard to get half as much, and here was the leader of the free world saying *everybody* would get half as much.

Or at least that's how his adolescent sensibility understood it. He didn't see why this emboldened him until much later. Carter had accidentally made explicit the American secret. All that optimism was a cover for a country in stasis, and possibly a country in decline. Why not choose a dying vocation? Why not plateau early? There was nothing behind the country's rainbow insistence of itself, its everywhereness of itselfness.

This belief buoyed him until he met Victoria.

CHAPTER 6

O f all the accidents. I finished my afternoon matcha and then tripped on the porch and landed hard. Forced to correct shoulder dislocation against the boulder in the front yard; two neighborhood kids watched and yelled encouragement. I am now known as "the baddest bitch."

The teacup survived.

I asked Juan whether my solitude would be interrupted by the festivities on the 4th. He said local anarchists light fireworks on the 3rd, but the cops shut it down pretty quickly. Everyone else goes to Twentynine Palms.

Even with ibuprofen the shoulder and collarbone are going to be sore for a day or two. I directed Juan's cunnilingus. Required micromanagement—for an alleged musician he has difficulty with rhythm.

Juan said there are abandoned mines in the park, though none close to the running trail. (Extractive capitalism—so primitive.) Every now and then a couple of teens will injure themselves exploring the ruins. I asked him what the attraction was; apparently a Halloween thing. People looking for ghosts, which he found interesting. I told him that word was forbidden at my previous company. "Interesting": the mark of unthinking.

Juan rubs his right earlobe when he's talking about the desert. Also when he's high.

He was curious about the Post-its. I explained Big Mike's technique, using the genetic editing column as an example. (Too many gaps.) He replied that he's all natural and held a bodybuilder's pose at his reflection in the sliding door. Said he's not going out like his aunt.

You already have cancer, I told him. Your body successfully fights it off. We carry death in our genes from the day we're born.

He said I bummed him out.

Most people have a hard time with it. Men especially.

We were quiet for a bit. He pointed out the orange haze in the sky. The summer fires, on the other side of the mountains.

P.M. session:
- 6 in clarity
- 3 in productivity
- 6 in focus

No closer to eureka. I thought it would have happened by now. I must build my edifice, my new statue against the sky.

———

Perhaps more bile would help—the latest cut of the takedown documentary is on the laptop.

At first Jeremy was skeptical; now it's a "masterstroke." He even tried to get some of the investors to commission their own: "It's oppo research, turbocharged. None of the participants know who's funding it, so they give us all their best stuff. Anyone doing a real exposé will get scraps."

As long as nobody leaks it. NDAs don't mean what they used to.

Because nobody wants to see me thrive. All this is the same glass cliff.

Not even Black Cube can help me. They could excavate a mountain of dirt on the muckrakers, the embittered ex-employees, Elena's widower . . . It won't stem the tide.

Remember, PrevYou is over. In the past.

That is to say, none of this would have happened if Elena were still alive. How the world's premier oncologist contracts a bronchial infection on holiday is beyond me. This is why you don't take vacation.

She was *weeks* away from cracking it. Two months at most. She said a year, but public-sector vets sandbag everything.

The fact is I believed in her, even when she didn't. I know greatness. She possessed it in spades. And look at how easily everyone believed me, how much they needed to believe she'd cracked it, how confident they were in her abilities. "I just connected the dots," I'd said. "Dr. Corral has cured cancer."

Jubilation. They knew we could do it, and we did do it.

Yes, there were a few more dots to connect. But I could buy us time.

That's all this is. Timing. People will accuse us of malfeasance, of ill intent. You want real monstrosity, consider those who make an actual medical breakthrough and hoard the secret for themselves. That French family of obstetricians—the Chamberlains. Chamberlens. Invented the modern forceps for safer deliveries, then sat on the tech for generations. Lining their pockets with the francs of grateful mothers.

Meanwhile.

Meanwhile.

Juan said the fires reminded him of childhood. He was maybe twelve and woke in the night to the ringing of a smoke alarm. His father collected him and his sisters, and they waited at the end of the drive for the fire trucks. But his mother wasn't there. Juan tried to run back in to rescue her, but his father held him back. Then he told them the truth.

She was at his friend Mario's place. From the tone of his father's voice Juan gathered it had been going on for a while. As the house filled with smoke—the culprit was a faulty dryer—Juan didn't feel anger or sadness. He discovered a newfound appreciation for his mother. She kept a clean house, attended mass three times a week, balanced the family's checkbooks, and sent ten percent of their income to relatives in Copper Canyon.

And at night, she got hers.

—

Henry had a wandering eye—the price of marrying so young, I suppose. For weeks after the funeral, the cryptic voice mails from Rose. Samantha. Gloria. Danielle.

They didn't know. I should have called them back. Called every one of them: "Aneurysm. In his final moments he didn't think of you."

Guy was always supportive. Ever loyal. Deeply incurious. All the qualities one seeks in an ideal partner. And, he would say, in a good American.

He was dense that way. And so *sensitive*. Bridling at any mention of the obvious: moral compromise is in the soil of the land. These are table stakes. Accept them and move on.

Juan asked about my parents. I gave a précis on life in Tacoma and their public records research firm. My first window into how a business is nurtured and grown. In their case, finding opportunity in the hidden bureaucracy of the state. Making a living from what others ignore.

Most of their work entailed tracking down title deeds for real estate closings. Commercial and residential. My clearest memory is Mother working the microfiche reader, a hulking taupe unit she fed reels of photo negatives. For hours she would twist the speed dial as images whirred on a vertical track like a sepia-toned slot machine, her eyes skimming the twelve-digit ID in the corner of each card. I didn't realize her deftness with the machine until my own summer at the reader, earning four dollars per hour.

—

The work was punishingly dull, so the field attracted its share of autists and loners. The type who, like Father, didn't mind daily trips to the secretary of state offices in Olympia, staffed by dead-enders aggrieved by ineluctable offenses from fellow dead-enders (no tuna in the breakroom, Jeanine), the previous customer (what do you mean, you don't know the DBA name?), or life in general.

Mother and Father didn't undercut the competition, nor did they find an underserved market. They simply applied the customer service experience from tenures at REI to a public-sector backwater, and this insight, paired with the small-business owner's usual workaholism, vaulted their little concern over the industry's low bar. They pulled clients from sleepy competitors and enjoyed double-digit YOY growth, hiring remote workers in four-fifths of the counties in the PNW.

When their Wagoneer hydroplaned and collided with another vehicle, they died instantly and, it could be said, happily, big-picture-wise.

Juan has a theory. Everyone carries a charge of bioelectricity, like a lower version of the electric eel. Some people produce more, which can disrupt nearby electronic devices: cell phones lose service, laptops malfunction. These people are ambulatory versions of Walden Pond.

Juan is convinced he's one of these people. "Predisposed to the natural world."

I told him his phone works fine.

He said he was "being metaphorical."

When I first met Guy he talked incessantly about composition. But he never progressed beyond fiddling with those tiny baroques in his Franklintown apartment. Why live in a grotto if you don't create the work.

By the time he moved into my UES place he'd given up any pretense of an artistic practice, happy to become my booster and full-time support system. The ease with which he did so says quite a lot about his artistic commitment. There was also something incomprehensible to me about his ability to transition so thoroughly. As if his bedrock certainty had been Styrofoam all along.

This wasn't in itself rare. I find most people incomprehensible.

Despite the suitability of our arrangement, and despite my real affection, there persists a slight pity.

This also wasn't rare. I find most people pitiable.

I will reach the Zone of Utmost Throb. Tomorrow I will run farther.

CHAPTER 7

"You may wish to wake up, Mr. Sarvananthan."

A crystal disc floated above with a burgundy coloring at its center, flecked in black. It looked foreign, almost otherworldly, yet with a familiar shape. An experimental satellite, that was it. He was dead, suspended in the atmosphere on a slow medivac to heaven. Turns out a lack of belief wasn't disqualifying. A welcome surprise. And ahead of schedule!

"Ah, there we go, sir."

A female voice, solicitous but on edge. The floating disc resolved into an object: a glass with a remaining drop of last night's digestif. He was looking at it from under the coffee table where he'd passed out. Which meant he was awake, which meant he was alive. How terrible.

He shifted a few microns and found his frontal lobe gift wrapped in high-grit sandpaper. His foot made an exploratory nudge and touched the leg of the piano bench.

"Shall we get started, sir?" The staff member stood somewhere behind him.

The exploratory nudge was in error. His foot now knew he was conscious and tattled to his leg, groin, and torso, who all followed with vociferous complaints of recent abuse. This was too much knowledge. If only he could return to dreamless sleep. Now he must confront the daylight hellmouth of consciousness.

"I'm awake." His voice was miles away.

Guy took three deep breaths. The sandpaper loosened around his brain. He tried once more to move and found his shoulders and knees had swelled in their sockets. His entire mechanical had been degreased and now abraded against itself with every shift and inhalation.

His let his head fall to the side. Someone had folded his trousers and set them near the piano bench, topped with a rectangular mint wrapped in teal foil. He directed his eyes toward his shoulder and was relieved to find it still covered in white piqué. He flexed his ass and felt underwear.

"Espresso," he said. "And breakfast."

"Mr. Averman requests all Quorumites dine in the veranda before the kickoff session. This will"—here she must have consulted her tablet—"engender an esprit de corps and shared magnanimity."

"Okay then."

He felt her retreat through the soft thump of the carpet. Today was Saturday.

A group noisily approached the alcove. He rotated the axle of his neck and glimpsed a huddle of white jumpsuits with "Arthur's Folly" sewn across the backs. They looked like a hip version of NASA, angrily debating "subduction zones" and "cyclonic circulation" while pointing at each other's laptops. The group disappeared behind an unmarked door.

He let his head fall to the left. Outside, the staff were bustling about, wiping down loungers and tilting umbrella canopies eastward. A dozen jogged toward the pool carrying padded gym mats. A bronzed youth with a backpack-mounted vacuum hoovered up flower petals from the stone pathways. It must have rained. The kid prodded a resistant clump of petals, then bent and shoved a handful down the vacuum tube. Another calmly slingshot ice into the trees, evicting crows to a copse at the edge of the lawn.

Jessica was by the pool speaking into a walkie-talkie. She checked her watch and waved her arm in an "over here" motion. Averman broke the surface, gasping and woo-hooing. He slapped the water, then swam laps breaststroke. The early morning exertion reminded him of Victoria, which, along with the scurrying about of the staff, produced a rising motion sickness. Guy focused on the Sauternes glass and the black dot of amaro. When did he drink amaro?

He pulled his hand up, which felt weightless; he saw he had time to shower and change before breakfast. He needed to abate the demons with a blisteringly hot shower, several stimulants, some hair of the dog, and the godsend of blood thinners.

He scuttled out from under the table by working his shoulders and hips in a jazzy motion, which confused his brain into cooperating.

Now. The move from the horizontal to the vertical. This would determine everything. He sat up slowly, testing how his skull handled a frankly incredible feat of physiology. His central nervous system had strapped itself to a madman's gyroscope. When he swallowed, the crackling in his ears resounded with thunder. Motor oil sloshed the retinas.

He could manage.

If he could sit up, he could stand. If he could stand, he could walk. And if he could find a path through the outer lawn, he might reach his patio without encountering a fellow Quorumite. He grabbed his trousers, wobbled upright with an economy of motion, dressed, ignored his gut's carnivalesque, and allowed the incline of the world to deliver him toward the exit.

The outside was full of outside air, and for this he was grateful. Overnight showers had cleaned out the dewpoint. It tasted like the very essence of rude health. The sky was a different matter. It had descended on him like a street hustler, fat grey swabs just over his shoulder, tapping him on the back. Needling him. What had he ever done? He spun around and saw nothing.

The motion addled him a bit, so he plopped down in his patio chair. And Weiss was right about the cross breeze. An unpleasant coolness tickled his arm hairs into an upper body quake.

His corporeal *Exxon Valdez* brought forth unwelcome thoughts of Victoria. At the moment he didn't feel anger—surely more of that was forthcoming—but a general incredulity. She was audacious, sure. It was a fair portion of her attractiveness. But her decision to keep him in the dark stung, and stung deeply. Deception required distance. Instituted a shallow, one-way intimacy. He wasn't so naïve as to believe couples shared a single reality. Every relationship held a few grenades of truth in abeyance. What Guy couldn't comprehend was just how separate their senses of their communion had been. Since PrevYou, if not from the beginning. He hesitated to let this line of questioning spiral out, lest it end in questioning everything. He was much too hungover for that. Nor could he see what possible benefit it might provide.

And Jeremy. The import of his latest update buzzed the doorbell of his lizard brain. Culpability. Incarceration. He knew not to ask how much worse it could get.

Roark approached from the far end of the path, pausing to assess each residence. Now *he* had a good story. An easy story. Perhaps that was Guy's problem: Victoria had created one for him, which he mistook for an actual life. And now that his story had ended prematurely he was left with . . . all this.

He could create a new story. But what would that even look like? Reinvention was a young man's game. It required learning the names of politicians beyond those you ran into at NYPL fundraisers. It required reading up on domestic policy and deciding if it affected you personally. It required thinking about money, which meant thinking about everything.

Guy waved, tried to offer a morning greeting.

"I was going to ask how you slept," Roark called out. "But it looks like you didn't." He kept a respectful distance owing to Guy's soiled presentation.

"I was in my cups. I may still be in my cups. I'm climbing out of my cups."

"My neighbor woke me at six. An oilman from the Lone

Star state, hasn't left his suite since check-in. Some crisis in Riyadh."

They watched Bax's flotilla circle the yacht in some kind of celebratory ritual. A faint beeping.

"Let me guess," Guy said. "You're looking to swap."

"I'm casting about. No firm commitments." He indicated the patio tiles. "Your veining's off too."

Guy checked; the grey and gold lines of the marble flooring didn't align at the seams. Now that he saw it, he couldn't unsee it, but also didn't care and couldn't understand why Roark did. What with all the what have you, and whatnot.

"My journey continues," Roark said. "And I'd recommend a washup. You look terrible."

"I feel worse."

Roark ambled off. Guy went inside and studied the bathroom wall display. He selected warm yellow lighting and the monsoon setting at the highest temperature.

The shower's fall bar vaguely insulted. Its literal function of holding on suggested a figurative "holding on," a steadiness in the face of the inevitable accumulation of infirmities. The reduction of one's faculties, and the slowing path from point A to point B. His infirmities would be elective, speedily applied, and with a minimum of suffering. With a minimum of feeling.

The water boiled his pores and scrambled his adrenal priorities. Guy inhaled deeply and steam cleaned his brain, then dried himself, wiped the mirror, and inspected the old facia: jaundiced eyes, spider-veined nostrils, a nascent blotchiness on the chin. Not terrible. The micro fillers and injections of

the past decade upheld their end of the bargain. A flip-book
of his red carpet step-and-repeats would show an unchanging
structure, firm of cheek and free of crow's feet.

He remembered when he first realized he had a face. It
was during a family holiday in the interior, maybe Kandy,
and he was sent to his parent's room to retrieve a bracelet or
some earrings. This involved rooting around in his mother's
jewelry box, a wooden contraption with nested drawers. At
some point he caught his reflection in his mother's vanity
and felt a profound dislocation. He was alive, and this was
his face. This was the thing his mother and father looked at
when they looked at him, and it was the thing from which he
spoke when he spoke to them. He opened his mouth wide,
then his eyes. He vocalized nonsense sounds: "Ho wha . . . ho
wha . . ." The sounds grew louder ("HO WHAAAAA! HO
WHAAAAA!") until his father shouted for quiet. Guy tried
it now, repeating the nonsense. The words unconsciously
cohered into solfège, the do-re-mis reprising a melody
from—where? An early piece. He couldn't remember which.
Gretchen praised it once; he'd transcribed a bit of the score
on a postcard for her.

He put on clothes and put in Visine. Made a final accounting
of his person. He heard a soft rush: someone had slid an envelope beneath the door. He unfolded its single sheet of paper
and, in the milliseconds between seeing the words and understanding their meaning, felt the page vibrate with rude clamor.

Jeremy. With updates. Or no, now that he read it again,
or actually read it: Jeremy with no real updates, but increased
urgency. Guy dry swallowed and placed the letter behind

Averman's books on the shelf. Let Jeremy do the worrying. Let him canvas the empty waters and consider the legal fallout. For today, at least, Guy could not be touched.

He walked to the main building, nodding at Quorumites also en route to breakfast. Runners circled the outer path with unjustifiable high spirits. The MIT kids sat cross-legged in the grass, angling their laptops out of the sun's glare. Averman's voice vibrated into Guy's bladder from hidden speakers in the landscaping: "Today is the day! Remember why you're here! Let's save the world, everyone! Today is the day! . . ."

The veranda had been flipped to a banquet setup, with large round tables extending to the lawn. Guy took a seat next to Benatti and Roark and motioned to a waiter. The two men were deep in argument.

"A tiered solution is always best," Benatti said. "What's gained by an end-all be-all approach?"

"Take disease," Roark said. "Immunology isn't a class problem. You invest in vaccines, not that neo-Marxist bullshit. The poor aren't different than you and me."

"Yes they are," Benatti replied. "They die before we do." He futzed with the vamp of his loafer, turning a gold Roman coin in the penny slot.

"No retirement for them, then." Roark sipped from his green tea.

Guy ordered eggs and toast, a double espresso, four ibuprofen, and a Bellini.

Roark continued. "You know what you have to watch out for with retirement: low T."

"You don't take the supplements?" Guy asked. He still

sounded like Tom Waits, but now with a pubescent pip. Benatti and Roark gave him a look and let it pass.

Benatti retrieved his cigarette case from his breast pocket. It was timeworn and monogrammed with his father's initials. "The doctors say I'm fine in that department. My T levels skyrocket after I close a deal."

"And the smoking?" Roark asked. "When the doc gives me that judgmental stare I'm sent right back to Mother Superior."

Benatti shrugged. "My sisters ganged up on me, pulling all these photos of my *nipoti* from their purses. Said if I don't quit I'll be dead in five. Everyone crying, real hystrionical. I offered them a compromise: no smoking before breakfast."

Roark turned to Guy. "I was telling our Neapolitan chimney here about a devilish drainage matter with my Meadowlands project."

Guy knew about it in outline. A development epic in scale and modest in originality. Roark envisioned a residential and commercial district on the wet expanse east of Hoboken, an insta-city with decades of tax abatements. He'd waited patiently until advancements in infrastructure dovetailed with the right starry-eyed investors. The whole ordeal reminded Guy of Michelangelo, who, after outliving his patrons, friends, and a much younger wife, embarked on ever crazier projects he knew he'd never see to completion.

Benatti leaned back in his chair. "It sounds like a migraine. Why bother? You're like Howard Hughes, if he waited until his eighties to build the Spruce Goose."

"The difference," Roark said, "is that nobody cares about giant aircraft. Whereas all I have to do is put up I beams. If the financing collapses, they'll have to chip in public funding—they can't have an eyesore on the landscape."

"Have you been to New Jersey?" Benatti asked.

"The unofficial motto is 'Too big to abandon,'" Roark replied. "It's about momentum. And, in a larger sense, preventing inanition."

Guy didn't know the word. "Your investors are on board with that," he said.

Roark finished his tea and stood. "Great moments in history begin with men lying to each other and hoping for the best." He buttoned his linen suit jacket and checked his watch. "I'm off to look at more suites. Let me know if you hear of anything. Remember: unbroken veining."

Benatti flicked his cigarette onto the grass and rolled another while summarizing last night's festivities. Guy concentrated on his intake. The eggs filled his stomach, the caffeine tuned up his heart rate, the juice feinted at nutrition, and the prosecco calmed his senses. He had smoothed out the first wave. They were never too terrible. You had to watch out for the next one. It may be provident to vomit. A reset, as it were. But no: he must retain his toxins. Stick to the program.

Two men behind them complained about their grandchildren.

"They want to be *personalities*. All of them work just as much as we did, but it's not compounding. There's no investment in the future."

"You have to let them make their mistakes."

"It's the rude awakening I fear. Like Elkann, faking his kidnapping."

"Chip them. Tie it to their inheritance."

"No, my guy says they're easy to hack."

The other sighed. "Dynasties are wasted on the young."

Guy thought of his piano students back in Philadelphia, watching their ascendance from confident teens to Phi Beta Kappas and ultimately successful members of society. White males who graduated and with a straight face became corporate consultants at twenty-one. A few sent him holiday cards, and occasionally he meet an old student for coffee. None of them still played. This didn't surprise him, nor did their guilty admission of not "getting into classical" as purportedly educated adults. Their parents hadn't paid Guy to instill a love of music, and he knew he wasn't a good enough teacher to make his own passion contagious—a passion which had cooled as a consequence of having to teach piano.

No, he was never surprised by his tyros' provincial tastes. But more than once they paused and said, now that they thought of it, they put on Keith Jarrett at the last dinner party. That was something, right?

It was. He'd assure them, hug them goodbye. His former students would return to New York, to San Francisco, to London. Their memory of Guy Sarvananthan would settle in the depths of their unthinking selves, perhaps surfacing when a TV commercial used a bit of Barber, or when their toddlers unwrapped a toy xylophone.

He didn't bristle at any of it, nor did he endorse the cliché of society's growing cultural illiteracy. It wasn't important whether anyone appreciated the music. A moment was enough. One of his students might be walking to their car, reviewing their grocery list, when a snatch of Bach floats from a nearby window. They are short-circuited, an open vessel for the music to fill and flood. The notes reach across the centuries to connect composer and audience. Across space, too: the notes connecting their ears and brain to the ears and brain of everyone else on the planet, all of us ourselves capable of short-circuiting in the very same way, possibly by the very same snatch of Bach. Of pop melody. Of birdsong.

The point was, it needn't be good. We'll all die someday. We can all have our moments of earthly feeling.

"You look sallow, friend," Benatti said. He licked a rolling paper, tucked it on both sides, and lined it up with others on his plate. They were impressively uniform in thickness.

"I'm trying to jimmy the lock on death's door."

"Jimmy? What does this mean."

"Never mind. How would you like to go, Bennett? Heart attack in the seraglio?"

"In my mind's eye I see a car crash on some rural drive, late at night. It's romantic, no?"

"Very."

"Chances are it will be these," he said, holding up a cigarette. "But not cancer. I have a terrible habit of smoking in bed. Some night I'll fall asleep and *fwoosh*."

"Not so romantic."

"Well, there's a history there. I've been reading up on it. Edie Sedgwick, Ingeborg Bachmann."

Guy faintly recognized the first name. Before he could ask, Averman swooped in.

"Gentlemen! Are we ready to change the world?" He wore

another teal jumpsuit, constructed from a nicer cotton than the staff's. A waiter handed him a brown smoothie, which he swallowed in one gulp. "Insect protein, it's the future. Female cicadas."

"I saw you at the pool earlier," Guy said.

"Training. I'm taking the grandkids free diving in Mexico. You ever do it?"

"I hate the ocean," Benatti said.

Averman beamed. "They keep you young, that's a fact. They play every sport. Every sport." He motioned to the north. "We're putting in a football pitch on the mesa over there. And a funicular right to the top. There's a caldera, you know—a mountaintop lake. Cleanest water you'll ever drink."

Guy then heard Averman's voice behind him, which jarred for a moment until he remembered the speakers. He thought of the muezzin's calls back in Colombo, broadcast from wooden poles throughout the city. He never learned the words. Still, the exposure to the adhan burrowed deep, and he could hum it now, as a sort of parlor trick.

Averman caught his expression. "I recorded them before everyone arrived. Just a little mantra to keep us focused. When it's difficult to see the trees for the forest as we get into the weeds. Ha ha!"

Guy winced. "I'm not at a hundred percent yet, Arthur."

"I heard you went aboard Petra's schooner." He straightened his posture. "I'm disappointed, Guy."

"Disappointment is popular these days."

Benatti motioned toward the residences. "I've been meaning to ask. Why white? It's hell on the eyes. Too reflective."

Averman scratched his wrist. "Not white. A proprietary mix."

"It looks white," Benatti said.

Averman crouched down. "Let me tell you a story. After I bought this island I camped out for ten days. Solo. Just a tent, some paracord, a lighter, and a buck knife. I wanted a relationship with the land, you see? When they picked me up I'd created a cairn trail to the peak and carved the floor plans for the first dozen structures, including this one. Broke my big toe. Somehow contracted giardia."

"What are you saying?" Guy asked. Averman's cheer was spoiling the mood.

"I added a drop of my blood to every gallon of the exterior paint. They call it International Averman Eggshell."

Benatti ground out his cigarette. "Still too reflective. How are you feeling about the turnout?"

Averman brightened. "I'm feeling great. Just great. We're going to accomplish so much today." He turned to Guy and snapped his fingers. "Jessica's been liaising with everyone's money managers—just a bit of due diligence. She's getting mixed signals from your people."

Guy suppressed a cough and tried to read Averman's expression: the picture of sun-kissed equanimity. But Averman was undoubtedly reading Guy's expression, had noticed the suppressed cough and taken it for a poker tell, and was now thinking of Victoria, upgrading her disappearance from accidental to premeditated, hypothesizing motives and spinning out possible scenarios. Guy knew this was Averman's true talent, the ability to take each input and imagine credible second-order effects, third-order effects, and so on and so on, keeping a mental warehouse of hypotheticals for every subject and interest.

What if he came clean? About the fraud, the betrayal, his own downgraded circumstance? It was a mad impulse. His sphincter's automatic response kept it from becoming anything more.

Guy finished his espresso and cleared his throat. "We're, ah, changing firms. Spontaneous decision. I'll send Jessica the info next week."

Averman took this in and smiled. "All's well, then." He patted Guy's knee, stood, and looked past Benatti to another table. "If you'll excuse me." He continued his rounds, back-slapping his way to the amphitheater.

Benatti pocketed his cigarette case and checked his watch. "You still do tennis? I'll need to get my blood pumping between the sessions."

Imagining his body in swift ambulation triggered acid reflux. "Let's play it by ear."

"You're in. All these other fucks golf. It'll help you to sweat out Friday night."

"I may do more than sweat."

"Purgation is necessary on the road to paradise."

• • •

AVERMAN PACED THE amphitheater stage as everyone filed in. He waved at a few people, thumbs-upped someone in the first row. Jessica rolled a whiteboard behind him and conferred with staff, who then filled the samovars and beverage dispensers under the giant painting. Guy spotted his negroni dot, faded to a pale pink, and then saw the brass plaque below the frame. Mehretu, that's what it was. He could see why Averman chose it for the Quorum. Vague enough to be welcoming, simultaneously urban and utopian—a reminder of their purpose. V's art advisor said they missed the boat on the artist. The queue was epic, and she preferred queer collectors. Averman must have bought at auction. Or not: a second glance at the plaque revealed Oikoi's logo and fine print on provenance. The start-up managed rentals for cash-strapped museums, a bit of fortuitous timing amid the reputational whitewashing post-Sackler. V was a recent member: she gifted him an Idris Khan print of Beethoven's sonatas, hanging somewhere in the Aspen place. The Oikoi angel investor was the red-haired guy in the fifth row—what was his name? Foy? Ferrin?

The Mehretu was on loan from MoMA. Eventually Guy's small contribution would be seen by hundreds of thousands of tourists. Included in monographs and gift shop prints. It was just a fleck, nothing really. And inarguably something. A piece of the work, and a little bit of him.

He took a seat in the back row next to Benatti and Mary Ellen, and close to a wall vent pumping out bergamot-scented oxygen. Benatti tried to show them his mistress's Amazon wish list—lingerie, naturally, but also practical items like dehumidifiers and label makers—but the screen made Guy nauseous. He was about to ask if they saw Roark when the man's voice filtered into the room.

"By the window—there. No, not by those assholes. By the window." A burly staff member wheeled in a sleek, silver hospital bed with Roark regally ensconced among its linens and pillows like a necrotic Dionysus. He wore a paisley dressing gown, silk pajama bottoms, Scandinavian house shoes, and a pulsometer clipped to his thumb. With its blinking green lights and elongated shape, the bed resembled an open-top fighter jet.

Benatti put his hand on Roark's forehead, who batted it away. "What happened to you?"

Roark pushed a button and raised his backrest. "It's minor, totally minor. Slipped on the grass during my reconnaissance. Just a sore hip and a broken rib."

"I'm no doctor," Mary Ellen said. "But it seems like you should be resting."

"Nonsense. I'm not going to stay in my suite while you decide how to spend my money." He gestured at his minder. "You. Turkish coffee."

Benatti put up two fingers. The staff member nodded and left.

Mary Ellen leaned close to Guy. "Listen, is Gustafson leaving the PrevYou board? I may want him for something, but he's been ducking my calls."

He felt a prick at the small of his back. He inhaled something ripe and foul: the bergamot air was mixing poorly with the lavender crop-dusting. Before Guy could respond, Averman called the session to order.

"Friends! Welcome to the very first session of the Quorum." He put up a hand to still applause that was not forthcoming.

"A couple years ago I was at Sun Valley—some of you were there—and I had this flash of insight. We've signed the Giving Pledge. Signaled our optimism for the future. Half or more of our fortunes put toward education. Or public health. Land conservation. The arts. In short, ensuring the world we know and love stays the world we know and love.

"But what's so great about the status quo? There's still disease. There's still poverty. We can do better. The brilliant minds in this room have achieved some pretty remarkable things. Jessica here reminded me you lot oversee more employees than the entire population of Chicago."

Averman stepped to the side, where a staff member delivered him a Quorum Nitro. He glugged half and handed it back. "Now we're going to achieve the impossible, and achieve it together. This weekend we will formally confirm our decision to pool our fortunes and decide which global ill to eradicate once and for all!"

Polite applause. Guy heard a variation on this speech when Averman conscripted Victoria.

"This first session is about mapping the territory. Jessica will transcribe our contributions, and then we'll discuss hierarchies and priorities in the afternoon session. Tomorrow is implementation. Monday A.M. will be our declaration and action plan."

A hand went up in the second row. "Yes?"

An anemic man in a sleeveless fleece vest stood up. "Can we start by addressing your insidious influence campaign? I would hardly call the proceedings unbiased."

"Jesus, Mike. Calm down. What are you talking about."

Mike pointed to the annex. "Your iceberg sculpture. Clearly you want to steer us toward climate change. Or arctic preservation. Or . . ."

"Okay, that's fair. An oversight, and totally accidental." Averman motioned to Jessica and whispered in her ear. She dashed from the room. "Jessica's moving the vitrine to my suite so it's out of sight. Happy?"

Mike nodded and sat down.

"That brings up a good point, actually," Averman said. "Climate change is out of scope. We're only limiting ourselves to the problems we can solve with our resources. Anything that involves the public sector is a nonstarter. Might as well flush our money down the toilet."

Scattered laughter. Jessica returned and handed him a printout.

"I thought I would start with a reminder of why we're all here. God and the markets have been very good to us, and I know we are all grateful. But life is still difficult for too many people. In the last twenty-four hours there has been, let's see here, a shooting in a mall in Houston, a corruption scandal in Sweden's board of agriculture, a tanker hijacked off the Madagascar coast, and—Jessica, I can't read this—ah: bombings in Afghanistan." There was more to read, but Averman handed the paper to Jessica. "Okay, that's probably enough. Let's dive in. Everyone got their Quorum Nitros? Just signal to the guys back there if you want one."

Jessica uncapped a marker and wrote *ILLS* at the top of the whiteboard.

"Right," Averman said. "I thought we'd begin with an

overview of the problems at hand. This is a brainstorm. There're no bad suggestions. We'll prioritize and organize in the second session."

Four men spoke at once and then deferred to Roark. "We're to list, what? Global pandemics?"

"Everything. Like heart disease, for example." Averman replied.

Jessica wrote *HEART DISEASE* in the top left corner.

A voice from the third row. "World hunger?"

Jessica wrote *WORLD HUNGER.*

Guy figured he'd come this far. "Jingoism!"

JINGOISM.

Benatti yelled, "Famine!"

"Isn't that the same as world hunger?" Roark asked. A chorus of assenting murmurs.

Wright called up from the second row. "World hunger is a distribution problem. Famine is agricultural."

"Gentlemen." Averman put his hands up in a conciliatory gesture. "Again, there are no bad suggestions. We'll sort everything in the second session."

FAMINE.

"SIDS!" Mary Ellen yelled.

"Malaria!" someone shouted.

Momentum gathered: "Alzheimer's! Influenza! Cerebral palsy! Women's education! Recidivism! Rising oceans! The migrant crisis! Diabetes! Earthquakes! Wage disparity! Racism! Blindness! Domestic abuse! Nuclear armament! Nuclear stockpiling! Opportunity for the less affluent! Drug patents! Ennui! Urban zoning! High-speed internet access!

The Great Barrier Reef! Food deserts! Healthcare reform! Religious extremism! Crohn's disease! Meningococcemia! Carbon emissions! AIDS! Female genital mutilation! Apathy! Child labor! Deafness! Corporate monopolies! Tax reform! Flesh-eating viruses! Infrastructure! University endowments! River-borne diseases! Mudslides! Marfan syndrome! Wildfires! Sexism! Opioids! Locked-in syndrome! Gambling addiction! Lyme's! Lack of potable water! Tuberculosis! COPD! Syphilis! Deaths of despair! Mass transportation! High blood pressure! Bee extinction! Monogamy! Pneumonia! Mass incarceration! Mass migration! Pornography! Fibromyalgia! Diarrhea! Cirrhosis! Bacterial infections! Poor hygiene! Illiteracy! E. coli! Car accidents! School shootings! Xenophobia! Holy wars! Preterm birth complications! Sugar! Terrorism! Diabetes! Unemployment! Depression! Norovirus! Fracking! Oxygen depletion in the oceans! Nuclear waste! Mortality! . . ."

Guy was impressed by Jessica's speed and penmanship. A Quorumite paced behind him in short laps, calling out morbidities while staring at the carpet. Another Quorumite stood in the fourth row flailing his arms in a loose, jerky motion while swinging his hips. It must have worked; when he called out "cellular degeneration," his neighbors nodded in support.

This was what Guy was after. Inside this room was pure possibility. Unfiltered agency. The belief that whatever troubled one's soul could be met and met head-on. The world could place its finger on you, but only a finger. He looked around at all of the eyelids stretched open. A feeling of euphoria came over him, and then a sudden fatigue. He leaned his head against Roark's gurney. The old man absently patted his hair.

Jessica stepped back from the whiteboard, which had transformed into a dense cloud of macro- and microruination: Satan's to-do list.

Averman clapped. "A great start. Some of these might be out of scope, but I'm confident we'll whittle down to the most impactful solutions." Jessica pressed a button on the whiteboard panel. A printer behind her began spitting out pages. "Please review these over lunch, so we can—"

"Diabetes is listed twice," someone called out. "Middle left, next to kidnapping."

Jessica located it and brushed away the word.

"We could probably combine ennui and depression," Wright said. Averman nodded at Jessica, who found the former and erased it. She reprinted the new board.

"I'm proud to announce we'll be getting some help before the afternoon session," Averman said. He asked the MIT kids to stand. "Our friends here are loaning us their university's quantum computing network and AI to, well, to—"

The female MIT kid spoke up. "It will fashion the list into subthemes and organizational questions to impose a hierarchy and guide our thinking."

The short MIT kid added, "Think of it as a million objective research assistants. For example, it'll look into up-to-the-minute epidemiology and ask, Would prevention cost less than a cure? Or, um—"

"Does solving the female education gap require negotiating with terrorists?" the first one asked.

Averman clapped again. "Yes, exactly. Thank you. Jessica, why don't you give us a preview."

Jessica retrieved her tablet as a screen descended from the ceiling. A projector behind the samovars whirred to life, showing everyone her tablet desktop. This always struck Guy as mildly invasive, like looking in someone's underwear drawer. She closed a document with the session's agenda to reveal a window of open tabs. Including the ProPublica homepage.

Panic. Guy skimmed the headlines for PrevYou or Victoria Stevens. Nothing. What if it autorefreshed, with a headline font reserved for the outbreak of war? Everyone's phones would ping a second later. They'd ask him to explain, but of course he couldn't explain. They'd conduct a spot vote of no confidence and toss him to the sharks.

Pestilence. That's what he was. Pickled and lurking. He felt both light and heavy. He fished around in his pockets, found two small blue pills, dry swallowed them both, then took a pull from his flask. Goddamn you, Victoria.

He ignored Mary Ellen's questioning look. The screen filled with a new application branded with the MIT logo. A string of words began running down the page.

Averman nodded to Jessica. "All set? Okay. So it's, ah, computing now, and will be ready by three." He motioned to the doors. "Take a printout as you leave and we'll see you at the second session. Lunch is buffet style."

The crowd gave Roark deference, allowing him to exit first. Guy positioned himself near the bed and touched the handrail to feign steering.

In the hallway Wright jogged up and took a photo of Roark.

"Can I help you?" Roark asked.

"Sorry, man, Brian made me do it."

Guy had met Roark's husband once or twice. Lead counsel for Human Rights Watch, something like that.

"I'm fine," Roark said. "Don't get in the middle of this."

Wright tapped at his phone and read a text. "Brian told me to say you downplay the severity of your ailments. And to call him." He looked up. "And I'm not in the middle. Brian's a friend." He gave a thumbs-up and walked off.

Guy tuned out Roark's grumbling as they rolled toward his suite. He enjoyed these windows into others' relationships, for the obvious voyeuristic thrill as well as the perspective they gave on his own implosion. Victoria was thoughtful, the kind of partner who would remember the anniversaries of his parents' deaths. And diagnostic. Constantly diagnostic, in fact, and much like Roark's husband, he could see Victoria casually informing him of some innocuous character trait. Where Brian seemed to do so out of a concern said trait may at some point prove harmful, Victoria shared the insight purely as a data point. She didn't think it warranted response, other than perhaps a confirmation of its veracity.

Wright had once remarked, with diplomacy and after-party honesty, that Guy and Victoria's marriage held a certain coldness. Guy understood this as simply an outsider's view of the somewhat transactional nature of their union. The fact was they had married late in life, and she possessed the widow's permanent trace of mourning. Late one night, after a few fingers of Macallan, Guy had even confessed to Wright they were not each other's great loves.

Still, he had believed they were strong, whatever that meant, on a day-to-day level, whatever that meant. They rarely argued and never fought. He knew he made cohabitation difficult at times, veteran as he was of single living, who arranged things *just so* and for a purpose he never thought worth making explicit. V's inevitable slights were minor and manageable. And PrevYou's rise, propitious in so many ways, also removed the obstacles of each other from their lives. She returned home just enough for them to not take each other for granted, but not so much that long-standing peccadillos enervated or riled. No surprise that the cure for their plateaued relationship turned out to be sudden, stratospheric wealth.

And now? Everything was poisoned. Victoria's four-dimensional duplicity retroactively destroyed whatever connubial half-bliss they once shared. Forget being each other's great loves. The last sixteen years now felt like a one-way street ending with a cliff.

This was all too much knowledge, too much self-knowledge. Victoria had invaded his brainpan once more—a telltale sign of demonic sobriety. He patted Roark on the shoulder and wandered off before the old man could respond.

A folded set of tennis whites and sneakers had been set outside his door on a teal tray. He tossed them on his bed and stopped at the bar cart. Why not? He enjoyed the fantasy of sweating out the liquor while its cousins whitewater rafted his circulatory system. He poured a double of room-temp gin. Perhaps it would break the blood-brain barrier quicker. How odd it was that most of the civilized world was room temperature, except for these hairless bipeds moving around, thirty degrees warmer than everything else. Had their ancestors been cooler? Warmer? He still knew so little.

At the courts Benatti was playing doubles with staff, impressively returning serves with a cigarette between his lips. The slow pocks of a single's game reported through the high fence and semitransparent tarp separating them from their neighbors. Closer to the jungle's edge, Mary Ellen and two other female Quorumites perched on folding chairs while staff filmed their repartee and held a fuzzy boom mic above their heads.

A line of racquets leaned against the fence; Guy chose the closest one at hand.

"My wobbly friend!" Benatti waved him over and dismissed the staff. "I'm warmed up. You want to volley first?"

Guy raised his right leg and rotated his ankle, then did the same with the left. "I expect I have thirty good minutes in me. Use it however you like."

"Let's play, then."

Guy netted his first serve and cleared it on the second. They had an easy rapport. Benatti wasn't very good, with a skewed forehand he kept overcorrecting, but he wasn't interested in winning either. This suited Guy just fine. He preferred that sweet spot between aerobic exertion and a good rally.

He'd inherited his father's interest in the sport, a vestige of British colonialism with thin but long-standing ties between the two island nations. His father liked to pantomime Frank Hadow's deep lob after dinner. Hadow owned coffee plantations in rural Uva, before everyone switched to tea, and the Wimbledon champion's dismissal of both the sport and old Ceylon did nothing to deter his father's hero worship—nor the fact that Hadow's win occurred when his father's own father was in diapers.

As for Guy, he loved John McEnroe. The coiled phenom's near-perfect performance provided much-needed distraction during his last year at Curtis. His colleagues considered a love of sport eccentric bordering on transgressive, save for the musicians' obsession with ping-pong, while off-campus such fandom was assumed. Guy didn't care for McEnroe's back talk to the line judges but understood it as a larger impatience with the world. Guy couldn't relate. In his first years out in the wild, his graduating class—only the second of the new composition program, with all the expectations that implied—established their names and accrued commissions. A handful of institutions came through for him, but never enough to live on or string together something so lofty as a reputation. His memory of that time reduced to hotel afternoons with Gretchen and weekends at his downstairs neighbor's, splitting a case of Yuenglings and providing color commentary of the Opens.

Guy knew his life sounded glamorous—four weeks in an Italian castle, working on a solo cello piece! But he had to find a subletter, or eat the rent; cancel piano lessons, his only source of stable income; and find a cat sitter for his tabby, who scratched visitors. He slowly retreated from the alumni events until his connections dwindled to Gretchen and a library clerk who let him check out scores and records.

Guy blinked and became middle-aged. Devoid of even the pretense of glamour.

As for McEnroe, there was pure talent. At first he looked too skinny. Didn't have the serve of the power baseline guys. But to watch him play was to witness physiology meeting its most well-suited expression. This must be how Victoria felt. Her preternatural gifts all but determined her choices in life.

Benatti held up a hand and paused for a hacking cough. Stopping was a mistake. Guy's side burst into flame and his knees clocked out. He loosed wet effluvium onto the service line. Staff ran off for cleaning supplies.

Guy and Benatti gathered themselves. They eyed the yellow puddle.

"Is that normal for you?" Benatti asked. He walked to the bench and grabbed his cigarette case.

"It is lately. I'm under high-alcohol palliative care." Guy dropped his racquet on the court. His shirt clung to him with sweat. "Call it a draw?"

Benatti winked and lit up. He lit a second cigarette end to end and handed it to Guy.

Guy inhaled and immediately felt better. "I asked; we're not supposed to smoke on the island."

"That's why I don't ask," Benatti said.

Averman crossed the lawn, trailed by staff. He checked in with Mary Ellen's group and waved to Benatti and Guy. He yelled, "*Es muss sein!*" while energetically pumping his fist.

Benatti hmphed.

"It's from Beethoven," Guy said. He'd forgotten that Averman knew about his erstwhile career. "Some marginalia in the sixteenth string quartet. Means 'it must be,' which most people take for a line about fate."

The phrase was a common toast at Curtis. Gretchen read

a novel with the line in it, this was the late eighties; from her explanation it seemed the Czech writer had completely mis-read the composer's intention.

Benatti returned the wave. "My father said people who invoke destiny don't deserve their wealth."

Staff returned with a bucket and towels.

Guy took the tobacco deep in his lungs. "There's some debate among musicologists. Some think he was writing to himself—cheering himself on, if you will. Others say he was upbraiding his maid about some financial matter. The more romantically inclined think the note was autoreflexive: it was Beethoven's last piece."

"A swan song."

"Even that's arguable. It wasn't the last thing he worked on, not technically."

Benatti scrolled through his phone. "I will check in with my sister now." Guy took this to mean there was news about the merger.

"See you at the next session."

Guy asked a staff member to have two negronis delivered to his room.

He hadn't thought of Beethoven's op. 135 in years. It was fine, not to his taste. Gretchen often invoked the last movement's inscription—"The resolution reached with diffi-culty"—during their combative state of the unions.

Back in his suite he sipped his drink and contemplated a shower. The mild exertion had left him flop sweated with the musk of all he'd ingested these past twenty-four hours. It felt good on him, a miasmal marker of achievement. Cleanliness was for the virtuous. For those interested in betterment. He felt ripened.

He picked up the pills from the side table. It was unlikely the two he'd taken that morning had metabolized. Better top up. He punched in Brahms's first piano concerto and splashed cold water on his face. Then he changed into a polo, yesterday's trousers, and black horse-bit loafers.

Bolted the negroni. Time for more.

CHAPTER 8

Keeping this diary still feels foreign. Though "keeping" isn't correct; it does not accumulate. An impermanent record, then.

Still. Maintain your candor.

Juan said I should do interviews. Tell my side of the story. But PrevYou *is* my side of the story. I've been showing the world my side of the story for nine years.

The public wants—what. Talking points. Canned responses. My riposte will not be verbal, but majestically capitalistic. Globally transformative. It will change the fabric of daily experience.

And I will deliver this riposte soon. Any day now.

Something clicked in my stride this A.M. A small but fruitful alignment.

There is satisfaction in achieving corporeal harmony. Once felt, it can never be forgotten. A pop song of the body.

—

I wonder how close I am to Truckee. Half day's drive, maybe. A visit would be the sisterly thing to do. It's Daniel's offseason, which means shifts at that hardware store. Or general dogsbody if the ski resorts have enough work.

I could risk it—he's more or less off-the-grid. Three years sober.

Guy was always squirrelly around Daniel. Did they have AA in Sri Lanka. It sounded like his dad was a fan of the bottle. When he was passed over for advancement: go for the arrack. When their first visas were rejected: go for the arrack.

I'll visit Daniel. After.

What became of my teenage diary. It must be in storage at the condo.

I once told Guy about it. A black leather-bound number with gilt edges. A gift from Grandpa Hochstapler. He told me to track my ideas and to play devil's advocate. "Argue with yourself on the page."

Either he planted the seed, or I got it from a documentary, but I had the sense even then that future biographers and MBA students would consult my entries. This proved highly motivating. At least until my brief crush with Kevin . . . Anderson. Jones. It's immaterial. I wanted to record my emotions, of course, but couldn't see a way to do so without compromising the integrity of the object.

Grandpa said, "Don't give them anything they can use against you."

The idea came during a Sunday 5K: reserve the impolitic

and highly personal material to Post-it notes as a pastor might bookmark bible passages. Incidentally, this was the actual first use by the inventor of Post-its, which was the kind of entrepreneurial history I would have written in the diary, had I wanted to call attention to the Post-its and my highly personal emotions.

The plan was to deliver the curated portrait of my teenhood in accordance with the more public (but no less manageable) portrait of adulthood when the time was right, immediately after removing the incriminating neon adhesives.

I haven't thought of that diary in years. Not during the First Flush, and not when the first profile writers came calling.

These are exactly the kinds of thoughts that lead to eureka.

I don't believe I've mentioned this yet. Juan speaks in the same pitch and rhythm no matter the subject or, it seems, his feelings toward the subject. As if all of life was of equal interest to him. Fascinating.

He showed me videos of his girl in LA. I didn't tell him about the suspicious postproduction.

He said he might be in love. When I asked what that word meant to him, he paused for a bit. Said it's a language with endless idiolects. You can never attain full fluency with another person, but you can share productive miscommunication.

It's a nice thought. I told him he should also be clearheaded about it. In a long-term relationship, one defines the terms and settles the territories. And then sticks to them. Things collapse when one partner redraws the boundaries.

———

He worked the shoulder a bit with the foam roller. There is still residual soreness. After our session I popped two white-heads on his back. Highly satisfying.

There's a tennis court on the property, and I found a ball dispenser in the storage shed. During midday break I practiced my forehand and paid Juan to reload the hopper.

He was very chatty. Kept wanting to show me YouTube videos. "Stuff that'll blow your mind. Life-changing shit." I told him not to bother; I have no interest in changing my life. I have been the person I wish to be since eighteen.

He pushed back, tried quoting Lincoln. An approximation of our exchange:

Me: Do you know the speed of a tennis serve at the professional level?

Juan: Isn't it, like, a hundred miles per hour?

Me: Roddick once hit a hundred fifty at the Davis Cup.

Juan: That's very fast. We were talking about new ideas.

Me: Agassi was on the receiving end of these hundred-milers for two decades. You know what he said? The ball looked huge to him. His kinesthetic response and perceptive faculty were so high that it all traveled in slow motion.

Juan: Impressive.

Me: Say you're Agassi. You're one of a handful of people on the planet with this concrete ability. A friend says, "Have you heard of bowling? Why not give it a try?"

Juan: I like bowling.

Me: Every minute Agassi bowls is a minute lost to tennis.

Every movement not put toward a serve or a return is a lost movement. Or worse, a counterproductive movement.

Juan: And you're Agassi.

Me: For the purposes of the metaphor, yes. Outside of the metaphor, he hit a tiny green ball for a living. I'm 100 times his net worth.

Later we drank lemonade on the porch. "You have to add the lemon rinds," I told him. Then I told him to masturbate: I wanted to see the motion of his arm muscles at work. He rain checked: "Indica dick."

I will have to scare up a sizeable angel round and blitzscale the first few years. A real idea demands it. Restraint in the early stages may suffocate it later on.

This is what nobody understands. A lack of capital should never get in the way of advancing society. Look at Edison. Astronomical debt. He knew what it really meant: a vote of confidence.

On the porch Juan monologued about the age of dinosaurs. I thought of my last birthday present for Guy: an ancient cricket—a katydid—preserved in amber. Scientists say its wings produced an E natural, the planet's first musical note, over 150 million years ago. He was very impressed, though he suggested we donate it to the Museum of Natural History. As if he was ashamed to own it. I told him shame blunts ambition.

———

I had Juan get me a postcard. He selected a touristy image of a large saguaro in Ray-Bans and polka-dot boxer shorts. It appeared to have no meaning beyond a childish zaniness. This was confirmed by Juan's THC-enhanced giggling.

I wrote to Guy *All will be well* on the back and addressed it to the Manhattan place. It will tide him over until I rescue us.

Though I wonder if Guy's still in Manhattan. Surely he knows I'd never actually kill myself. Would he fly to SF and join the search party. No. He'd stay at home and await my call.

Perhaps he's absconded to Sri Lanka to ruminate at a beachside hotel in Galle. Though it's the start of monsoon season; he hates the rain.

It's all temporary. I will reach Utmost Throb on my next run.

Must ideate methods for nurturing exhaustion and hallucination.

CHAPTER 9

Guy entered the amphitheater with a burst of serotonin, a result of the voided stomach or the exercise or the negronis or the nicotine or whatever was in the blue pills. Averman consulted with Jessica and the MIT kids while groups of Quorumites milled about, talking low with their hands covering their mouths. Guy detected a current of insurrection.

Mary Ellen waved him over.

"Maybe you can answer Gerry's question."

She was with a trio he recognized from that morning's running group. They all looked like men who rose with the sun.

"You went on Bax's little sloop last night?" Gerry asked.

"Affirmative."

"Did she mention if they'd sailed to the spaceship graveyard? Or are planning to?"

Ah, Gerry Laughlin. He and that white filmmaker competed for increasingly esoteric deep-sea records. The newest concerned the area in the South Pacific where outdated shuttles were sunk after a controlled descent. "She didn't. You'll have to ask her yourself."

One of the others nodded at Guy. "This might sound indecorous given your wife's work, but I think the Quorum needs to address implementation strategies *before* we narrow down our causes. What if we put our money on cancer prevention and there's another Carrington Event?"

"You mean a solar flare?" Mary Ellen asked.

"It caused untold damage, tons of cases of skin cancer. And that was a hundred and sixty years ago. Imagine the effects today. Satellites, emergency systems."

"I keep a couple astronomers on retainer," Gerry said. "They tell me it could happen at literally any time."

The third guy spoke up. "Not to mention the unquantifiable problems. Loneliness is worse for mortality than a pack-a-day habit."

"That doesn't sound right," Guy said. The man flinched.

Gerry looked annoyed. "So? What's your solution? We sink our fortunes into a cause we can't measure?"

The third guy played defense. "You're so certain of the metrics we *do* have? How do we know a group isn't inflating their misery? Some beau geste effect to get more attention than is warranted?"

The second guy cleared his throat. "That's not the only problem with Averman's methodology. What about rollout strategies?"

"You're talking advertising," Mary Ellen said. "Marketing. Paid media, earned media."

"Yes. A good agency can sell this as transformative, a once-in-a-century opportunity, instead of, of . . ."

His friends piped up. "Social Darwinism?"

"White saviors?"

"Collective delusion?"

"Um, sure. Take your pick."

Mary Ellen waved her hand at a bug or at the trio's suggestions. "You presume transparency is necessary. Why not circumvent the hoi polloi? They needn't cast a vote when it comes to their deliverance."

Guy caught the transgressive tone in her voice. "Like those secret sterilization programs," he said. "With homosexuals and the disabled."

"But you know," she said. "The other way."

"It would save time and effort," Gerry said. "Who knows how many people would continue to suffer while the ad agency developed its campaign."

"That's not even the real problem," Mary Ellen said.

"What is the real problem?" Guy asked, playing dumb.

"What if you cure malaria, and in so doing empower a dictator bent on ethnic cleansing?"

Gerry pointed at the MIT kids. "I think that's what those three are trying to solve."

"I don't mean knock-on effects," Guy said. "How do we implement anything without buy-in from heads of state? Our little gathering is inherently antidemocratic."

The three men blinked. Gerry said, "Well, sure. But only temporarily."

Averman clapped. "Everyone! Let's get started. We have some exciting updates to share with all of you."

They took the same seats as the first session. Guy didn't see Benatti. He nodded at Roark in his mobile bed; the old man had dozed off.

Mary Ellen leaned over. "Gustafson's not answering my emails. I need to ask you about him later."

The MIT kids projected dozens of charts on the large wall. Jessica helped them with the focus.

"Victoria and I are through," he said absently.

"Really?" she said. "Huh. Okay."

Averman walked to his marker on the carpet and put his hands up like a Baptist preacher about to sermonize. Before he could begin someone leaped from the first row and joined him. Guy thought he might be the lead runner from the morning group.

"Arthur! We're all very much looking forward to the progress we're sure to make in this session. But some of the others and I have concerns we feel it's best to express presently."

Averman blinked a few times. "Presently as in 'soon,' or presently as in 'right now'?"

"Right now. This will only take a moment."

Averman leaned against the wall and made a "go ahead" gesture. The MIT kids and Jessica paused their work and held their positions.

"Thanks, Arthur. Hey, everyone. A few of the guys and I wanted to address an issue with our decision-making framework. I'm sure our friends from Cambridge here have some brilliant things to show us, but before they do, let's ask ourselves a simple question." He held for dramatic effect. Mary Ellen snorted. "Are we overindexing societal ills and underindexing the specific groups saved?

"Economists at the RAND corporation once calculated the cost of a human life to be about ten million dollars. Obviously this an oversimplified average. Why would a *Fortune* 500 executive be worth the same as a toddler? Or reverse that. If potential life matters more than experience, we might say the executive has a decade left on earth. A decade of decreased capacity and increased senescence. He's already accomplished all that he's meant to.

"But why focus just on age? We have other demographic markers. Nationality. Longevity. It'd be hard to argue with an endowment for, say, Ashkenazi Jews with graduate degrees in their late twenties. They live forever, they have a proven track record of thriving under adversity, and they gather in stable geographic regions."

Averman put his hand on the runner's shoulder. "Great points and some amazing insight here. Thank you. We'll tackle all this in tomorrow's A.M. session, and I don't want to get off track—"

"If I may?" The MIT female said. "We have something that may square the circle here."

The two other MIT kids whispered it wasn't ready. She ignored them and gave a more polished version of the pitch Guy heard last night. She projected the software onto the wall. "This will guarantee our bequest's constant maximum utility and accommodate known unknowns and unknown unknowns—"

Gerry cupped his hands around his mouth. "Hey, Averman! I didn't commit twelve billion for an algo cooked up by these chalk-fingered, desexed robots."

Mary Ellen leaned over. "Guy. Your nose."

"My what? Oh." A thin line of blood glistened atop his polo

fabric. He tipped his head back and stood. A staff member handed him a stack of napkins.

He exited as the MIT female said, "Our classrooms switched to smartboards years ago . . ." A globule floated in his nasal cavity, resistant to his attempts to swallow it down. He twisted a napkin and plugged his nostril. Raised voices escaped the amphitheater. He decided to wander.

There was a backstage quality to the buildings during the session: staff sweeping floors, refilling ice chests, removing a dead lizard from a pool. The Asian staff member from last night trundled boxes across the circular drive while mumbling into his phone.

Guy walked and tried to shake the floaters from his vision, wandering toward the jungle, where he was met with a cacophony of birdsong, far louder and more pluralistic than he would have thought possible. Fine, no jungle. He turned and followed the signs for Astrid's Beach, named for Averman's daughter. Or maybe granddaughter; old-fashioned names were coming back.

The dark line of the jungle gave way to a dark smear on the horizon, giving contrast to the light blue waters. He descended the wooden staircase to the sand, kicked off his loafers, and waded in up to his knees. The water was bathtub-warm and calm. Swells rose at the edge of the sand shelf. The curling waves had a hypnotic effect, each one a closing hand beckoning him forth.

Curiously, everything was silent. The ocean was just a big bowl of water. Happily dumb, following the moon without issue or worry.

There was a measure of relief to Victoria's betrayal. It confirmed his long-held, almost inherited skepticism of good fortune. "God doesn't give with both hands," his mother would say. When people brought up her deceased husband, or asked how they were managing: "God doesn't give with both hands." She didn't indulge in reminiscences—people were surprised by how little she mentioned Sri Lanka—and gave up cooking biryani at home, only making lamprais on Christmas at her son's request. Her assimilation was accumulative; she treated her non-white customs as burdensome. Guy resented this at first. Thought she was turning her back on the past. He was wrong twice over: his resentment was purely adolescent, and her forbearance entirely driven by grief.

At some point in their first year his mother sat him down. "Remember," she said. "Your father imagined this place as one of unlimited potential. His passing doesn't change that." It was their duty to fulfill this potential. Days became sites of work, of chores and checklists. And slowly, eventually, they fashioned an American life. It wasn't until Guy's late-stage accidental affluence and its bountiful laxity that he saw what was hidden at the time: a functioning American life kept you too busy to register its liabilities. Call it denial, call it compartmentalization; success demanded partial blindness.

What was the name of their cemetery? St. Luke's? That sounded right. When she collapsed his second semester at Curtis he didn't know what to do, and he asked the director of the funeral home to reprise his father's service. Same casket, same flowers, same wake. Most of the local diaspora showed up. He swapped out "The Last Post" for "Hey Jude," his mother's favorite. The piano had been tuned by a moron, but he trudged through, stiff upper lip and all that.

He and Victoria had never talked about their plans. He always pictured a mausoleum on the grounds of the Hudson Valley estate, something marmoreal under an old elm. Now? Cremation held a certain appeal. Where embalming felt secularly pharaonic, being rendered to ash was modest. Sustainable. Ahistoric. Burn him up and sprinkle his ashes into the coffees of friends and strangers.

Guy walked farther into the sea. Bits of seashell were loosely scattered as if art-directed. Did Averman have this *groomed*? The sand appeared to shimmy, the water became a million temporary shapes with glowing edges. He fell casually and floated on his back. His clothes felt heavy, but he was able to keep his face and chest above the surface. He inhaled through his mouth and blew through his nose, shooting the bloodied napkin straight up. It landed on his forehead and rolled off.

Pale sky filled his vision. He could be anywhere. Let the current carry him out to a pleasant beige finale. A composer's tradition of a sort. Schumann's attempt. Hugo Wolf's attempt. And what of the accidental drownings: the young Linley, that old Spaniard Granados. Sure. Why not be inclusive.

It was incredible to think he would die. Actually die. He wasn't leaving behind any children or blood relatives. No unfinished business came to mind. Would it be Monday? Ah, to die on a Monday. He laughed, then caught himself, as if he had whistled in a graveyard. But who was there to offend.

There was Victoria. Out there, plotting a comeback. He would make her a widow twice over. A fitting rebuke and, he hoped, a bit of salt in the wound. Who would marry someone with two in the ground?

He dipped his head back to look at the horizon. Green and purplish striations danced above the line where water met sky. Or danced below. Whichever. The blue pills must have kicked in. He sank into the low-level euphoria.

He couldn't begrudge Victoria. She followed her nature, could not help but be who she was. There had been subterfuge when they first met.

The Allentown wedding must have held four hundred guests. After his commitments—a ho-hum German program with a pinch of Ligeti—he tried talking a bartender into a to-go bottle of Riesling. Victoria appeared at his side in a navy knee-length dress and asked for another seltzer with lemon. She turned to him and complimented his "performance." Then she said he slouched during the Bach, and, when it became clear to Guy he was being flirted with—which Victoria later told him anyone else would have gathered immediately—she held a hand to her mouth, mock-conspiratorial, and said her paperwork with the Universal Life Church had been lost in the mail. The marriage she had officiated wasn't officially valid.

An exchange of secrets is the quickest method of seduction; Guy swooned. It wasn't until years later when he shared the story with Wright that he learned Pennsylvania didn't require an ordained minister. The Quakers had ensured witnesses sufficed.

Subterfuge was one thing, betrayal another. She had the idea for PrevYou long before they met—at the deathbed of her first husband or her grandfather, depending on who was asking. Was it a fraud from the beginning? There must have been a decision. Some crossing of the Rubicon. He couldn't see her launching the company—the cause—knowing it would never work. The sheer amount of labor. Of passion! What was the point if it was all a lie? Maybe the point was never the point. The point was to simply keep going. This was what alpinists and Ponzi schemers shared: the commitment to continue on, despite all.

Perhaps she saw no end, apart from everlasting glory.

There was an element of sociopathy there, and naturally she'd been accused of it (and worse). Guy never gave it any credence. Who contemplates their loved one's pathologies amid the good times? Or—if he were being clear-eyed—amid the decent times?

He sensed movement. The Japanese ambler stood a short distance away, bare-chested, in a black speedo, sketching on a large notepad. He had the torso of a lifelong swimmer. Guy got to his feet, corrected his balance, and approached. The man smiled and angled his notepad to show an ink drawing. Guy couldn't focus his eyes on it.

"Impressive."

"Thank you." The man flipped through the pages to show portraits, landscapes, pointillist clusters. Guy had a vague memory of an electronics company founder who maintained a daily vlog of his drawings. Maybe this was him.

"No Quorum for you?" Guy asked.

"I'm disinterested," the man replied. "I won't be around for the implementation of . . . whatever they agree to implement."

Guy realized he was fully clothed. If he didn't address it, perhaps the man would assume it an eccentricity. These people were so forgiving.

"I know your wife," the man said. "I know her well."

Guy fixated on the horizon and the intensifying green. The man spoke about promise, about pain, about the destruction of capital. Guy attempted to occlude reality by focusing on the striations.

After a spell the man's voice broke through again. "You know," he said. "The song of the humpback whale can travel thousands of miles across the ocean." He gestured at the water, as if Guy was dense. "But it's imperceptible to our ears. All that music . . ." He checked his watch, its face positioned on the underside of his wrist. "Nice speaking with you."

The man waded to the beach and walked barefoot up the steps.

The striations danced over the water, the sky, his person. His ability to remark upon them and cogently separate them from his thoughts—that is, the ability to think at all, and think of Victoria—that spelled trouble. Guy needed to arrest time. Derail his faculties, get beyond himself.

He returned to the veranda and grabbed a terry cloth robe from a lounge chair. Benatti's unmistakable voice was regaling a small crowd at the bar, and Guy entered to see him drinking champagne from a staff member's ballet flat. Other staff members cheered as the remainder dripped down Benatti's chin. He returned the shoe with exaggerated gallantry, slipping it on the foot of a tittering redhead. Guy ordered a

Gibson and, not finding Jessica, requested cocaine from the blondest staff member.

He took a bracing mouthful. Cold, briny, salubrious. He made a peace sign to the bartender for another. "High spirits around here," he said to Benatti.

Benatti winked with sarcasm. "Didn't you know? We're a third of the way through the Quorum! A third of the way to saving humanity!"

The crowd laughed, which drew reproachful stares from the bartenders. None of them had drinks in hand, but there was a feeling like everyone had done shots before he arrived.

A staff member turned to Guy. "You missed a pretty memorable session, sir." He looked familiar. The one who handed him a napkin for his bloody nose.

"Oh?" Guy instinctively inhaled. Dried flecks and a lingering saltiness.

Benatti distributed cigarettes. "One of the casino guys spit on the MIT boy. The ponytailed wunderkind."

"What do you mean, spit on him? In front of everyone?"

"He yelled 'sic temper tyrannis' and let it fly," Benatti said. "Which I do not understand. The boy's a lightweight."

The staff member raised his hand. "I believe Mr. Lurie was referring to the algorithm, sir."

"So now Averman is running private mediation between them," Benatti said. "We're killing time before dinner."

"No news from your sister?" Guy asked.

"Holding patterns, she tells me."

"What's your plan?" The blond staffer returned and surreptitiously handed Guy a baggie.

"My plan," Benatti said, holding out his hand. Someone handed him the champagne bottle. "Explore the island. There's a rumor Bax's people have sneaked ashore. In a beach hut, running the conclave."

There was little chance the Quorum within the Quorum existed, and if it did, zero reason for Bax to insert herself. But a drive would be beneficial. Put some distance between himself and the man at the beach.

Guy finished his drink, picked up the refill, and pointed at the fulcrum of the veranda, where the open doors afforded a view of the line of Jeeps in the circular driveaway.

"Let's take one of those." He motioned Benatti toward the passenger side. He needed to drive, to transmit the brain's electricity into the ganglia of his nervous system, to express its motor function in beautiful concert with sensory input. The groinal thrum to executing a complex task.

The cup holder held his coupe glass perfectly. He cinched his robe tight and started the vehicle. The redhead and the napkin guy jumped in the back. Benatti passed them the bottle; they sipped furtively, like teenagers raiding their parents' liquor cabinet.

When was the last time he drove? Fifteen years? He pulled at the gearbox, which was different from the Volkswagen his father had taught him to drive with, and finally managed to reverse out. Benatti raised an eyebrow.

"A bit rusty," Guy explained.

"I only drive Italian. Wouldn't know how to navigate this piece of shit."

He managed first gear and exited the drive, scraping the

side mirror on the entryway column. The dashboard map indicated a straight shot down the narrow road, past the airstrip to a remote patch north. He accelerated until the thick foliage blurred and the crunching gravel fell into a satisfying rhythm. Car noise fell away as they sailed over ruts, their passage through the jungle like an arm through a shirtsleeve.

He ignored Benatti's animated talk about a dealer in rare Alfa Romeos. The back seat badinage concerned Averman's promise of student debt relief for the top quartile of staff. Such quaint problems! He thought of the Quorum's whiteboard. There was generational culpability in nearly every item. Maybe he'd been born at the wrong time.

The two kids moved on to discussing a herpes outbreak among the grounds crew. They might be the last generation. How freeing, to feel so doomed. To justifiably blame everything on one's elders.

He put a hand out to the warm air. Guy could drive this stygian path forever, could forever live in this exact state. Inside every tempest was a temporary calm, a marshaling of forces before the next onslaught. If he could laze inside this calm, pickle his insides, he would never have a blue thought ever again.

The redhead mentioned a Quorumite whose name sounded familiar. Maybe one of the finance guys? She'd created Google alerts on the attendees—"as a hobby"—and she'd just received news of an impending divorce.

"There goes his invite," Benatti said. When the other staffer asked why, Benatti explained that, depending on the settlement, the Quorumite's reduced net worth might drop him below Averman's threshold.

"So he'll be kicked off the island?" the redhead asked.

"No, nothing drastic," Benatti said. "When Arthur finds out he'll treat the guy like he has—what's the word, bedbugs?"

Guy sunk the rest of his cocktail and tossed the glass into the brush. News alerts. He hadn't thought about that. Would someone scoop ProPublica? Wasn't that what journalism was, people scooping each other in pursuit of the most sensational story? How did he ever think he could get away with all this?

The redhead tapped his shoulder. "Can I ask a personal question? What's it like being a billionaire?"

He put his hand out to catch the breeze again, but his fingers caught the leaf tips of the mutant roadside shrubbery. Like sticking your hand in a box fan. "It's difficult to relate to others."

"My therapist says I have the same problem."

Guy motioned for the champagne bottle and, when he turned his head, made the error of turning his arm along with it. The Jeep swerved and dipped into a culvert, sending red-brown spray up the passenger side. They casually flipped onto the passenger side, then fully capsized. Benatti had somehow ended in the fetal position, with the redhead's bare foot on his cheek. The napkin guy laughed, then cried, then laughed again. Guy hands were at ten and two, out of habit, and he was suspended in air by his seat belt, which he'd put on also out of habit. Fuck. They hadn't been driving that fast, but he felt like he'd missed his chance to be thrown from the vehicle. Plenty of tree trunks for a quick exit.

He unbuckled, twisted his legs free, and positioned his head on the padded roll bar. The four of them were splayed like toddlers in a crib.

"That dragonfly came out of nowhere," Guy said. "Everyone okay?"

Italian blaspheming indicated Benatti's annoyance but lack of injury. The redhead murmured her assent. Guy lifted his head to verify; she was bleeding from the forehead and likely in shock. The other kid said in an endearingly apologetic tone that his ankle was broken.

The dashboard display beeped and a recording of Averman's voice informed them help was on the way. Benatti opened his door and rolled onto the dirt. Guy watched his feet move to the front of the Jeep, past the culvert to the tree line, where he urinated with angry force while slapping at mosquitos. Guy's stream had long ago weakened to hangdog dribbles.

They extricated themselves and waited in the road. With the ocean breeze blocked by the greenery the full heat of the sun pricked their skin. Guy let the mosquitos buzz his ear canal and watched a writhing black fly stuck in the trail of blood on the redhead's brow. She gave him a dazed smile and propped up the other staffer.

"Roark's taken a turn," Benatti said. He fished around the Jeep for his lighter. "The fall, it exaggerated his heart condition, so he's confined to his suite. Which has bad marble, or something?"

Guy shivered. "Is he going to die?"

"Who knows. He is ninety. Ninety-one?"

"Mr. Jefferson is ninety-three," the redhead offered.

Benatti nodded. "At that age, you cough wrong and it's over."

Two Jeeps pulled up, followed by a truck with a tow bar. They were quickly surrounded by people assessing injuries, asking where it hurt, and distributing bottles of lavender-scented bug spray.

Guy felt a general soreness, nothing acute. There would be a bruise where the seat belt pinched his side. Maybe a broken rib. He accepted a vitamin booster shot.

Benatti waved off any help and requested a new car.

"You're continuing on?" Guy asked, nodding toward the upside-down Jeep.

"That's nothing. I once crumpled a '68 Spider on a test track. Papa said nobody could have survived the crash. But I'm lucky, you know?" A new Jeep arrived. "Coming? I'll captain. You drive like a Roman."

Guy looked down the road. Bax's cronies would be focused on injecting agita into the Quorum, which seemed onerous. The heavy air sapped his energy.

"Heading back. Good luck with the conclave."

"Such a softie." Benatti motioned for the staff member to get out and drove off.

CHAPTER 10

Grandpa Hochstapler once told me I was a cannonball, and youth was for amassing saltpeter. That's what this time has been. Another amassing of saltpeter.

But effort has not yielded tangible result. One cannot force eureka, but one cannot ignore the ticking clock. I am off-grid but still terrestrial—when the news breaks, people will find me. They'll read a headline, skim a tweet, and throw their heaviest stones. They'll line the property with their placards and chants, destroy any chance of concentration.

Why can't they see the bigger picture. The American Century was built by white men: less than a third of the population. Imagine the prosperity if anyone else had taken the wheel.

The only chance of thriving in the next century—of even surviving the next century—lies with people like me.

Could it not be argued the truly innovative organization falters in equally innovative ways.

A.M. session:

- 5 in clarity
- 3 in productivity
- 7 in focus

A troubling downward trend

The boy's been researching me. Asking pointless questions. What was Stanford like. Did the governor really detect a lump in a PrevYou booth. How did I get all those people to invest.

His last question was easy: one-on-one facetime. That's it. Powerful men always assume whomever they meet has been vetted. The challenge is getting in the room. Don't bother with the handlers, the assistants, or the managers. They're paid for excessive diligence.

Go through the nephews. Help them with their career, then press for an introduction.

And warfare. Men love it when you frame your work through the vocabulary of war.

He's very naïve, of course. Thinks the Giving Pledge is just reputational laundering. Even quoted scripture at me. Some story about the donated pennies of a widow meaning more than the surplus of the wealthy.

Small-dollar donations do play better, as every populist knows. But if you want to achieve anything, you need capital and vision.

I told him Jesus's parable sounded dictatorial.

—

Juan talked meditation: "Every mountain was once a valley. Every valley will someday become a mountain." That's not how geology works, but I take his point.

He's young still. He doesn't understand. All life is pressure. Every building is held up by its foundation. The tectonic plates of the earth grind against each other every second of the day. To push back is to be of the world.

Not to say I haven't attempted to relax. How many vacations were scuttled by last-minute fires. Guy said they were excuses, and he may have been right. But I still felt—still feel—the work deteriorate without my presence. Complacency. Regression. As the vacation approached, the feeling, located behind the stomach, in the spleen, would spike and spike.

I did play hooky that one afternoon, at Guy's urging. A matinee near the Emeryville campus. I don't remember the movie. I do know that I was halfway through the red-carpeted lobby when one of the assistants texted that AmEx flagged the ticket purchase for possible fraud. That was my sign from above. The algorithms were telling me to go back to the office.

The A.M. run was dissatisfying. Pushed another half mile. The shin splints persist. The blisters distract.

I am noticing the landscape more, which may mean I am thinking less. Is there a corollary between the two. Something to consider.

The new idea must be mutable, must be resistant to hidebound thinking down the line.

Remember the booths' second-order effects and the Year Four windfall. It may have been Jeremy's idea. He had been circling the data-licensing aspect, which was obvious enough: if booth patients in a given neighborhood regularly receive healthier results, that's a valuable datapoint for property owners and realty firms. (Neighbors with low BMI do wonders for resale value.)

Jeremy's breakthrough was treating it as an end run. Soon after initiating a short-term license with RE/MAX he quietly assembled a skunkworks with his logistics guys. They cross-indexed patients' health graphs with the property listings and market frothiness in midsize cities. Once they ID'd which properties to buy, we killed the realty contracts and then officially got into real estate. We accumulated the portfolio and published the data on the company blog—THE 50 BEST US NEIGHBORHOODS YOU'VE NEVER HEARD OF, not the most elegant headline—and watched the prices skyrocket. Then we flipped the inventory and banked the profits.

It wasn't sustainable, but it bought more runway as we scaled up the oncology personnel.

Medical and engineering—they're to blame. They had every resource. Blank check after blank check.

What did that lab tech call me. A martinet. Well, sure. You have to exert pressure. If it were easy, humankind would have found the cure decades ago.

Even an enthusiastic employee will not deliver their best, not at first. You must break down the troublesome propriety.

And our perks were second to none. Denmark-level health plans. PTO vouchers for up to four protests per annum, and leave for additional days on a case by case basis.

I accept partial blame. I left an open flank and I was attacked. It is not unreasonable to speculate the Cancer Society's Innovation Award would have provided the necessary Teflon.

This evening I dismissed Juan after cunnilingus . . . Conducted a late P.M. session with the Post-it grids. An hour in I was spooked by a flash of yellow in the backyard. It was only when I approached the screen door that I realized it had been my own hand movement, reflected against the black of night.

Critter or not, my BPM wouldn't settle. I opened the door and walked to the property edge. Satellites and planes sailed above the indiscernible grounds. Everything below the ridgeline was pure black.

I ran a circuit of power poses. If there were any animals or malefactors about, they were sufficiently cowed.

My categories may be too subject-based. Perhaps a conceptual approach would yield result.

What did the advertising people say. We had to use the pillars of Fear, Uncertainty, and Doubt. A confused customer was a faithful customer.

It is unclear whether I am making enough progress. The ideation is fine but lacks true insight. May need to augment the asperities.

—

The new goal: strategize complexifiers for the public sectors. Consult the blue column of notes near the living room window. Push harder. The Zone of Utmost Throb awaits. You have days, not weeks.

CHAPTER 11

Guy walked the lawn, keeping the residences to his left. Quorumites excitedly debated whatever conclusions they'd come to in the remainder of the second session. He passed a group playing bocce and dragging the MIT kids' algorithm; another huddle discussed "overflow capital," presumably in the event they cure a global ill and still have a few billion to spend. From one of the patios a distinctly Texan voice screamed, "I am being rational!" When he concentrated there appeared as if by magic various staff going about their duties: polishing the buildings' teak trim, sweeping sand from doorways, wiping every surface.

He spotted Wright on a bench, facing the bay and tapping his phone.

"What happened to you?" Wright asked.

Guy brushed at the dirt and blood stains on his clothes. At some point he'd lost his robe. "You should see the other guy. It'll be high time before he besmirches Gustavo Dudamel again."

Bax's deluxe paperweight floated before them. Its armada circled in ritual fealty.

"How was the rest of the session?" Guy asked. "Still thinking water rights?"

"Hell no. I'm pivoting to microloans." He nodded toward the bocce court. "Take these idiots out of the equation."

"Averman would say microloans are out of scope."

"I would reply the Quorum is a process."

Guy waved over a staff member and ordered a scotch. Wright ordered a Quorum Nitro.

"So how's yours doing, really?" Wright meant the Stevens Foundation. "You guys moving to Stamford if the progressives take Albany?"

Guy never followed the political side. He wondered what would become of their grant recipients. Maybe he could fob some off on Wright.

"Steady as she goes. You?"

Wright outlined their scholarships and mentoring programs. A true believer, without a doubt. Guy silently mouthed *bless you*, then *fuck you*.

The scotch was peaty, acerbic. He coughed and Wright patted him on the back.

• "Easy, tiger. You've been burning the candle at both ends."

"What's the Russian proverb? 'Eating increases the appetite'?"

"That's about abstention."

"Respectfully disagree." Guy pointed his glass at the yacht. "Are you going tonight?"

"Thinking about it. Bax said I could feed the giraffes."

"Let me ask you something. What would you do if you weren't doing this? Career-wise. If you had to change course."

"Why would I do that?"

"If you had to. Fired tomorrow. A coup, whatever."

"Shit, I don't know." He scratched his chin. "Practice law again? No, Cynthia would hate that. I could make a run at politics, if I find the right district."

"She'd prefer politics over law?"

"She'd prefer I be home more. My three-year-old puts his hand to his ear when Cynthia mentions daddy." He mimed the gesture, like he was receiving a phone call. "Why do you ask? You thinking of composing again?"

Guy shook his head to pretend he was thinking about it. He hadn't completed a piece in over two decades. Even at Curtis he knew music composition was in decline, like throwing confetti into the void. Now the void was so much bigger, had moved forward, was practically on his toes. Could you push back on it? Don't ask him. He's just the money guy. He'd commissioned new work from John Luther Adams, David Lang, a bunch of others. So much of his life spent assembling meaningless beauty for diminishing audiences. But he didn't feel like a vestige of the past. More a harbinger of things to come. Everyone should prepare for diminishing audiences. For diminishing everything.

Wright started talking about his fantasies for bottom-up education reform. Guy tried to follow and ordered another scotch. The dark smear on the horizon shaded pink as it met the falling disc of the sun.

• • •

HE CAME TO in the dark, with the sounds of laughter and music behind him. A few Quorumites smoking cigars. Wright was gone. His rocks glass was still in hand with—ho ho!—a finger of liquor remaining. He drank the rest and stood. He'd missed dinner.

He swatted at a beetle on his crotch, then saw it was just a stain. The gesture did provoke a concupiscent urge, though that might be from the car accident. The proximity to death and all that, like the way mourners fumbled to enjoin genitals after a funeral.

He rolled the glass down the lawn and watched it drop out of sight. Then he stumbled toward the lights and music coming from the veranda. Most of the tables were empty, though a few lingering Quorumites nursed sherry or coffee. A small crowd near the pool fist pumped to electronic music, tossing glow sticks in the air. Guy thought he recognized some of Bax's flotilla; the DJ looked like that Goldman Sachs exec.

He ordered a drink and a dinner roll, then wandered the tables until he found Mary Ellen and a handful of others debating Quorum protocols.

One of them pointed with his dessert fork and a speared morsel of chocolate cake. "You have to allocate to the First World first. A rising tide lifts all boats."

"Good news for boat owners," Mary Ellen said. She clinked her vodka tonic with Guy's drink.

"Who doesn't own a boat?" cake guy asked.

"I'll tell you what I hate," someone else said. Guy remembered he did something in solar energy. "Those dystopian movies. No imagination. They focus on the underprepared, the people who have to live like nomads to flee the zombies.

Or whatever. Why not show the smart survivors? Living a half-mile underground. Or in their Kiwi bolt hole."

"They can't show that," Mary Ellen said. "Too optimistic."

Cake guy spoke up, spitting bits of food. "It's not dystopian at all. The First World's dystopian future is just the present for much of the Third World. Global catastrophe simply adjusts the median."

"My granddaughter calls them EBPs," energy guy replied. "Earth-Based Problems. She says it's a fait accompli her generation'll live off planet. Or at least the ones with the foresight and the resources."

The talk moved on to terraforming Mars and the challenges of wilding a property in Easthampton. Guy turned to Mary Ellen, who was almost vibrating in her chair.

"Successful day of power brokering?" he asked.

"Both my competitors in the European market are coming in under their quarterly projections. So yes, a good day."

"Chin-chin."

She wiped at a grass stain on his knee. "You've been through the wringer."

"Sightseeing is all. With Benatti. Any takers on your piss bench?"

"Plenty of butts. Stellar ROI."

"Good for you."

The men at the table got up and wished them good evening.

Mary Ellen checked her phone and then slid it to the center of the table. "I'm tired of business talk. Tell me something new."

Guy thought back to Gretchen. She had a parlor trick she used to pull with prospective Curtis students after the campus tour.

"Got a pen?"

She borrowed a Bic from a bartender. Guy asked her to lay her left hand on the table, palm up. He wrote *ut* on the ball of the thumb, *re* below it, and *mi* at the joint, then continued down the other fingers.

"Medieval singers learned music notation through what's called the Guidonian hand. Do, re, mi, etc., except they didn't have 'do,' they said 'ut.' And 'ti' wasn't added until much later."

He finished. She looked at her hand.

"It's a memorization technique for their tone system. Also known as the gamut"—he pointed to the gamma symbol on the top of her thumb—"where we get 'run the gamut.' Now these aren't all the tones, just six of them: a hexachord. But you get the idea."

"Show me how it works."

"If you were a choir boy in Renaissance Italy, you'd look at your hand and you'd know the relationship of the hexachords to the tones."

"Are you going to sing for me?"

"No, and you should be thankful for that. But study your hand and you'll be sight-reading in no time. Wait." He wrote *ee la* on the top of her middle finger. The flesh was springy; he wrote slowly and with care. "Done."

"It's like a spiral. Going inward."

"Inward, downward, all the same."

On the lawn a large gathering circled a firepit, from which

rising sparks were visible even at a distance. The dance crowd chanted something about being around the world.

Mary Ellen exhaled upward, sending a wave through her bangs. "Want to come to my place, see my etchings? Maybe elicit an orgasm?"

•   •   •

HER SUITE WAS exactly like his, save for a larger desk and a grid of monitors.

"I wouldn't let on you have such a nice workspace. People are swapping for the smallest amenities."

She put a hand against the wall and kicked her shoes off. "How do you think I got this one?" She walked over the bar and poured them drinks. He felt newly adolescent, and teetered on his heels, unsure of himself. Sex with Victoria was routine, which wasn't to say joyless. More a long-running Broadway musical, with tight choreography and dependable results. Now this new person. A novel feeling, almost nostalgic. Let it come. It confirmed he was still capable of feeling new feelings. Or, at the very least, feeling old feelings once more.

He removed his shirt, wincing at a pain in his side, and then pulled his pants and underwear down. His deflated cock was crowned by a wiry nest and darker than the rest of his body.

Mary Ellen handed him a glass, then sat on the bed and removed her stockings. "Think you can perform with all that booze in your system?"

He handled his crotch like he imagined people at the grocery store assessed fruit. A stirring, if not to life, then something half-alive. He reminded himself he would be dead soon, and this stimulated more physiological cheer. "To be determined."

She removed her blouse and bra to reveal two nearly symmetric scars under her nipples. She lay down on her back, her feet dangling off the side of the bed. Surprisingly petite.

Mary Ellen clasped her hands behind her head and looked at the ceiling. "Oral sex would be nice."

He kneeled before her. This position always felt faintly ridiculous, almost simian, with his testicles swinging freely in the air. He'd prefer to be supine with Mary Ellen straddling his face. But she looked comfortable. He tried to push her up on the bed; she resisted. So he dug in his knees and began, finding a rhythm she liked and ignoring the pain in his shoulder. She grunted and exhaled almost legibly, guiding him toward alternating deft flicks on the clit with slow laps down to the perineum and back. He hummed a Caroline Shaw piece; his cock replied metronomically.

From his foreshortened perspective her body filled his vision, abstracting into fields of color. The line of her mastectomy scarring resembled a closed eye, and when she pitched her shoulders up it became a fold, or a closure of some kind, such that if he wanted to, if he wanted it enough and if he asked with confidence and respect, Mary Ellen might allow him to reach in, to find an internal inside the internal, if that made sense. He knew—had decided, and felt it necessary to remind himself as he worked his tongue—sense was no longer the point.

He was distracting himself. Eventually she gripped his hair

and moved his scalp back and forth on his pate. He knew not to vary his method. She came, with less movement than he expected, and dug her fingernails into his hairline.

She scooted up the bed and retrieved cigarettes and a lighter from the nightstand. She lit two and held one up. He stood, and his knees cracked so loudly they both looked away. He accepted the cigarette and joined her on the bed.

"That was a nice surprise," he said.

She ashed into a rocks glass. "When life hands you lemonade, say thank you."

"*Thank you.*" He indicated her desk. "No rest for the wicked? I don't think anyone else is working." He paused. "Except for Roark's neighbor."

"Can't be helped. We're due for a market shift, and that's when large-cap companies fall prey to active inertia." She looked to see if he followed along. "You know, there's a change and we react with more of the same. And more aggressively. That's doom. Accelerated."

"So that's what it takes, huh?"

"Something like it. You also have to be raised in an environment suitable to the flowering of your talents."

"Unless you're a Jamaican bobsledding team."

"Don't take career advice from Disney movies."

They smoked in silence. Under the tobacco he could smell the saltiness of their exertion.

"Do you think Averman will pull this off?" Guy waved his cigarette, indicating the Quorum.

"The implementation will be difficult. He'll run into the tontine problem."

"The French noblemen thing."

"At one point, yes. A group of individuals puts in capital, lets it accrue compound interest, and agrees to withdraw funds only at a predetermined time. Usually it's when the last individual is left alive. He gets the pot."

"That sounds like a lottery."

"Historically it's been used to build war chests, grow insurance companies. It really only works if you have tons of buy-in. With the size of the Quorum it's bound to fail."

"You think we'll start killing each other?"

"Nothing that direct. But think through the incentives. We reach consensus this weekend, picking—I don't know, famine. Why wait until everyone's dead? Why not divest our fortunes immediately? Benatti's fifty, and he's been on the Mediterranean diet since birth. He'll outlive Greta Thunberg."

"What about a tiered system? We give some now, and more as more people pass on."

She blew smoke toward the ceiling, where it clung like morning fog.

"If that were effective," she said, "it would already be in place. The answer is there is no answer. The only solution I see is, someone with a high moral flexibility starts killing off the Quorumites. Starting with the youngest."

"I think this was a *Twilight Zone* episode."

Mary Ellen wasn't listening. She gestured in the air as if she were writing on a blackboard. "But you wouldn't want people to think there's a serial killer targeting billionaires. You'd spook the market. And your victims would retrench, sleep in panic rooms, beef up security detail. No, you'd have to space it out. Make it seem like natural causes."

"Wouldn't that be the same—"

"Exactly. You're back to the timeline problem. I'm sure there's an equation for this. The shortest window to kill everyone while avoiding suspicion, balanced against the lives lost from delaying the implementation of whatever program we deem most viable."

"Your pillow talk is rather macabre."

"And sport fucks are better seen than heard."

"How do you think tomorrow will go? Session-wise?"

"Weiss is convinced we'll stalemate on Monday. He wants to hold the next Quorum at his ranch in Wyoming next year, which is laughable."

"Because?"

She propped herself up on her elbow. "There won't be another Quorum. Don't you know why Averman's doing this?"

"Reputational laundering, same as everyone else."

"Yes and no. He's got a ticking time bomb with his workforce."

Mary Ellen explained that Averman's fifty thousand warehouse workers were attempting to unionize after finally realizing they had leverage. While their demands weren't unreasonable, Averman believed he was being astroturfed by a Toronto-based competitor.

"Why would they care?" Guy asked.

"Take your pick. Market share, bad press, bruised ego. Averman looks anti-union, which is very damaging for his brand. The whole thing is pretty funny, since he's been so anti-automation, and the Canadians eliminated something like ninety percent of those same jobs out of their supply chain."

"How does he know it's the Canadians? Not just some grassroots thing?"

"I think his PIs."

Guy gave a blank look.

"Victoria doesn't keep private investigators on retainer? Surely she must."

"Probably?"

Mary Ellen slapped the bed. "PIs are the best! You have to get some. It's like next-level Wikipedia. You cannot imagine the satisfaction of learning the pornographic habits of your elementary-school crush."

He balanced his cigarette in an ashtray on his nightstand. "When I said earlier Victoria and I were done, it's more like she confessed PrevYou's a fraud. Then she faked her death. Or not."

She stared at him for an uncomfortably long time, her pupils oscillating. "A joke. I saw her at Arianna's thing last week—"

"This all happened Friday. No, Thursday."

"Shit . . . What chutzpah. Good for her."

"Good for her?"

"I suspected something when she rolled out that ad campaign. 'We are PrevYou,' with all the user testimonials? Straight out of the Philip Morris playbook. Definitely a red flag when your ads show 'everyday Americans.'"

"It was all a scam, though."

"Eh. A scam is just innovation without scalability."

"I don't think her problem was scale."

"No shit. That's what's so admirable. She should have taken Pfizer's offer. Nobody would have found out. Or, they would have, but she'd be indemnified." She looked at him as if for the first time. "Is this why you're such a mess?"

"Principally, yes."

"Cheer up. It's a righting of the world. Your natural state is . . . different from this."

"It doesn't have to be." He stroked her hip. "This is nice."

"Easy there. I have plenty of suitors. And you were fine."

He recoiled an inch.

"So sensitive," she said. "What's your plan?"

"I'm taking it day by day."

She went to the bathroom and called from the toilet. "You know what your problem is? You're an adult, pretending to be an old man, and acting like a child. Take your drubbing and move on. You can live to a hundred if you want to."

"In this economy?"

"Ah, the quitting type." She returned to bed. "You really don't realize how easy it is—making money. Opportunity is everywhere."

He must have made a skeptical expression.

"You remember when the Russians shot down that Korean passenger plane?" she asked. "In '82, maybe '83. A couple hundred people died, including a US congressman. The Russians thought it was an American spy plane."

"Okay."

"I'm in fourth grade. I don't understand why my teachers

are suddenly so nice to me. My dad tries to explain—the Cold War, communism, spycraft—but he wasn't, let's say, geopolitically literate.

"So I'm asked to give a speech. At assembly, about dead people I've never met, from a country I have no memories of, in front of classmates who flick snot at the stage."

He imagined it. Mary Ellen with a cartoon character's oversized head, dressed in a navy cardigan and plaid skirt. Staring down the freckled boors.

"The speech was whatever. I think I used a Lincoln quote." She considered it. "It was on a banner in the hallway, next to a trophy case. Anyway. I wore a red and blue ribbon, and at the end I told everyone it was for the US and South Korea." She tucked in her left knee and brushed some fuzz off her left foot. "I sold those ribbons for a dollar each to every adult in that school, except for the janitors. Even did a brisk business with a folding table and a sign at the Piggly Wiggly."

The pat tale of pipsqueak hustle reminded him of Victoria. "I suddenly feel very lethargic," he said. "And increasingly sober."

"Don't fall asleep. I want you to do something else." She bent her leg toward him, curling and uncurling her toes.

"Take my foot in your hands. Yes, like that. No—don't suck. I want you to trim the nail on my big toe."

Guy inspected the nail. It was painted a matte red, somewhere between crimson and burgundy. A little long, but not noticeably so.

"You have a clipper?"

"Use your teeth."

"You want me to bite it?"

"Yes. Bite it." She leaned back and closed her eyes.

Guy had never been one to notice toes. Hers were attractive enough: small, like a child's. He regretted never playing with children's toes, the fleshy worms—he'd assumed it would come up at some point, but it never had.

He navigated with his tongue to establish a marker and tasted beach grit. The polish was tasteless, but slick. He remembered wrapping Christmas presents with his mother, how she demanded precision running the orange-handled scissors down the long sheet of gift wrap. That sweet spot of finding the correct angle, applying just enough force, and maintaining even speed.

He took the edge of the toenail between his teeth for an exploratory clamp. The bottom row pushed against her skin in an attempt to slip under and gain purchase, which freed more beach sand into his mouth. Perhaps his teeth were too large for the job at hand. A new strategy was needed. He adjusted his body to relieve the pressure on his neck and tilted his head accordingly, moving the nail toward his incisors. There it was: solid purchase on a Goldilocks amount of edge. He looked up and met Mary Ellen's passive stare.

"I 'hink I gaw i'," he said. She blinked in assent.

He bit down. It was like a nutcracker: tough at first, then pliant. He bent the foot away at an angle, shearing the ridge with miniscule bites. Mary Ellen remained silent, though he noticed her other foot arched slightly. He gripped harder, creating a vise. At the corner he lifted up, removing with it a triangular scrim of polish. The exposed line of white like coconut meat. He released her foot. She raised her leg straight up in a graceful, frictionless motion, such that her foot was above her face; Guy had never thought before how the hip was a hinge, and the body a truly odd assemblage.

She judged his work and nodded. "Good."

The nail trim idled on his tongue like an omakase serving. Should he spit it out? Would that be uncouth?

"Happy to oblige." He swallowed and reached for the glass near her side of the bed. He took a quick swig before realizing it contained her cigarette ash and dry retched like a dying cat. Mary Ellen's laughter didn't help. Guy stumbled to the bar and chased the black sludge with mouthfuls of vodka.

Mary Ellen's laughing doubled upon itself into a coughing fit, and it sounded like she might vomit. She settled her breathing and smiled at him. He felt confident, standing naked before her with the vodka bottle in hand, backlit by the bar.

"That may have been better than the oral," she said. "Okay, out with you. Tomorrow's a new day."

"No morning quickie?"

"Some of us have businesses to run. I have a Zoom call at six."

He found his clothes by the bed and dressed.

"I love watching a man put his clothes back on. Especially the belt."

"I'm not wearing a belt."

She put on a sleeping mask and turned away. "There's always room for improvement."

• • •

GUY OPENED HIS eyes and did not immediately regret it. Mary Ellen pointed toward something like possibility. If not with her, then someone else. Fucking: it provided . . . not quite purpose. A function.

He was a pariah—so what. He didn't kill anyone. And even if he did, what about those women who marry guys on death row? Yes. He could still be loved.

Unburdening himself of Victoria's secrets also curbed the suicidal impulse, however temporarily. And Mary Ellen took it well! Perhaps he might tell Benatti and seek his counsel. Now, Guy wasn't insane. He'd be smart about it. If Averman got wind, Guy would be instantly escorted to the hangar. A latchkey kid on the school curb.

And yet. The news would break. Any minute now.

Guy showered and dressed. A linen blazer, with a jaunty pocket square to match. He assessed himself in the full-length mirror. Skin, dried out. Lips, a lunar surface of crags and craters. Eyes—he looked away. Not yet.

Enough of this self-reflection. He did a bump off the bar spoon. Walked over the envelopes slid under overnight and headed toward breakfast. Through the annex's large windows he spotted Averman at the jungle's edge, plucking fruit from a mutant tree's branches. Averman bit into what might have been a peach, then dropped it. He pulled down an apple and did the same. He was reaching for an orange when a tanned gentleman in a doctor's coat passed Guy and said good morning.

Roark. He deserved a visit. Maybe he'd have some wisdom to impart. Breakfast could wait.

The doctor directed him to Roark's new suite down the

hall. So the old man had completed the swap before his tumble. Good for him.

Averman's muffled boosterisms rose in volume as he passed the windows of the corridor. The looping exhortations were predictable, yes, unoriginal, yes. Still, he detected an ameliorative effect.

Perhaps he'd been rash in opting for the accelerated exit. Here he was, surrounded by the wealthiest people in the world, whose sole criterion for admission was a public declaration for helping others. Who better to finance his next move? And who better than Guy to receive it? He might not be financially savvy, but he retained the best wealth managers money could buy. Or had retained them; surely they'd honor a longstanding client. And what was Guy really after? A bridge loan. Enough to maintain his lifestyle while he—well, he didn't know quite yet.

He knocked and entered Roark's suite. Blinking consoles surrounded the hospital bed like android kin on death watch. A technician in teal scrubs sat quietly in the corner, almost in the dark, counting out dosages for a silver pillbox.

Roark looked bruised but alert. His silk evening gown had taken on a curious volume, as if it were a weighted blanket crushing his torso. An IV line snaked into one sleeve; pulsometers clamped two of his fingers. His other hand rested on a stack of crisp bills. He flicked the corner in a slow ostinato, which sounded to Guy like an alighting songbird.

"Always carry cash, my boy. I know it's become an affectation, but it's soothingly tactile. The key is to have the notes ironed."

"You seem chipper. People say you died yesterday."

"I'm not going anywhere." The ostinato quickened. "And I must ensure the sessions don't descend into calamity. It's a real risk, the closer we get to the end."

"I assume the doctor ordered bed rest."

"No time. Being wealthy is a full-time job, you know." He considered something. "But this little setback could prove advantageous. Demand a face-to-face with my eldest while I convalesce, that sort of thing. Get her up from Coral Gables and away from that swarthy charlatan."

"I don't think you can say 'swarthy' anymore. Charlatan's still okay."

Roark ignored him. "I've been nourishing their marital strife by increments. If I can get her in the city for a few days, really lay it on thick, maybe she'll finally leave him for someone suitable."

"How is he unsuitable?"

"For one, he begins sentences with 'To be fair . . .'"

"What a monster."

"The trick is working both sides. When it's just him and me in the room, I fake senility. Then they argue, it becomes a question of his perception, and she has to choose between husband and father."

The technician appeared with a paper cup of pills and a glass of water. Guy leaned forward but couldn't ID the capsules. While Roark dry swallowed them Guy noticed the man's bare shins. Varicose lines cabled down the hairless expanse with subdermal rudeness. The technician returned to her spot in the corner.

"So back to Manhattan tomorrow?" Guy asked.

"Hoboken first. Pressing business."

"The Meadowlands."

"The very same. My newest albatross."

Roark explained that his engineers had calculated weight tolerances for the usual demographics, assuming the fifteen thousand residents and staff represented a cross-section of ages and backgrounds. Lately sales had hit a wall; only retirees were buying. In most cases swapping four thousand children for senescent Boomers would not be a problem, beyond additional emergency parking for ambulances. But Roark recently learned corners had been cut with the synthetic bedrock—at least figuratively—and the anchoring columns, which were supposed to be contracted by the people behind Venice and Amsterdam, had been subcontracted to a Kansas City upstart. When Roark reached the occupancy needed to turn a profit the entire neighborhood would begin listing and quite possibly slide into the marsh.

His tone grew professorial. "Bribery and subterfuge are part of any major development, and I pride myself on transparency with my team about the acceptable amount of both. What gets my goat is the bribery and subterfuge they don't tell me about. How is that any basis for trust?"

"So what's the plan?"

"At first I thought, rebrand the residencies. Easy. Starter homes for young families. Or put in some amenities, attract the DINCs."

"Dinks?"

"Dual Income No Children. Dream tenants. But they've all decamped to the second-tier cities."

"I don't know why you bother. Why not hand over the reins?"

Roark took this in, or pretended out of respect. "The brain becomes lighter with age. That's the cruelty of time: you lose weight in precisely the wrong places. Thankfully reason and judgment are the last to go. I'll lose motor function. Piss and shit myself. But I'll always know when I'm being fucked on a deal."

There was a moment of silence, or near-silence. The technician flipped a page of *Celeste*.

"You look like hell, by the way," Roark said. "Get a good night's sleep tonight, hmm?"

"I haven't had a complete REM cycle since Victoria left."

"You should say 'disappeared.' 'Left' implies agency."

"The board thinks kayak accident. CFO says suicide." Guy thought the ease with which he could say this last word indicated his own belief in its impossibility.

"You say otherwise."

"I do. She's out there, somewhere."

"And you're here. No desire to track her down."

"I need . . . time."

"You must know how you sound. Denial, and all that."

"No, it's not—well, maybe. I don't know. I think . . . suicide demands regret. Doesn't it? Overwhelming shame. She doesn't have it in her."

"You may be right. But that's not unique to your better half. Our group, we have our levers of personhood set differently than the general population. I've long believed dedicated accrual to real titanic amounts of money—that requires total self-assurance. To a degree the average person would find off-putting, if they ever saw it up close." He nodded toward the technician across the room. "Sure. We make mistakes. And we learn from them. But they're external to people like us."

"You have a few loopholes in your logic there."

Roark thinned his lips into a deep-sea trench sucking in all light and warmth.

"Appeals to logic," Roark said, "are a refuge of the weak. I'm talking hard truths here. Speaking of. If she has passed—if she is gone—this weekend takes on special import for you."

"Her legacy, you mean."

"Correct. Honor her commitment." He sat up, with effort, to try and gain another inch on his perspective looking down at Guy. "And get me into Averman's conclave, goddammit."

"I don't—I mean, I haven't—"

Roark flapped his hand, curling the pulsometer tubing around his index finger. A benedictory gesture. "Forget it, you wouldn't have access anyway. Focus on the Quorum."

"I'm not sure I can," Guy said. "Honor the pledge, that is. It's complicated."

Roark raised an eyebrow. "You know, I saw you perform once, before you met her."

"Really? I haven't played since—"

"A sonata, during an evening with the beneficiaries of the Allegra Foundation."

Guy remembered. A small commission with a fortnight in Florence, living in an ancient villa with another composer, a translator, and two poets. These last two residents dominated the communal dinners with arcane questions about taxes and

S corps. He had never met anyone who complained more about money.

"My first trip to Europe," Guy said. "I was still in Philly then."

"Your piece was nice. A little meandering, but nice."

"Roark, you know I've always considered you a father figure—"

"Stop talking. I know what that look means. My boy, I already have a son. He took bronze in the Olympic biathlon and clerked for Sotomayor. You . . . do nothing. Whatever hardship you're going through is best experienced alone. Otherwise how are you to learn?"

The bent corner of the stack's topmost bill. The space-age tubing. "At my age I think I've learned all I can. Or learned all I will. Maybe all I should."

"Nonsense. Add new wrinkles to the cerebellum. Look at the Meadowlands. It may collapse, it may not. But it's not my legacy. I've got half a dozen developments in the works. When my time comes, I'll be at a groundbreaking. A ribbon-cutting. You'll see."

"I have the feeling my time is now. I'm spent. When you saw me play, I was so full of possibility—"

"Christ, give it a rest. You'd think the guy with the catheter would be wistful. Don't look backward. Waste of time. Why revisit less evolved versions of yourself?"

"They say it helps you prepare for death."

"They say that, huh. What's to fear, I ask. My last moments will be full of the knowledge I've provided for my family. For future generations. For thousands of strangers. That should guarantee a pleasant exit."

Guy made an agreeable face. He should have known. For all their abstract largesse, the Quorumites were in practice quite mercenary. How else would they have come so far.

"All this death talk has made me hungry," Guy said. "I'll see you at the next session."

Averman pressed a button for a top-up of painkillers. "Fine, fine." He closed his eyes; a bubble sat on his lips.

Guy backed out of the room and into the too-bright day. He ran into Wright outside the veranda.

"Coming or going?" Guy asked.

"Crashing. I pulled an all-nighter at Bax's." Wright's broken grin distracted from his bloodshot eyes. Guy checked the man's nostrils for white residue, but Wright misread the gesture and blew his nose.

"I take it you did well," Guy said.

"Total flow state. I cleaned up: two Pateks, a Bugatti, and a fifth of a Basquiat."

Guy whistled. "Did she show you the harem?"

"I asked but she demurred. My theory is they're just for marks."

"What could she want from me?"

"Maybe she's looking to diversify. Big money in cancer."

Mary Ellen passed them, carrying a fruit plate to a table poolside.

"So what did you two talk about?" Guy asked. "Objectivism for urban youth?"

"Ha ha. She just bashed the Quorum all night. Said whatever global ill we address will be more endemic—no, *systemic*, than we think. Ineradicable." Wright mouthed *call me* to someone behind Guy. "Otherwise someone would've solved it already."

"I thought retirement made one more optimistic, not less."

Wright shrugged. "If tomorrow's a wash, we'll do another Quorum focused on implementation. Everyone's invested."

Averman slapped them both on the back, startling Guy.

"Gentlemen! Another important day." He emanated chlorine and mouthwash. His jumpsuit looked different somehow; a thicker cotton than yesterday's.

"Morning, Arthur," Wright said. "I'm off for a catnap before the next session."

"While I have you, a question." Averman lowered his voice. "Did any of Petra's people come back with you last night?"

"What do you mean?"

Averman put his hands up in an "easy there" gesture. "I'm not here to police anyone's behavior. But there's a rumor she's sneaking her people onto the island."

"Why would she do that?" Guy asked.

"To sabotage all our good work, of course."

"I didn't see anything," Wright said. "It was just me and the boatman."

Averman's look hovered just above suspicious. "I'm . . . sure it's just a rumor."

"Most rumors are." Wright headed to his suite.

"What did you get up to last night?" Guy asked.

Averman monologued about a bonfire somewhere in the jungle, where an "intimate coterie" traded stories about their first proxy fights. "We bonded. Went deep into the ancient ways."

"Sounds lovely. I'm just going to get some—"

Averman sighed. "You know, I wish Big Mike was here. He worked with Victoria, no? This is very much his scene. No doubt we'd be further along by now."

Jessica appeared and whispered in Averman's ear. He swore, then excused himself, and they ran off.

Guy filled a plate at the buffet. His appetite was back, and in force. He wanted a tropical fruit. No, all the tropical fruits. Every pastry. Various yogurts and custards. He ordered an Irish coffee from a waiter and sat at Mary Ellen's table, next to a distracted Benatti.

"Somebody's hungry," she said.

"Hungry and alive. Feeling very positive."

Benatti scrolled on his phone. "Gold's acting very funny this morning."

"So I've thought about your predicament," Mary Ellen said.

Guy looked at Benatti, who was ignoring them. "Oh?"

"You only think everything's over because you've convinced yourself everything's over. I say, find yourself a medium-size city with good public parks. Become an office manager. Work admissions at a community college."

He considered it. A furnished one-bedroom in an old Victorian. Rented by a cardiganed dowager who lived on the parlor floor. He'd take up the piano again, do the Sunday crossword. Weekly bingo in a church basement.

But he'd still be himself. Would still lie awake at night with his brain, his thoughts. He needed more than a new life. A philosophical framework, that was it. Perhaps a religious awakening. The comfort of blind zealotry. Can one manufacture such a thing? Maybe he could concuss himself.

"I'm not sure anonymity's an option," he said. "I could run the other way, sell my story to Hollywood."

"Forget it. Nobody has sympathy for the wealthy. We write business books, self-help. That's it."

"What about the formerly rich?" Guy replied. "A classic fall from grace."

"That's not grace," she said. "More a fall from lassitude."

Benatti looked up. "What are you two talking about?"

Mary Ellen lifted her chin and looked past Guy. "Looks like Weiss is on the warpath."

Guy turned and blinked, then found himself on his back with blood dotting his shirt. Again. The sucker punch had exchanged his thoughts with palatial slop, thick and pulsing. His nose bludgeoned into jelly.

Weiss stood above him with balled fists. "You motherfucker! You know what your wife has done? You know how fucked I am?"

Guy sneezed more blood and rose to his feet. Ah, that's where he first met Weiss: the last round of PrevYou investment. A party on Sand Hill Road.

Benatti had positioned himself between them. Mary Ellen righted his chair and addressed Weiss. "You need to relax," she said. "Fighting isn't going to help."

"Fuck it's not," Weiss replied. He was still vexed, but less confrontational. "This asshole's asshole wife just cost me an eighth of my net worth."

Benatti looked to Guy for explanation.

Weiss spat. It landed on Guy's arm. "I'm going to sue the both of you until—until you're nothing. Until you're less than nothing."

People noticed the scuffle. Whispers, questions. A respectful and rubbernecked distance. Guy tapped at Weiss's spit.

Here it was, everything out in the open. The news will spread, everyone will recoil, and then—what? Collapse. Mob violence. Stabbed to death with silver-plated cutlery.

A great lethargy overcame him. "Go ahead," he told Weiss. "Sue away."

A screeching of metal on metal rang out from a few tables away. One of the bankers had leaned on the samovar station while looking at his phone. Guy thought the man's slackened face would drip off and land on the terrazzo marble.

"I've been shorted!" he yelled.

Across the room another Quorumite dropped his plate. "Me too!"

The sudden, polyphonic hum of dozens of vibrating phones. Weiss read his screen with horror and seemed to forget Guy as he slowly sat down.

Averman jogged in. Sweat rings pooled at his neck and armpits. "Everyone, everyone. If I can have your attention." He must have had an earpiece in; his speech echoed through the PA system on a brief delay.

"There's a hurricane. We're to evacuate immediately."

CHAPTER 12

Still no eureka.

Remember. All you can do is endure.

I noticed a return of my natural smile while performing my A.M. routine. That's a positive sign. It has been, what, eight years. The media trainer cycled through all those clips, pointing to the lines in my cheeks. A marionette's mouth, she said. And nobody controls Victoria Stevens. She made me say it, over and over. Nobody controls Victoria Stevens.

Juan wanted to sit on the porch after our session. Brought up the more apocalyptic-minded message boards he's been reading. (I would have thought he'd be more hopeful afterward.) He said when the end comes, he'll go out happy: he has a cache of MDMA reserved expressly for the purpose.

"Comfort, that's what it's about. You don't have to look at the sun as it explodes. You don't even have to feel sad."

Guy brought up the topic sometimes, usually around the

anniversary of his father's passing. I always assumed we'd die of natural causes a few months apart, despite our ages.

I gave Juan my opinion of the end times: an unencumbered elect will circumvent the worst of it; that's all humanity required. His face registered disgust.

The Post-its may be encroaching upon my abilities. Are they a record of progress or a testament to stalled thinking. If they vitiate the process even a fraction of a percent, they must go.

Nipples are still sore from today's run. The shoulder's better.

Took a good hour to revert to my base heart rate after the collapse a few yards from the porch. I lay on my back and considered the sky for thirty minutes before I had the strength to reach the house.

No Zone of Utmost Throb today. I did encounter a new state in the outdoor shower which may be worth transcribing. Well, not in the outdoor shower. Outside of it. I turned on the water and looked at the water. The cold silver beads.

Then a childhood memory returned. Standing at the back of the tub, waiting for the water to warm. Obsessing over the state change between *dry* and *wet*. Convinced if I jabbed a finger into the flow quickly enough I could outsmart physics. Fool the porousness of objects. Retrieve a dry pinkie and exceed the speed of wet.

I tried it again at the outdoor shower today. Same result. Of course. But I did entertain the possibility, for a moment or two. Wonder what that means.

—

The next run will be *the* run. You needn't wait until tomorrow. Thoughts gather. Inspiration mounts.

Credit goes to Grandpa. I liked basketball, but he said I was built for distance running: "With your lungs and your red blood cell count—nobody can touch you."

I have prepped the magnesium water and assessed my main runners. The insoles are shredded at the edges but otherwise fine. I relaced out of habit, sending blooms of red sand under the synthetic grommets into the air. The ghosts of past runs. Failures. No, not failures—rungs on the ladder.

Last index card. I have forced a new phase.

I retrieved the box fan and the extension cord from the closet in the spare bedroom. With the fan on its highest setting I freed the Post-its. They piled up between the living and dining rooms, where I created an indoor funnel. A neon-colored tornado.

Onward, Victoria.

CHAPTER 13

Guy took a seat with his Bloody Mary outside the main entrance, where just two days ago Averman had welcomed them with Panglossian ambition. To his eye the storm still looked a ways off—more a roving purple smear than serious threat—but he toasted the strange new cast of light. And gone was the lavender: the hurricane's emissary of displaced air returned the island to its natural scent. Something confused and riotous. It aided the general feeling of caffeinated reset.

He also toasted the staff, presently routing Quorumites to a line of Jeeps. Such industriousness. They had agency within the teeth-gnashing panic. They could get on top of things.

Jessica stage-managed from the hub of the circular drive, one foot on the fountain's edge, while she paged through a laminated booklet of line items. She spoke calmly into a headset: "Grounds crew and kitchen to the loading docks . . . Toss the fondue tower . . . Handcuff the weather crew if you have to, we need answers . . ." He caught a flash of Averman sprinting between residences farther down the steppe. Apparently the storm was supposed to turn east, or perhaps just peter out, and Averman had downplayed the risks by invoking his sixth sense for impending disaster. Guy figured the man couldn't help rolling the dice.

The Quorumites were to board the Boeing Business Jets hangared at the airstrip. They'd land near Averman's resort in the Bahamas. Or maybe Florida—Guy wasn't paying attention. The Quorum was over; the spell broken.

Objectively the weather threatened the leadership of a healthy percentage of the market. Someone had deduced this vulnerability and bet against their escape. He bolted the rest of his drink while passing Quorumites conducted business on their phones. These people would depart safely, dictating a short squeeze from the cabin, and go on to do all the things people with options go on to do.

Nothing good awaited him in New York. The entire mainland, in fact. Lawyers. The press. Vituperation. Protests. Jail. And what could he do? What should he do? He could simplify. Become a shape of fewer sides.

He didn't need to go home. Bax's yacht? Sail the seven seas, finally learn how to play craps. Find companionship with a Mona Lisa, or an approximation of companionship. It wasn't so pathetic—Brahms frequented brothels, didn't he?

But no. Once the fraud was public Bax would jettison him forthwith. If there was one thing Guy knew about libertarians, they hated the poor.

Perhaps the option of no options. Of stasis. Take his chances here, on the island. And why not. Better the devil who pelts you with hundred-mile-an-hour rainfall. There was enough drink to complete his slow-motion seppuku. He'd ride out the end a soused Robinson Crusoe, blind to his public collapse and deaf to the recriminations. He would opt out, just like Victoria. How fitting: as in so much of their relationship, he'd follow her lead once more.

The white gravel drive took on a sickly pallor under the massing clouds. Stones kicked up by frantic staff pocked ankles and car tires. Drivers honked and shouted out names.

"You're off to New York?"

Guy looked up. Benatti had changed into a black tracksuit. He slung a leather weekender over his shoulder. Averman had told them to leave their luggage; it'd all be swiftly returned.

"Unsure," Guy replied. "This was more of a one-way ticket." Guy finished his drink, bit the celery, and tossed the glass into a hedgerow.

Benatti didn't seem to hear. He retrieved a pair of monogrammed aviators from his pocket. "Miami for me. Scouting new artists."

They watched the commotion. The wind toppled a pile of coolers and ejected tilapia, fanning out like playing cards. Staff members regarded at the pile, whispered to each other, and ran inside.

Jessica continued with an ASMR monotone: "Bax isn't our problem . . . No, the *Kiki* Smith; the David Smith's too heavy . . . Leave it, insurance will cover it . . . Someone tell Mr. Averman Big Mike's daughter had a girl . . ."

Benatti dropped his bag and lit a cigarette. "Everyone's pissy that Arthur was so cavalier. But it's very Arthur, is it not? Turns out Kitakata shorted everyone. Look: first out." He pointed to a Gulfstream clearing the tree line, sharply white against the clouds.

"I thought we weren't allowed to park for the weekend."

Benatti hummed to himself, then stopped. "I'm already down eighteen percent. And the merger's at risk. Be glad your wife's little going concern is private." He cocked an eyebrow. "Or is it all smoke and mirrors?"

Guy touched his nose. Still sensitive, but not fully broken. "Not worth going into all that right now."

Benatti placed a hand on the balustrade. His pinkie ring caught the light and blinded Guy. In the flash he saw a long, reddish scar running up the side of Benatti's hand. A scabbed-over burn, maybe a birthmark Guy hadn't noticed before. For a second it gave the impression of an inhuman, unfinger-like organism—a sunbaked lizard, boiling on the limestone, exhausted. The alien image pulled him from the scrabble and tumult. When he looked up everything appeared faintly ridiculous.

A driver honked and waved to them. Another Jeep was ready to depart.

"Find me at the Grand Prix next month. We'll live it up if you're not broke. Or suicided." They shook hands. *"A presto."* The genial Italian bounded down to his chariot, stopping to hand Jessica his card and deliver an overly familiar peck on the cheek.

The sunlight changed again, some dip in wattage. How fast did hurricanes travel? Was it a question of minutes? An hour? Averman said they needed to leave ASAP, though it's reasonable to assume he was erring on the side of caution. Wouldn't want the jet to be struck by lightning. Was there lightning in a hurricane?

Averman's voice boomed from the speakers: "Friends! Wheels up in twenty. It'll be a tight clearance, but we've got the best flight crew in the world!"

Two staff members ran by, speculating whose name would be listed first in the headline should one of the BBJs crash. Papers sailed the lawn, caressed the trunk of a palm, caught their breath, and made for the cliff.

Jessica swiveled and pointed at Guy. A staff member appeared with a tablet bearing a video call from a sunburned Jeremy Halloran.

The normally hale CFO looked like he hadn't slept in days. He was bare-chested and a shade lighter than the orange raft he was sitting in, surrounded by oxygen tanks and tactical equipment. Jeremy reported improved morale: a second shoe had been found. Behind him divers fell backward into the water while others boarded in a seemingly endless routine. Jeremy continued on, all locker-room boisterous, then set his device down to zip his wet suit. Guy's screen filled with cloudless blue and drops of sea spray. He held the tablet up to contrast the local bedlam.

Then Jeremy again, in extreme close-up. "Despite our optimism," he whispered, "we must accept that Victoria will not be present with regards to that other thing: the, ah, revelations. Without her—without a CEO—the hydra of press, legal action, and criminal charges will swallow us whole." Jeremy sneezed, then sneezed again.

Without her. Guy knew she'd sit out the conflagration, had assumed as much. A small part of him did imagine her reappearance at the last possible moment. Liberty leading her people.

"We'll need a sin-eater," Jeremy said. "Possibly several. For now, get to the war room in the East Coast HQ. I can only guarantee so much protection. From what I gather of your, let's call it, reaction to events, you seem incapable of protecting yourself." He wiped mist off his camera.

"Noted," Guy said. "Well, you're right about one thing." He Xed out of the call and felt a deep well of ambivalence. If such a thing were measurable.

The staff member who'd handed him the tablet had gone. He looked around and saw Mary Ellen in an idling Jeep, tapping feverishly at her phone.

He jogged down, ignoring Jessica's command to get in Benatti's vehicle.

"Hey, I—"

"Hold." She finished her email. It took a second for her to recognize him. "Yes?"

"Where are you going next? Can I join you?"

The driver whispered they were holding up the line. Mary Ellen's expression told Guy his offer was ill-advised.

"Not feasible. Did you think this was, what, the start of something?"

He took a step back. The drivers behind them tapped their horns. "We have so much in common—"

"Stop. We're proximate, not compatible. Do you know what I've had to overcome? The condescension? The backdoor maneuvering?" The honking crescendoed. "Whereas you . . .

you haven't even been to space. You did nothing to get here."
She signaled to the driver. "Earn my respect, and maybe we
can fool around again. And quit with the aw-shucks interloper
routine."

They sped through the gate, then braked. Mary Ellen
leaned out the window.

"Hey!"

"Yeah?" Guy replied.

"Is Gustafson still on PrevYou's board?"

"Um, yes. Or . . . maybe? I don't know."

She groaned and the driver gunned it, swerving around
an overturned golf cart half in the ditch. The last Jeep in line
ferried the MIT kids, who gave him a confused look. Two
shuttle buses full of staff brought up the rear; that Asian kid
made eye contact with Guy, waved, and took a photo of him.

And then quiet. The distant caws of jungle birds. Puttering
jet engines. Guy walked up the stairs, past the boxes and
crates. A pile of teal-colored jumpsuits lay discarded at the
sign-in desk; Guy imagined a trio of defiant staff cavorting
naked through the campus. He walked through a puddle of
colorless syrup, creating a Velcro sound from his sticky shoes
on the cement.

A relief: they hadn't packed up the bar. He made himself
a gin martini with the dregs from the ice bin and toasted the
airstrip. It tasted of Windex for some reason. No matter. As
he lowered his glass the first jet roared and cleared the runway.
The second one must have been heavier; its wheels clipped the
canopy and took a few branches with it. The jets flew toward
the ominous, bubbling horizon before turning north.

He padded onto the lawn to get a look at Bax and co. He assumed they would have left by now, but Bax was still in port. And staring straight at Guy. Or in his direction: she stood on the top deck with a pair of binoculars fixed on the island as her crew scurried about, tying down lifeboats and shipping crates. Circling jet skis cheered them on. The faintest sound of classic rock. Past the yacht Guy made out a midsize cruiser at full throttle; when it turned he noticed a teal stripe down the side. More of Averman's staff, headed to the nearest port.

The storm arrived. Rumbling gales tossed pool chairs. Windows cracked and spidered into a busy mosaic. Bax's yacht wobbled, then pitched as if held by a giant hand from below. A wave crested its lowest deck, then the one above. The armada disappeared behind greenish crests.

The rain soaked him in a second and ruined his drink. Perhaps a nap would rejuvenate him, provide the clarity to plan the rest of his day. He grabbed the bottle of gin and found a couch nestled in an alcove. The storm whistled, then moaned, then whistled and moaned. The atmosphere was womb-like, happily conducive to relaxation. Lights flickered and went out.

He awoke twenty minutes later, stood, and stretched. The drumming rain sounded closer, but not stronger. A thin flood of seawater and palm fronds nudged his feet. A scent of aloe, or something fresh and cold like aloe, permeated the hallway. He took a pull of gin and sloshed toward his suite.

The windows lining the hall had shattered, and the wind pushed him sideways. Helpfully the broken glass was being carried downstream. And what was this? Cut limes? Perfect.

He bent down, inspected them for shards—the tiniest glistening fragments, nothing a robust digestive system couldn't handle. He forced a slice into the bottle. Now if he could find some ice he'd be in business.

The wind picked up *again*, deafening all. Guy yelled a few nonsense words but couldn't hear himself. This was more like it! Rain cut into the hallway through the open windows in wet spotlights. Where did one hide in a hurricane? The bathtub? Was that only for tornadoes?

The walls turned a stippled shade of pink and appeared to spin. It was nauseating; he stopped to focus. The pink cohered into serifed letterforms, first upside down and then on its side. He tilted his head: GENITAL MUTILATION. The words sped down the corridor and disappeared. He turned to the window and saw a lawn projector held taut in the air and umbilically tied to the ground. So there was still electricity somewhere, via backup generator. A pause in the wind dropped the projector to the flattened grass.

His room was flooded but unharmed: intact windows, upright patio furniture. The sky had darkened further, with an approaching curtain of blacks and blues. After another pull he was stopped by the awesome sight of Bax's yacht, now really swaying from side to side. The pitch looked sick-inducing even at this distance. It was difficult to believe people were aboard. An awful, subterranean noise broke through—a child's yawn, a failing train brake—and the deck rose vertically. The massive vessel succumbed to physics. Guy felt his bile collect; he closed his eyes, concentrated on the sound of the wind. When he looked again the yacht was almost peaceful, perfectly capsized in parallel to the shoreline. Through a crack in the dome a perfect spray of sand arced into the ocean.

He closed the door and locked the patio, put a robe on over his wet clothes, grabbed a few pillows, and hopped in the tub. Then he remembered his gin. He retrieved it from the bedside table, next to—ahoy!—an ice bucket with a few fat residents. Closed the bathroom door, brought everything into the tub, and toasted his good fortune.

Being fully dressed in a bathtub felt lightly transgressive, like ditching class. Which, granted, he had never done, what with the certainty of outsize parental censure were he ever caught. He hadn't done a lot of things. And now here he was, foggy with high-proof botanicals and snug in what looked like Carrera marble. With an end in sight, truly in sight. No more hypotheticals, no future conditional.

The caves at Lascaux—that was on the list. And not the replica they trotted out for tourists, but the real thing, accessible through assiduous decontamination protocols and substantial donation. The birth of Western art! He'll have lived a complete life without bearing witness. An incomplete life, then. Incredible to think it could ever be otherwise. Had he really fooled himself into believing he could see it all, do it all?

Bugger to all of it. He poured the gin into the ice bucket, swirled it about, and took a good, long sip. The alcohol produced an involuntary shiver, then a cough. Or not just the alcohol—there was a foulness to the air. A gas leak? Something wrong with the central air? He coughed again and couldn't stop.

This was it. A few inhalations and then sleep. It would be

easy, like stepping off a curb. Should he take his shoes off? It felt important to wiggle his toes one last time. As he decided about the matter of the shoes, the wind cut out. A temporary reprieve. He caught his breath and sat up. The tub was pleasant enough, but he didn't want his last image to be that of a walk-in shower.

High ground. There was an idea. Absorb nature's bounty in his final moments. Expire with an ocean view. It would take every ounce of courage to leave his toxic cocoon. Or if not every ounce, then most; he was unsure how many ounces he had left.

He stood and measured his balance. With one eye closed he could—nope, that first step sent him right to the floor. He took it hard in the shoulder, heard a pop in one or both of his knees. Okay, again. Bracing himself against the tub, he managed to stand. Battered, but nothing too serious. He grabbed a pillow and opened the bathroom door. Ankle-deep water nosed in, and then out again when he opened the patio door; the suite must be a few inches above the lawn. The air immediately cleaned his lungs. The cleanest air he had ever inhaled. He took a tentative step, whanged his hip on chair, and looked about for a way up. A trellis. There was definitely a trellis, and if the storm hadn't ripped it off he could scurry up and have a nice little spot to watch the show.

The rain lightened up. He dropped the pillow and continued around the building, pausing at the sound of a rhythmic beating. It sounded like a knock. Did someone else stay behind?

He followed the sound to Roark's suite. The old man was

bobbing about, face down, his magnificent robe open and undulating like a jellyfish. Pulsometers still connected his hand to the medical equipment. His white pate tapped against the patio doors with the current of the rising waters.

Probably died in his sleep, the lucky bastard. Guy raised his hand in salute. May the old man bob for all eternity.

Continuing on, Guy found the trellis near the residence entryway. The lawn was really slick now, sending him ass over teakettle once, then twice. Hearty muck pulled at his loafers with increasing tenacity; he took the hint and belly crawled the remaining few yards. The robe provided traction without weighing him down. A high-quality garment.

An unimaginative landscape architect had stuffed the trellis with orchids. Its petals formed an almost gelatinous skin over the wooden frame. His first handhold brought back a palm covered in viscid, purple-brown flora; his second slipped and dropped him into a nascent puddle reeking of humid sperm. He wiped his face; the gesture amplified his shoulder throb.

This was about as bad as he could imagine. And he was wetter, more soaked through than he'd ever been. On the other hand, he had a bit of liquid courage in him, and the hot wind was more balm than lash. It was only fifteen or twenty feet up. Surely he could accomplish this one final task.

Guy planted his feet astride the dark bilge. He shook the trellis. There was give, but it seemed secure enough. He wedged a foot into a diamond cutout and tested its weight. It held. He took a deep breath and scrambled up, figuring he had less chance of a slip if he hustled. He had exactly enough upper body strength to pull himself over. The roof had absorbed the morning sun and was warm despite the rain. He rolled toward the middle of the building, near a gurgling drain and a squat HVAC unit. Someone had carved "BAX" into the metal sheathing.

• • •

NOT TERRIBLE, AS catastrophes go. The earth had cleared its throat, then sent the hurricane west. It left a sun-shower and the intense scent of petrichor as parting gifts. The air felt clean and empty.

He inspected his ankle, expecting a bruise and finding a swollen violet bloom. An exploratory flex—ah, blinding pain. And not just his ankle. A generalized ache forded his gin moat and charged his inner sanctum. Still alive.

When had he last experienced extreme weather? They'd missed the recent spate of tristate blizzards. When the forecast predicted anything mildly deleterious Victoria's assistants prepped the jet.

He thought of his first summer in Minnesota, when the KARE 11 anchors reported tornadoes with the casualness of commuter traffic. Even the on-camera eyewitnesses were resigned to it: your roof gets ripped off, you call your insurance guy. During the first heavy storms he and his mother hunkered in the basement until the Knutsons said the metro area was safe. ("Twisters like farms.")

The pain would not subside. Ankle be damned, shoulder be damned, corpus be damned. He must climb down and locate alcoholic redress.

But first he must attend to the exigent demands of his bowels. His short gastric fuse would not allow for first-world civility: he rolled toward the roof's edge—screaming as his ankle twisted with each revolution—slid his trousers down, and nudged his ass over the side. The position recalled the calisthenics routine his father insisted upon before laps at the Colombo Swim Club. He stretched and almost reached his toes, which aided a forceful evacuation. If he was counting silver linings—including the literal one, to the south—he didn't require much wiping beyond a sacrificed handkerchief. He dropped it to the lawn and pulled up his torn pants. Was the old swim club still around? There was a donation at some point—either a preservation grant or a raze-and-rebuild capital fund—and a thank-you note pinned to the corkboard in the Foundation's kitchenette. Maybe they'd installed an on-site plaque. That would be nice.

Large birds circled Bax's yacht and cawed excitedly, in contrast to the lack of birdsong from the jungle. He stood with some difficulty and loped across the roof for a better look at the behemoth.

The onboard zoo was paddling toward the remnants of Averman's dock with varying degrees of success, like the bleating inventory of an incompetent Noah. He spotted several boars, the bristles of their oddly equine faces glistening in the light; an actual giraffe, fighting an underwater hindrance of some kind; the shells of a half dozen armadillos, like dark fingernails on the ocean surface; and, closest to the deck, a thrashing over what he hoped weren't human corpses.

From somewhere deep inland a column of smoke thinned

and went out. He tried to orient himself. Was that the hangar? Or something else? Perhaps some staff had remained behind to get a jump on recovery efforts. Well, shit. Guy wanted the island to himself. He felt as though he'd found an empty row at the theater, only to be joined by loud strangers at showtime.

It was a big island. He could keep to himself, stay inebriated, empty his mind. This made him giddy and he thought, improbably enough, of Franz Ferdinand. The story had been drilled into him by a high school teacher who called Bosnia the center of the twentieth century. The archduke survived the first assassination attempt due to a bomb thrower's poor aim, and then survived several other attempts as separatists lining the motorcade lost their nerve. Ferdinand insisted on giving his speech as planned. How alive he must have felt! His enemies bested, his wife by his side.

His luck ran out, of course. They took a detour on the return route, where his vehicle stalled in front of one of the separatists and erstwhile cowards. The assassin didn't need to be told twice. He approached the open-top vehicle and shot the presumptive king and queen close enough for all three to make eye contact. Guy's teacher went on and on about the intimacy of it. How the spark for the powder keg of Europe was lit by three people within spitting distance of one another.

He found the trellis, figuring it to be the safest way down, but misjudged how much weight his ankle could support. He fell down the wall and landed on the soggy lawn. No worse for wear, though now his left arm sported a deep rash from bicep to wrist. He tucked in his torn shirt—right, that's sorted—and hobbled toward the main building.

It felt good to be ambulatory. It felt terrible to be ambulatory. He just needed some painkillers. And a handle of something high-proof. And a California king.

The residencies were flooded and their windows blown in. Floating glass caught the sun, like a preview of his migraine. At the steps to the main building he was met with a strong breeze of spoiled meat and ammonia. It was quiet save for the orbiting midges.

He tried the kitchen first. It looked abandoned in a hurry, with pots and cutlery scattered across the countertops. There was a soft buzzing from the row of fridges. Perhaps they ran on a backup system? A cold pét-nat would do just fine. He opened a fridge door and found rows of small plastic bags with red liquid and timestamped labels. Averman's blood—he must have gotten into injection cycling, the Lance Armstrong routine. But the light was off, which meant the electric was out. No generator here.

He followed the buzzing around the corner. A jeroboam of red wine had crashed to the floor and attracted a cloud of black flies. At least someone's having fun.

Jessica's room. She'd have something.

Averman would have put her close by, between the veranda and the amphitheater. He tried a few unmarked doors. Custodial closet, linen closet . . . bingo. The windowless quarters were spartan and free of personality. He waited for his eyes to adjust and stumbled toward the bathroom. The medicine cabinet had only Q-tips, children's Tylenol, and a large bottle of biotin capsules. He swallowed a handful of Tylenol and continued his search. Something golden on top of the dresser caught the light: a large brass bowl with thin handles. A spittoon. Its inscription claimed it as property of Gerald Averman of Perth, 1901.

The closet was empty save for a flashlight, a black evening dress, and rows of teal-colored tote bags. He pocketed the flashlight and brought one of the bags to the hallway for inspection. There was a cartoon drawing of Averman printed on one side, giving a thumbs-up and declaring, "WE DID IT!" Inside he found an exit survey, a combination pen-voice recorder, Averman's wife's magazine, a water bottle, and a Rolex Daytona with "Quorumite" written on the dial.

Guy stood and listed to the wall. His ankle was disquietingly large. He slung the tote over his shoulder, retrieved the spittoon, and headed for the staff residences.

Also flooded, with a thick waft of sewage. The staff building was the only one with a basement, and he descended its stairs on a hunch. There might be a generator, one with a simple enough mechanism for him to initiate a restart. The water was knee-deep here, and the flashlight too dim to be of much use. He sloshed past gardening equipment and soaked cardboard boxes to the end of the hall. All the doors were locked. Through a small window he could make out a grid of white squares; using the flashlight they became ziplocked bags of sandwiches floating around, and, just beyond, two of Averman's staff in teal polos and white tennis shorts, face down. He gagged and turned, trying to shake the image as he fell up the stairs.

Outside he coughed and inhaled and coughed. No more basements.

The layout resembled a college dormitory: bunk beds, cheap standing closets, dry-erase boards affixed to the doors. He located a wall-mounted first aid kit and wrapped his ankle with a cold compress in gauze. The rooms turned up a fifth of Grey Goose, some bread rolls, and a travel-size spray bottle of clear liquid. Its label depicted polar bears in sunglasses. He also found a keychain Swiss Army knife, too diminutive to be of use.

But he had something better than a pocketknife, and more befitting these circumstances. A final bit of reconnaissance. Then he could lie in repose.

The water in his suite had turned brackish, with iridescent oil spots collecting in the corners. A new scent of rot. He retrieved the ski bag from the closet and removed his sword. The blade wasn't sharp, but it might be enough to clear brush. He brandished it at an imaginary opponent. Ceremonial, but still reassuring.

He exited through a blown-out window. If indoors wasn't an option, he would make do with raw nature. Bivouac like a real pioneer. Like a conqueror: the island was his by default.

The dormant volcano glistened with rivers coursing down its face. He thought of the mountaintop palace, the one in the hill country his parents insisted on visiting over Easter holidays. Sigiriya. A thousand years ago some king built it to lord over his dominion. The ruins were impressively preserved, with clear outlines of floor plans, antechambers, guesthouses, and plumbing technology his father said was centuries ahead of Europe. He also extolled the king's use of biological warfare, specifically the wasp nests installed along the mountain trail. What Guy remembered most were the murals of bare-breasted servants painted on the caves bordering that same mountain trail and also impressively preserved. Climbing the steps behind his parents, Guy snuck looks at the comically buxom friezes; they became foundational to his onanistic imaginary. His father joked that invaders got a pleasant final image before they were stung to death. Guy faked a laugh until he saw his mother's stern look.

He kept the volcano to his right and made for the trees. Surveying the downed branches and general destruction, he recalled something from Friday night: Averman's welcome speech, bragging about a priest blessing the island. How much of the holiness had been strewn about? Did it extend below the water table? Was the holiness now in the air and out to sea?

Averman had also mentioned a bonfire, which meant a clearing of some kind. It would suffice. He wasn't a compli-cated man. And the Tylenol was kicking in, thank Christ.

The jungle was a good five degrees cooler and eerily quiet. The canopy felt depopulated. Or worse: dense with fauna silently watching his tentative intrusion. He took an embold-ening pull of vodka and chased it with a few sprays in the mouth. It had no taste; probably a good sign.

He hadn't thought of the fatherland for some time. Apart from a perfunctory trip with Victoria—to satisfy her curiosity and confirm the rumors of Galle's high-end hospitality—he'd seen no reason to visit. All the relatives were deceased save for a few distant cousins. And the civil war had picked up about the time his postgraduate horizons contracted to a middling life in Philly. He could ignore the slaughter and the human rights abuses by simply turning off the BBC world news update when it came on local public radio.

This aversion became difficult after the First Flush—if difficult was the word—as appeals for repatriations swarmed in. Still. He was a composer, and a lapsed Catholic Burgher. He had no dog in the fight. What did they want from him? He gave a little here and there. The swim club. STEM funding for the university.

Of course he could have done more. If he had, would he still carry this late-stage guilt? He'd never known a martyr, but he imagined they rarely died with a smile on their face.

He took another long sip of vodka. Even these thoughts, he knew, were a distraction. The engine of self-regard revving once more, that old talent for rationalization. He knew he should be troubled by this, but at this moment, walking this path, stepping over felled branches, rotating the ache out of his shoulder—it was something he could shrug off without consequence.

Hadn't he seen the world? Hadn't he tasted every flavor? If he was to die bereft and soiled, then he had the right to pretend otherwise. Let everyone else have their deathbed grasps at moral clarity, those too-late attempts to make amends. Not him. There must be a little honor in staying true to one's fixed self, as dishonorable as that self might be.

V would know what to do. Or the V of a week ago—the uncorrected V. She helped Guy navigate the survivor's guilt during the foundation's initial disbursement, mollifying his anxieties (even if they were somewhat performative) and insisting the unfunded applicants would receive money elsewhere.

The world was chock full of philanthropy, she would say. *Accept what you cannot change.*

And the Victoria of now? She was incapable of change. Prided herself on it.

What would you say to her if she were here?

That was the question. He'd ask why. Scream at her for ruining their lives. He'd ask why, again and again and again.

Nothing she'd say would help. She was who she was. He would tell her he wished they'd never met. But that wasn't true. She saved him from a midlife rut, from a slide into complacency and depression.

That's all? You're not blind with rage?

What good would that do? Victoria was a pure product of America. An unstoppable object. He knew that from day one.

Forget the good it would do. Forget everything. You forgive too easily, always skimming the surface of life, afraid to submerge.

He'd lived well for someone so passive.

Submerge! Pop your ears! Burn your lungs!

His body had been through enough.

"Enough"—there's your problem. If your parents had been fine with "enough," you'd still be living on that dirt floor in Colombo.

It was poured cement. There were housekeepers.

Guy came upon the clearing. Downed palms formed a skewed tic-tac-toe grid around a bluestone firepit. One of the trunks had landed on a cord of stacked logs and scattered the firewood about. He kicked a teal-colored coffee mug, which ricocheted off a tree and disappeared into the brush.

A fine place to die. Primal, a site of ritual.

Ritual is important, especially after trauma.

Guy dropped the sword and tote bag and made himself comfortable. There was an ashy sludge in the firepit, but he could use the magazine for kindling and build up to the firewood, provided it wasn't too wet. He tore the pages into strips, balled them up, and laid them in the center of the pit, then assembled a teepee of short branches around it. He lit the paper using camp matches from the first aid kit and blew until it caught.

Some of the cave drawings were done by artists experiencing oxygen deprivation. They needed fire to light the walls while they worked, but this sucked up the O2. And produced powerful hallucinations.

He could still make a fire. That counted for something. During his first summer in the States his mother enlisted him in a ten-day camp at a dude ranch in South Dakota. It may have been North Dakota; the state was that unremarkable and his interest that minimal. His mother said the camp taught "American skills," though he couldn't see how lassoing calves or baling hay were tests of assimilation. He did gain respect for the Twin Cities' relative cosmopolitanism. He also learned, courtesy of furtive evenings with a delinquent chubby girl who went by J, the compromised merits of receiving a beginner's hand job. She improvised techniques with palms calloused from ropework. J's life was the stuff of antidrug PSAs. She enthused about St. Cloud's punk shows and whippet parties while she worked away at his cock; he would nod and stare at the stick-and-poke tattoos on her forearms, a line of cartoon skulls dancing with the rough motion.

He added branches to the fire and lay back. The clouds had burned off and left a pale bowl of evening sky. A falcon or a hawk flitted overhead. It was difficult to tell whether the bird was flying away or straight up. For a moment Guy couldn't place the axis of the world and became dizzy. He turned to his side and retched, but nothing came up. He forced down a bread roll and followed it with a drink and a spritz.

A large rodent moved beyond the firepit. Guy sat up. A bunny with filthy, matted fur ambled into the clearing, its orb-like body bouncing from side to side. Guy felt pure envy. Yes, the animal was confused, and likely in pain from the heat and the grit under its paws. It was thirsty and alone. But also alive in this strange environment, where no bunny had ever been.

The bunny registered his presence and hopped into the brush.

He added larger logs to the fire and rested his head against a felled branch.

Good night, sweet prince.

CHAPTER 14

Well past the previous threshold.

For the first seven miles you didn't notice your thumbs outside your fists. Slip them inside your curled knuckles. All of civilization at your back.

The sun-warmed earth beckons. Keep your head raised so the sweat trickles down the temples.

Out there is nothing but opportunity. A global GDP of $80 trillion. Every single ecosystem undergoing massive change. That's all the world is, constant change. The best time is now. The best time is always now.

Carve out your fraction of a percent. Surely they would grant you that.

Yes, you broke and checked your phone before the run. The news is out. Or their version of it. Trending in eighteen countries. Already dropped by our personal counsel. Plus that unctuous *Hang in there!* note from that skeletal pharma guy. How did he even get the number.

Don't get distracted. Concentrate on form. Your assemblage of bone and blood and muscle.

The first mouthful of battery acid. Remember: you can withstand pain longer if you curse. Remember: all those nights screaming in your soundproof office.

Fuck the journalists. Fuck the nonbelievers, the armchair critics. Fuck those without vision. Your heroes enslaved others. They hated women. They were anti-Semites and godless perverts.

The sweat is in the eyes now. Blink it away—don't wipe. The mountains become wavy and slick. It's like driving blindfolded. The sky and the ground refuse to define themselves. Giant floating Rothko shapes.

You will be absolved. Years from now you and Guy will joke about this "rough patch" as you toast the sunset at the Hudson Valley acreage.

A ghost movement just ahead. It's you, running, at your absolute peak. Leaving nothing in reserve. Entering the Zone of Utmost Throb. Victoria with total focus and zero attachments. An open vessel shorn of all that impedes eureka.

You can catch her. Ignore that hollow sensation in the teeth. Ignore the popping blisters, the raw skin flaying with each step. Ignore the razor blades in the calves.

Those stotting gazelles and their ostentatious displays. You know what they're doing. They're taunting the predators. *C'mon over. Attack my neighbor. She can't jump for shit.*

Those who provoke the most, survive.

More battery acid. Now in the throat and lungs. You are an apparatus of groaning hinges, taking the next step solely because you've taken so many already.

The caterwauling in the ears becomes white noise. Every

footfall touches down on even, firm ground, as if predestined.

An IRA prisoner on hunger strike once described death as having a smell. Is that what's in your nose. The cold burn at the edge of the nostrils. Not sulfurous. Sedimentary.

Gazelles at your left and right. Impossibly large and spectral. Leopards too.

The idea is at the periphery. It wiggles and glows. And another idea, a variation in movement and a reddish aura. And another idea, zigzagging in ochre.

More and more. They shimmy to the center of the field of vision. Obliterating. Beyond language. You've been screaming for the last half mile.

The gift of catastrophe! It resets the table. Erases memory. You are rich in gifts. You can tolerate the impermanence and the inconstancy better than anyone, so you will rise. You are pure invention. Your story will be heard through the fog because your story will be exclaimed at volume. And a story can be anything.

CHAPTER 15

A series of frustrated exhalations disturbed his sleep. A large dog choking, or a chorus of large dogs choking. The sounds came from behind, matched by the crisp trampling of several feet. Or paws. Or hooves. Whatever it was, it stopped moving and continued its forceful breathing. He wiped the crust from his eyes, registered the morning light. Swept his things into the tote bag, grabbed the sword. If he couldn't pierce skin, perhaps he could thwack his visitor on the head. Disorient it enough to escape.

The sounds were closer now, ten or fifteen feet away. Then he remembered: fire! Everyone hates fire. He crawled to the firepit and pulled out a club-like branch with a stump of glowing embers. Counted to three and leaped up.

Nothing. The brush wasn't terribly thick, so whatever was making the sound should have been visible. Save for the faint rustling of leaves there was no indication of company. Then another exhalation, a thrusted snort straight ahead. The product of a robust respiratory system inside a more robust beast unlikely to be dissuaded by the hot stick he now feebly held aloft.

The snorting repeated, but without any movement. An awkward detente. He screwed up some courage and javelined the branch toward the sound, then turned tail. He heard a riot of squeals and thrashing but dared not look. It charged through the firepit. That Blake poem about the tiger, life imitating art.

As he ran the tote banged against his ribs, and he was winded after thirty seconds. He risked a glance; nobody was chasing him.

But what a rush! Goddamn. Jesus. Whoo boy.

The trail opened to a switchback path down to one of the beaches. Had he been here yet? Incredible, these last few days.

He jogged the steps, bracing himself with the young trees lining the handrails and ignoring the hot pain his loafers sent to his knees. The tree line stopped a dozen yards from the water; a fine spot to collapse. He hoovered several bread rolls and then felt an overwhelming need to urinate. He could go in the water—or anywhere, really—but it was important to maintain discipline. Guy set the spittoon near the base of a palm tree and ejected a satisfying amount of deep yellow piss.

There. That's the bathroom. As for the rest? He could fashion a lean-to, something simple and functional. He took two quick pulls and started collecting fronds. After some trial and error he was able to hatch them together, imitating the intrecciato design on his loafers. It wouldn't repel water if the rain returned, but he could lie in the shade with his feet in the sand. He cobbled a frame of long branches, braced it, laid the hatching across, and stood back to admire his handiwork. A half A-frame with enough clearance when he sat down.

Next he emptied the tote. There were enough magazine pages for another fire if he wanted to risk it. It might get cold at night. Was it cold last night? He couldn't remember. And the boars? How to fend them off? Do those booby traps in movies really work? It seemed like a lot of effort, and he had limited supplies.

Aha! The magazine. He ripped out the perfume ads and opened their sample strips, then arranged a loose perimeter with stones for paperweights. Not the strongest deterrent, but good enough. He created a makeshift carpet of the remaining fronds and lay down. A persistent sting licked his knees, shoulders, neck, head, arms, and brain, but he felt otherwise comfortable.

The storm hadn't damaged this side of the island much. A decidedly pre-Anthropocene view. Pre-everything.

Guy Sarvananthan, the last man. The first man? Whichever—someone no longer in need of a name. Or a partner. Someone without individuation, without subjectivity.

Victoria was a monster. Sure. A profligate liar without a moral compass. Sure. But what did he want? What had he ever wanted? Did it matter if the love he'd felt was ultimately mistaken? It was real at the time, or real to him at the time.

Let the past be the past. It might be immature or cowardly, but look where he'd ended up. There was nobody to impress. Who cared if he engaged in a bit of magical thinking at his ignominious end. The arc of his life was complete. Foreclosed from possibility. This was freeing, in a way. He had nothing and wanted nothing. Who was it who said nothingness was its own form of perfection?

Victoria would profess the gospel of improvement until her dying breath. But why grow when there was no tomorrow? He had this Eden underfoot. This lukewarm spirit in hand.

A swell of generosity in his chest provoked a wet cough. Everyone should experience such liberation! In a macro sense, the end was assured and soon arriving. The younger generations wouldn't survive, and if they did, it would be under so much duress, and in such a blasted landscape, they'll wish they all went out like him.

This could be his posthumous gift: an inspiring way to die.

He thought of Ben what's-his-name—the Boston kid at Curtis. Struck by a taxi while biking. The funeral was one of those Quaker services where nobody talked except for the stammering, Chanel-clad mother who repeated anecdotes about his first recital. Afterward Guy saw the other composers huddled in the parking lot, sharing notes on tenure-track interviews. He'd become so estranged since graduation, so quickly and so thoroughly.

Ah! The unbidden memories. The intractable deluge. What could he do? Well, he could actively ignore the klaxons of his roiling mind. Actively ignore the vivid and the known, try to rearrange his self-conception and ease the downward slide. Soak the cerebellum with devil-may-care fecundity. Yes! Blithe reinvention!

The serotonin washed over him.

He drank again. A third of the bottle remained.

How she looked while sleeping. Those rare nights together. He would stay up reading and kiss her forehead after turning off the light. She would issue a murmur and a slight nod.

Sometimes he would kiss her collarbone and tongue the small bowl of skin behind it, a youthful gesture he repeated partly for the "round peg, round hole" satisfaction and partly to test his neck strain. Eyes closed, Victoria would murmur again and say, "The morning." A few times they did indeed fuck the next morning.

Now never again.

Mary Ellen had been a nice surprise. That long torso, that cotton-sock smell of her pussy. He idly pawed at his crotch and then masturbated in earnest. His shoulder creaked, but he soldiered on. Mary Ellen became Victoria, Victoria became Jessica, Jessica became Gretchen on their last Poconos trip.

That did it. His ejaculate was more theory than practice: one thick drop resting atop his tired cock. A breeze rose the gooseflesh on his arms.

He buttoned his sodden trousers. Now he really was king of the island. He let himself drift to sleep.

• • •

GUY AWOKE A few hours later to what sounded like fireworks. He walked to the water for a better vantage. Confirmed: fireworks. Timed to go off at the Quorum's conclusion, presumably. The storm must have damaged the launchpad; instead of shooting upward, the red and teal trails arced low across the water. Still, a nice light show against the early evening sky. Wind sent the smoke toward the beach, which commingled with a different, sootier scent in the air.

He turned to the water. The tide swept over his feet and

took the loose gauze from his ankle. It was still bruised, but no longer swollen. Here's to progress.

Guy removed his shirt and walked in. It was calm, just shy of warm, and dirty with kelp and plastic flotsam. He tried for a dead man's float, remembering to stick out his stomach and hold his breath. He should let the ocean claim him. Spend his last hours serene and boundless, carried on the scrim of the world until . . . What? A shark? No, he'd succumb to exhaustion first, falling into the big blue. A terrifying way to go. Perhaps he might buffet it with a little foresight: inhale deeply, count to ten, and be done with it.

His mother had gone peaceably. Dinner with friends, then a bit of television with a cup of decaf. She passed in her brand-new recliner, a brown leather number paid all-cash that enveloped her small frame. In her white pajamas, like a baseball tucked in a fresh mitt.

The firework residue rolled out to sea like a great grey lint ball. Lint. When was the last time he'd seen lint? And how had he become someone who couldn't recall the last time they'd seen lint? True, he wasn't the kind to pause and take stock. Life with Victoria was a dense and numinous present. There was no time for introspection or opportunity for perspective. On the rare occasions he was asked—for a softball piece on PrevYou, or in polite conversation at an IHO dinner—he professed modesty with a touch of wonderment: nobody could have anticipated how his life turned out, him least of all.

Was it ever thus? It was easy to be deterministic. Most billionaires were.

Perhaps he never meets Victoria. He stays in Philly.

Continues the piano lessons and mostly keeps to himself. Eventually he gives up liquor, makes a case of Schuylkill punch last a month. Then the tutoring dries up. A temp gig as an office manager becomes permanent. He's set up with a coworker's sister. They date, move in together, and marry. He gives her however many kids she wants. They move for her job, buy a house, support the local orchestra. At dinner parties he impresses their friends with his curry and hoppers. Myocardial infarction while mowing the lawn.

Or: He makes a final plea to Gretchen. She stands firm. In his desperation he emails her husband, confessing all, and it ends terribly for everyone. The husband owns a gun and shoots Guy in the stomach. *Dateline* does a lurid segment on the love triangle. The music world is shocked, shocked.

Or: He realizes the limits of his talent at Curtis and transfers out. Gets a musicology PhD somewhere in a niche specialty. Maybe the ravanahatha, which funds research trips back to Sri Lanka. A breakthrough connecting the instrument to Italian luthiers gets him a position in a nice liberal arts college. Northern Ohio. Western Oregon. Marries someone in an adjacent department who has, like, three cats. Each morning one of them sits on his chest to wake him. The university, swept up in the general decimation of the humanities, offers him early retirement. He takes it. On a Sunday, while his wife is at the post office, he chokes on leftover steak and dies in a fake Eames lounger.

He could see these other Guys. Hundreds of them, floating nearby, arms out, maybe twenty pounds heavier, all sighing at the onset of twilight. A choir of sighs.

He loved an island at night. Soon the stars would appear and he would be in infinite space.

He lifted his head to look around. The current hadn't taken him out to sea at all. He was maybe fifty feet down shore from the lean-to. In fact—yep, he could stand. This was still the man-made sand shelf. From here the bow of Bax's yacht peeked around the curve of the island. It had become a natural part of the landscape. Its contents and animal carcasses formed a trail, such that a spryer man could hopscotch from boat to land.

Guy waded ashore, picking strands of kelp off his thighs as he went and only losing his balance once. He took a long pull of vodka to get the saltwater taste from his mouth, then used the last of the spray.

That smoke smell was more prevalent. Should he make another fire? He could hike back to the residences and find some blankets. Fuck. He should have planned this better.

He finished the rolls and filled the spittoon. Applied ointment from the first aid kit to his rash, then stowed everything in the tote and set it in the corner.

Sitting cross-legged, the cross-hatching of the lean-to tickled his hair. He focused on the water. A wonderful vantage for the sunset.

Away from her, away from it all. Perhaps this was how it was supposed to happen. The symmetry of being born on an island and dying on one too.

People often develop cases of apophenia late in life. They see meaning where none exists. Coincidences become pattern. Patterns become ubiquitous.

Sounds delightful.

You should resist. The world always contains the same amount of sense.

But I want simplification. Oversimplification. Total inter-relatedness.

That way lies zealotry.

From where I sit there's low downside.

CHAPTER 16

!

CHAPTER 17

How long would it take to die? Perhaps Averman would send a plane first. If not to rescue him, then at least to assess the damage. Roark. Those kids in the basement. And him, down here. Would they know where to look? It may be prudent to locate a phone. He still wanted solitude, and he still felt suicidal—just not exceptionally so. The other, minor part of him saw the wisdom in a Plan B.

He walked toward the shipwreck, forgoing his polo shirt. If he were rescued, he would find her. Confront the immovable, inexorable Victoria Stevens. There were a million things to say and every one of them pointless. It was self-defeating to try to convince her of anything she hadn't already thought of herself, hadn't thought through or decided to never reconsider.

He reached the yacht and the wreckage it had sent ashore: poker chips, neon-colored pool noodles, house slippers. He tried to suss out a backpack or a go bag among the floating detritus. There was a black halo around the boat he hadn't noticed before. Some kind of toxic runoff.

Forget it. He'd search Averman's office in the morning. Guy returned to his lean-to and took another drink.

The beastly exhalations returned. He peered around the lean-to as a half dozen boars trotted by. They were extraordinarily stout, with grey-brown skin and mud patches on their stomachs. The one in front had large burns on its flank.

Boars had a strong olfactory sense—though maybe that's pigs? Boars too, surely. They'd smell the perfume samples and wander off. Unless it backfired: some trans-species pheromonal attraction. That seemed possible.

The pack turned and approached the tree line, seemingly deterred. Should he remain? He could make for the water, but clearly they could swim. And the sword was useless against multiple attackers. He should have grabbed the chef's knives from the kitchen.

He slid the vodka into the tote and shouldered the bag, then moved behind the lean-to, positioning it between himself and the boars. He crab walked to the spittoon and hoisted it by the lip. It felt nice and heavy. The urine sploshed, and one of the boars immediately stopped.

They charged without hesitation, bleating in near unison. He chucked the spittoon at the leader, which bounced and coated its back in glistening piss. More enthused squealing. Guy did a quick 360. Nowhere to go but up.

He scrambled up the tree, ignoring the cuts from the scalloped bark. The trunk swayed under his weight but held fast. His thighs burned, then everything burned. He paused until the boars circled the base, then found a last reserve of adrenaline and climbed. Gripping the stems of two sturdy-looking canopy branches he lifted himself onto the rough navel, clutched the tote to his side, and flipped onto his back. The recess was just wide enough for his ass; with some adjusting he could nearly recline. The boars, taking the escape personally, scratched and bit at the trunk in a rising frenzy. Surely there was better quarry than his ruined self.

Apart from the noises below he detected a crackling, like the popping of bubble wrap. The smoke smell had intensified—the jungle must be on fire. That's what drove his porcine malefactors to the beach.

His stomach grumbled. He stripped a length of palm and tried chewing it, without success. His dangling legs grew numb and lessened the pain.

Well, this was undesirable. Guy let out a sigh, then another with exaggerated volume. The boars paused for a moment before continuing their vain assault. One of them had rudely trampled his lean-to—despite the security perimeter—and was shredding his polo shirt.

He finished the bottle and tucked it by his side. He was safe enough. At this height it was almost pleasant.

He rooted around in the tote and found the pen recorder. Averman was fond of dictating his memoirs; naturally he assumed the Quorumites shared the habit. The device was slim, with a grid of dots on one side and a backlit display on the other. Guy tapped a button. The display read a full charge. A message in a bottle! Yes. Here was providence. Here was a thing he could do while the boars circled and butted.

"Guy Sarvananthan here—" His voice was cracked and slurred. Nothing he could do about it now. "Whoever finds this, please know that I had no prior knowledge of the actions and malfeasance of my wife, Victoria Stevens. I was made aware of the fraud only days ago, on—ah, Wednesday. No, Thursday, June thirtieth. If it provides any measure of solace to the victims, I apologize on behalf—" He clicked off the recorder and deleted the message.

"Guy Sarvananthan here. I will be survived by no children, no grandchildren. No nieces or nephews. There may be a cousin somewhere with some kids, I don't know. And the archives at the Curtis Institute of Music—I think there are a few chamber pieces. An unfinished symphony. That's my legacy. It isn't much. It could have been a lot more, I suppose.

"Goddamn you, Victoria. How could it end up like this? You were my city upon a hill. I was your, what—your poor and huddled masses. Yes. And you couldn't keep your promises. That's my naïveté. My blinding desire. I got to have a lifetime of . . . of mobility, of movement, and experience, and—and now it ends in shambles.

"I suppose I finally know you. Truly know you. You'd ask forgiveness for all this without admitting fault. Expecting me to adjust.

"I'm not sure I'm capable." He considered his present circumstances. Godless. Apocalyptic and bedeviled. And alone. "One last debasement. One final act of assimilation. But there's the question of dignity. If I have any left, I should preserve it. Right, V?"

He slid the recorder into the vodka bottle and replaced the cap. He sat up, gingerly, so as not to sway the palm too much. The boars squealed louder. Guy held the bottle like a football and rehearsed the throw. He wouldn't make it. The bottle would hit the sand and shatter.

Victoria. That wasn't love. It was idolatry. And why go on when you have nothing to worship when the end times arrive?

He opened the bottle, shook out the recorder, and deleted the message. Erasing it reminded him of that story about Janáček tossing his sonata in the fire.

The boars were still circling, still roughly exhaling. He leaned back into the navel and set the bottle on his stomach. The glass felt cool on his skin. He rubbed the waxy palm, imagined the atoms of the leaf comingling with the atoms of his epidermis.

He could almost see her. She would be alone too. Sequestered and scheming. It was still daylight on the West Coast. Perhaps she's on one of her runs, punishing herself while ignoring the oncoming fallout, the collateral damage. Incapable of even acknowledging it. He could see her perfect running form: the even footfalls, the tightened shoulders, torso bent forward. The coils and springs of her body. The rhythm of her breathing. Symmetrical inhalations and exhalations.

A landscape of nothing. Just an open void for her to charge through. He heard her breaths now, heard the counterpoint of her footfall on clean ground—no reverb to echo and distort. A steady percussion. He turned on the recorder and raised his arms, foregrounding her exhalations.

Out in the water, his hundred selves rode the current. He swayed his left hand to bring in their chorus of sighs, then adjusted to a low moan to complement the bass lines of the strengthening tide. Plus the feral and aleatory accompaniment from below: their inexhaustible energy creating the tones of a downshifting semi, then a stadium crowd, then an impotent howl.

An unruly, disjunctive piece. His own Late Style.

He conducted Victoria with his right hand, shaking off the ache in his back and sending her farther into her empty landscape. She was in pain too, overcoming it through habit and will. An expression devoid of emotion. A fixed gaze fixed. She started vocalizing nonsense—another voice for the largo—creating blistered harmony with the boars and his floating contingent.

The boars hit a new pitch. Easy enough to solve. He arched his neck and found hundreds more of his choir. And past them, catching the last bit of sunlight, what looked like three dots suspended in the darkening sky.

Rescue. Or the intoxicants disturbing his tired vision.

Either way. He was fine. Scraped out and ecstatic. He ignored the pain and the hunger and added his own dry voice to the orchestration:

do, do, do, do, do, do . . .
do, do, do, do, do, do . . .
do, do, do, do, do, do . . .

ACKNOWLEDGMENTS

With deep gratitude to Marya Spence and Mackenzie Williams at Janklow & Nesbit; Mark Doten, Rachel Kowal, Erica Loberg, and everyone at Soho Press; Jonny Diamond, Libby Flores, Chad Fugere, David Goodwillie, Amitava Kumar, Courtney Maum, Lincoln Michel, Kevin Nguyen, Kimberly King Parsons, Ben Obler, Scott Ordway, Justin Taylor, and Teddy Wayne, for their insights and generosity; the James Merrill House and its board, for the support; and Summer Smith, for everything.

Research for this novel included writing by John Carreyrou, Chrystia Freeland, Amitav Ghosh, Anand Giridharadas, Gideon Lewis-Kraus, Jane Mayer, Mark O'Connell, Ned Rorem, David Rothkopf, Alex Ross, and numerous business moirs that needn't be name-checked. The seed for The Quorum was planted by a Doug Stanhope bit.